A Secret Affair

Violet Hamilton

ZEBRA BOOKS
KENSINGTON PUBLISHING CORP.

ZEBRA BOOKS

are published by

Kensington Publishing Corp.
475 Park Avenue South
New York, NY 10016

First printing: July, 1991

Printed in the United States of America

Chapter One

"Oh, miss, 'tis a dreadful country, this. Not safe for man or beast," Polly Prewitt wailed as the coach lurched along the moorland track.

"Nonsense, Polly. No harm will come to you with a coachman and two grooms," her companion, Jennifer Dryden, replied briskly. Looking away from the window where she had been intrigued at the bleak prospect of Bodmin Moor stretching into the distance, she soothed the frightened maid, concealing her irritation. Her parents had insisted on the presence of Polly Prewitt, a village girl who occasionally obliged at the vicarage and would lend the proper note of propriety to Jenny's journey. Neither of the girls had been far from their Wiltshire village before, but while Jenny was relishing the new experience, she was finding her chaperone more of a trial than a helpful abigail.

Their coachman had insisted they cross the moor in full daylight for he warned it was the haunt of smugglers and brutal miners, not a safe harbor for travelers. His tales had roused Polly's fears but Jenny had paid little heed to them. She was journeying in style to Trevarris, her cousin's village on the coast of Cornwall, on the insistence of their neighbor, Sir Henry Ruston, who had provided the coach and drivers.

However, not even the comparative comfort of the coach nor the novel sights of the trip, could completely dispell the grim memories which accompanied Jenny. Her thoughts matched the landscape beyond the window. It was an inhospitable country, Bodmin Moor, with its brown barren furze, lowering gray skies, and buffeting winds. In the shadowy distance she caught a brief glimpse of some ancient stones, circles and crosses, relics of the ancient Celts who had bowed reluctantly to their more sophisticated conquerors, Romans, Saxons, Normans, and finally the hybrid English. Cornishmen considered themselves alien and Jenny could understand their strangeness, bred in the soil of this peculiar land. Since their coach had left the market town of Launceston, on the edge of the moor, Jenny had sensed the brooding quality of this westernmost edge of England, so wild, so empty, so intimidating, so unlike the green hedgerows and gentle chalk hills of Wiltshire. Her thoughts were disturbed again by the complaints of her companion.

"And I heard tell that if you strays off the road, the horrid mucky sands drags you down to a slow suffocating death. Oh, it's not for proper folks, this land. Why did you want to come here, miss?" Polly concluded.

You know very well why I've come, my girl. To

escape all the gossip and embarrassment at home, Jenny thought to herself. But she could hardly discuss that with Polly. Instead, she said firmly, "I have been invited to visit my cousin down south, by the sea, where it is very pleasant at this time of year, not at all like this gloomy moor." She hoped that would quiet Polly for a time, and, to reinforce her intention of not talking any further, she closed her eyes, feigning sleep.

If Polly did not take to Cornwall she could return to Wiltshire. Jenny was not sure she wanted her anyway, unused to an abigail of her own, and Polly would be a constant reminder of home and the unhappy events which had led to this journey. All the preparations, the distractions of travel had helped to divert her temporarily from her wretched situation. On Bodmin Moor the depressing memories of the days following Harry's defection flooded back into her mind.

She had been incredibly naive, not realizing that her fiancé, Harry Ruston, was tiring of her, his eyes straying to the doctor's niece, blond seductive Amelia Langdon, a recent visitor to their village. Amelia had succeeded in luring Henry, the very eligible son of the squire, Sir Henry Ruston, to elope with her in Gretna Green. And to add to Jenny's mortification, he had not even hinted to her of his change of heart, but had sent his bluff, kindly father a letter telling of his elopement. Sir Henry had been appalled and disappointed, Jenny's mother furious and disappointed, and her father tolerant and mediating. The scandal had both shocked and fascinated the village.

Jenny and Harry had been childhood friends, their

engagement a natural outcome of their longtime association, encouraged by Sir Henry and reinforced by Jenny's mother. Jenny had little vanity and few illusions about her own attractions. She considered her short mop of chestnut curls, hazel eyes which could turn to green under the stress of excitement or deep emotion, and a neat figure, passable but not outstanding. Jenny knew that most men admired cool blond beauties with limpid blue eyes, who flattered and looked up to men as superior beings—an attitude Jenny had never been able to adopt.

Still, Harry had appeared to find her brisk matter-of-fact approach endearing. He had often congratulated her that she had never suffered from the vapors like some girls and could hold her own in the hunting field. Obviously her mother had been right when she warned Jenny not to take Harry for granted.

Absorbed in helping her father with his parish duties, Jenny had not noticed how much time Harry was spending with Amelia, nor the excuses he offered for avoiding her. When he realized that he loved Amelia and felt only fondness for Jenny, he must have been torn between his heart and his duty, she reasoned. Jenny just wished he had told her of his feelings instead of sneaking off to Gretna Green. Harry certainly had been reared to follow certain standards of duty, honor, and consideration for others. If he was also carefree, heedless, and light-minded, his natural kindness and good humor made up for a want of steadiness.

Sir Henry had believed Jenny would remedy these

faults in Harry's temperament. Sir Henry understood that his son "lacked bottom," a hunting term which Mrs. Dryden would have labeled coarse but described Harry exactly. The elder Ruston had no hope that Amelia, a scheming hussy, he called her, would improve either his son's character or add to the well being of the manor.

Mrs. Dryden agreed. She had quite looked forward to Jenny reigning over Sir Henry's establishment with a mother's natural ambition. Of course, she would never have urged Jenny into a marriage which was repugnant to her, but she could not help preening a bit that her daughter would someday be Lady Ruston.

However, such worldly concerns never occurred to Jenny's father. The vicar was a truly tolerant and Christian man. He did not believe Jenny's heart had been broken and, unlike his wife, had never thought Harry to be a strong partner for his spirited daughter. He suspected her pride would suffer more than her deepest emotions. Still, it had been an unpleasant blow to his daughter's consequence.

After the first shock, Jenny realized that she was more shaken by Harry's method of rejecting her than the actual abandonment, happening as it did within a month of their wedding. Harry's kisses had been pleasant, but she had never felt a passionate longing for the ultimate act of love. Perhaps Harry had sensed that lack in her. She admitted ruefully that her father was probably right; her pride had suffered more than her heart. It was shameful to be dumped like an unwanted parcel, ignored and given only a perfunctory apology for such caddish behavior. Harry had not wanted a scene. He should have known Jenny would not create one.

Jenny's ruminations on her situation were interrupted by a cry from the coachman, as he sawed frantically on the reins. Jenny, roused from her unsatisfactory thoughts by the jolting of the coach, looked out the window with trepidation. Why had they stopped? She opened the coach door and, telling Polly to cease her wailing, stepped out onto the road to meet a scene of some confusion. Another coach, drawn by four coal black horses had drawn up just ahead of Sir Henry's. The coachman of this brillant vehicle and her own were engaged in heated conversation. Jenny feared they might come to blows and wondered if she should intervene. Before she could carry out her intention, though, a gentleman descended from the other coach and strolled across to the two disputants.

"What seems to be the trouble, George?" the stylish gentleman asked casually. Jenny believed him to be one of those elegant men of fashion she had read about, stars of London salons and the court. He was dressed in the latest stare, a black caped driving coat draped about him, and a beaver hat cocked insolently on his head. He appeared not to notice Jenny as she gave him careful scrutiny.

"Sir, this cove refused to give way when I had the boy sound the horn, and when we tried to pass him, he nicked our side wheel. Deliberate, I'd say," growled George.

"You were comin' too fast. Didn't allow me time to

move the cattle," protested the stolid John. "And you might have run me into the ditch."

"Well, no harm seems to be done. I think we had best be on our way. I'm in some haste to reach Truro, George," the gentleman insisted in a quiet voice which brooked no argument. As he turned, his glance wandered to Jenny, and his eyes roamed over her in what she thought a most insolent way. Then, as if deciding she was not worth an apology, he resumed his walk back to the coach and swung easily aboard.

With a few more mutterings, his coachman followed and within minutes had whipped up his horses and left them behind in a cloud of dust.

"Nasty, arrogant fellow," John complained, coming to Jenny's side and assisting her back into the carriage. "I'd like to have given him a taste of the dirt."

"Never mind, John. No harm done and we, too, must not dally if we are to reach Truro by dusk. Forget the pair, servant and master both," Jenny advised. She had not liked the way the elegant gentleman had dismissed her, but she smiled a bit as they rumbled away. Her pride was certainly suffering a great deal these days. Probably it was good for her, but lowering all the same. Rejected by Harry and by the lordly stranger. Her parents might have said it served her right as they were always reproving her for her domineering ways.

Somehow the little incident had placed her problem in its proper perspective, banished any remnants of self-pity, and Jenny felt a good deal cheered without knowing why. Perhaps the tonic she needed was at hand—new faces, new adventures, new decisions. Her mother's suggestion that she avoid the villagers' sympathy, their neighbors' innuendos, and the arrival of the newlyweds by visiting her cousin in Cornwall had been the right one.

Sir Francis and Amy Morstan, with their six-year-old daughter Barbara, would be eager to entertain her, she had been assured by her mother. And her father had reminded her that Amy had just lost a baby, the long-awaited heir, and Jenny could forget her own troubles by comforting her cousin. As usual her father had made her feel a bit ashamed, for losing a betrothed in no way compared with losing a baby.

As the coach put the last miles of Bodmin Moor behind them without further incident, the sun came out and dappled the landscape. A good omen, Jenny felt, as they rode toward Truro.

Chapter Two

Dusk was just beginning to fall over the ancient medieval town of Truro as Sir Henry's coach lumbered over the cobblestones of Lemon Street and came to rest in the courtyard of the King's Head. Jenny, accustomed to her small village and having no experience of larger towns except for a few visits to Bath, was agog at the sight of the bustling inn, a waystop for many travelers en route from the West Country to London. As Sir Henry's weary horses and equipage drew up, Jenny peered wide-eyed from the window, as curious as Polly at the sight of the variety of carriages, curricles, phaetons, barouches, landaus, and the huge mailcoach, all with drivers bawling commands to the bustling hostlers. Determined not to show her timidity, Jenny accepted John's hand as he helped her down from the carriage and thanked him for his care on the drive.

"Now, miss, Sir Henry bespoke a private parlor for you, and you had bests repair there soonest. 'Tis no place for a young lady here with all these jackanapes about. I understand there has been a mill nearby and all the swells in town for the occasion, some of them a bit bosky," he warned, conscious of his charge and her vulnerability.

Indeed, there did appear to be an inordinate amount of young bucks and gallants roistering about and they were not slow to notice Jenny as she drew her cloak about her and hurried, under John's protection, into the inn. But the burly coachman served as an intimidating guardian, and with Polly scurrying behind her it was obvious that Jenny was well chaperoned. Within moments she and Polly had been ushered into a neat bedroom overlooking the back of the inn, away from the tumultuous street scene. It appeared, though, they would be well advised to keep to their chamber for the sounds of celebrating, clinking tankards, loud voices, and singing drifted upwards from the taproom.

Having repaired the ravages of the journey with Polly's help, Jenny felt hungry. She set out to discover the reserved private parlor. Stopping a hurrying maid she asked for directions and was directed to a parlor on the first floor. As Jenny entered the room, she was surprised she was not alone, for a gentleman rose from beside the fire and drawled wryly, "I don't believe I requested your company, my dear, but now that you are here I cannot be so rude as to turn you away."

Obviously he did not recognize her from their encounter on Bodmin Moor, but she could not mistake the arrogant careless pose, nor the rather insulting glance he gave her.

Jenny's chin went up haughtily. Not for a moment

would she appear intimidated by this imperious man, for a gentleman he could not be and address her so. "I beg your pardon, sir, I seem to have mistaken the room." She continued in what she felt was her most dignified tone, "I believe our coaches met on the highway, and even then I thought your manner rather insolent." As she turned to leave, he crossed to her and laid a hand on her arm. "Oh, come now, don't take offense. I was mistaken for the nonce. I should not have impugned your motive. Obviously you are the most circumspect of young ladies, although maybe not long out of the schoolroom," he teased and smiled at her, his striking deep blue eyes crinkling at the corners.

Jenny had to admit he was quite the most handsome and elegant gentleman in his dark coat, linen cravat, and gleaming top boots, although there was a half-defiant air to the suntanned face beneath a shock of black hair. He just might be the type of man who would dare all and let the consequences fall where they may. A dangerous man, she felt, and one she had best escape as soon as possible. But there was a compelling quality to his smile and her best resolutions were weakened under the force of his persuasive tongue.

"If I promise to behave with the strictest propriety, would you dine with me? I fear I have wrested the last private parlor here and I suspect the landlord has given me the very one he should have reserved for you. So you see, it is my duty to act as your host," he explained outrageously.

Jenny, aware of his fallacious argument, knew she should have made her apologies and retired, but she could not resist the challenge in those blue eyes. And feeling a bit reckless and forward she accepted his invitation.

"Very well, sir. I do want my dinner and I believe I will have a much better one if you order it," she said simply, causing the gentleman to arch one eyebrow in surprise at the artless agreement. Not so would most of the ladies of his acquaintance have replied to his invitation. At first he had thought his fair intruder was no better than she should be, but on closer examination his experienced eye saw that she was indeed a lady, although a rather innocent one and very young, not his usual style. Still, he was bored and restless and perhaps she would offer some novelty of conversation which would amuse him. And they were travelers not apt to meet again, although the Earl of Trevarris had little difficulty in dealing ruthlessly with importunate women when he tired of their favors.

Escorting her to a supper table laid by the fire, he placed her in the chair and bowed extravagantly over her hand. "Let me introduce myself. Piers St. Robyns, at your service," he said, deciding she had no need to hear his title, which often had an unwelcome effect on chance-met acquaintances.

"I am Jennifer Elinor Beatrice Dryden, from Tidmouth in Wiltshire, where my father is the vicar," she blurted out, determined to let him know of the very respectable background from which she hailed. If she was prepared to behave in this improper fashion she must at least assure the gentleman of her credentials.

"Jennifer Elinor Beatrice . . . what a mouthful of

names for such a young lady. And what are you called at the vicarage? I know, you must be Jenny, and I shall call you that. Miss Dryden sounds much too formal for this impromptu and delightful rendezvous," he replied, gazing at her with a wicked glint in his eyes. "You may call me Piers," he added graciously.

Jenny, a little startled at the sudden intimate direction in which their new acquaintanceship was moving began, "I am not sure . . ."

"My dear Jenny, I have been thoroughly warned and I can assure you I will not forget the shadow of the vicarage which looms over us, protecting you from any evil designs I may have." He arose before she could protest and opened the door to shout for the landlord. Returning to the fire he looked down at her quizzically. "If you are going to flee, now is the time, before I order dinner," he mocked, daring her to take advantage of his offer.

But Jenny had decided to be rash. She could not resist a dare and, after all, no one would know she had behaved so recklessly. Father, Mother, Harry were far distant. Her face darkened when she remembered she no longer owed Harry her allegiance. She was quite free to flirt with other gentlemen if the mood took her, although she thought Piers St. Robyns was not one with which to be trifled.

"Now, what have I done already to earn such a frown of disapproval, Jenny? I promise you that I will behave with the most genteel propriety if you will dine with me," he pleaded humbly, which did not deceive Jenny for a minute.

"I doubt very much if you ever behave in such a

fustian manner," she admonished him, but made no move to escape. "And it is not your antics which brought about my frown, just a matter in my past," she said with what she hoped was a blasé air. She did not like being taken for a flat, country innocent who did not know how to go on.

If Piers St. Robyns was amused, he was wise enough not to show it. "Do I detect an unhappy romance, Jenny? You do not appear to be the kind of ninny who would fall into a decline over some cad's rejection. Not that I can see any young man rejecting you," he added gallantly.

Before Jenny could protest or explain, they were interrupted by the innkeeper, who knew the quality of his distinguished guest and had decided that a heavy tip would reward his personal service. If he was surprised to find the earl of Trevarris dining with the new arrival, he quickly masked the smirk on his face under the earl's admonitory glance.

"Miss Dryden has kindly consented to dine with me, Manvers, and you must come up with a splendid repast to honor the occasion."

"Of course, my lord. We have some tender pigeons and some fine jellies my wife has just concocted, the very thing," the landlord replied, not realizing he had confirmed Jenny's suspicion that this was no usual gentleman to whom she had trusted herself. She had little experience with peers of the realm, but she suspected few of them had the address and the sophistication of her new acquaintance. She must be on her guard.

The landlord bowed himself out and Piers,

ignoring the reference to his title, urged Jenny to tell him of her recent disillusionment.

"Now come, Jenny, you have intrigued me. Tell me about this blighted romance. The man must have been not only a cad, but amazingly foolish, some bucolic youth with no appreciation of your obvious qualities," Piers teased, quite enjoying this unexpected fillip to the evening which had banished his ennui.

"Well, Harry is certainly not a cad, just a very sweet, easily influenced young man. Besides, some of the fault was mine." Before she knew what inspired her, she plunged into a recital of her engagement, Amelia's conduct, and the elopement which had left her without a fiancé. Piers was gratifyingly receptive and sympathetic.

Privately he thought the young man had behaved foolishly to abandon such a charming girl for an ambitious hussy, but did not make the mistake of airing his views. "So that is why you have fled the sanctuary of the vicarage," he concluded, pouring some lemonade into her glass, for he doubted Jenny was accustomed to the fine claret he was enjoying and it was not part of his plan to befuddle her.

As the evening wore on Piers found himself enchanted with her naiveté and honesty. They were both rare commodities in the fashionable world of which he was a notable member. "And where are you escaping to?"

Jenny, aware that she had lowered her defenses and confided in a stranger, although he did not seem such to her now, had enough sense not to give her destination. It was all very well to enjoy this interlude, but she had no intention of ever meeting with this unusual gentleman again.

"Oh, I am off for an extended stay with a cousin. Do you live in London, sir?" she asked, determined she would learn something of her new companion.

"I spend a great deal of time there. As you might have suspected, I came to Truro to attend this mill, having regrettable taste for fisticuffs which must disgust you," he temporized, equally unwilling to tell her his true direction. After all, they were mere passengers, temporarily thrown together. He did not think it would be wise to pursue the brief acquaintance, considering what lay in store for him.

Jenny, sensing his withdrawal, quickly engaged him to tell her of London. He was a fascinating raconteur and the time sped by.

Suddenly she was recalled to the late hour and the impropriety of sitting with a strange man, exciting though the encounter had been. Giving a sigh of regret, she rose and thanked him prettily. "You have been most kind and forebearing to entertain me so well, sir, but I must retire now. We will be making an early start in the morning. Thank you for your hospitality."

But Piers, who had been dipping deep into the claret, was not about to let the evening end so tamely. If she had been a different type of girl, he would have tried to involve her more closely, eventually luring her into his bed. But realizing that would be a shabby recompense for her generous friendship, he desisted. Still, she should have some warmer expression of his gratitude.

"The thanks are all on my side, my dear. This has been an unexpectedly delightful evening. Since it is doubtful we will meet again, let me give you an experience to compare to your Harry's undoubtedly callow lovemaking," he drawled, and before she could protest he had drawn her into his arms and kissed her gently. At least the kiss had intended to be gentle and brief, but the feel of her quivering lips beneath his stirred his devil. As she responded, the kiss deepened, becoming hard and masterful. Jenny, surprised at her own warmth, for Harry had never evoked such a reaction, finally tore herself from his arms, blushing with mortification at her response. Of what had she been thinking? Now he would indeed think her the light-minded female not to have struggled and withstood his practiced embrace.

"That was unfair, sir, and unwarranted. But perhaps you thought I invited it by accepting your company. If so, believe me, it was not my intention and you had no right—" Jenny broke off in embarrassed confusion and ran from the room before he could offer any apology or explanation.

"Damn," he cursed. He had not meant to behave in such a boorish fashion, but she had been exceptionally appealing. Not his usual taste, but provocative in an entirely unfledged manner which intrigued him. He had not meant to insult her, but to introduce her to a taste of passion. He doubted if the faithless Harry had ever roused her to more than a few tepid blushes.

Well, she would soon forget the stranger who had taken such liberties. For his part, he had far more important concerns to engage his interest.

Chapter Three

Despite the dramatic conclusion of her evening with Piers St. Robyns, Jenny had not lain awake brooding over her behavior, which she knew her parents would have condemned. As she ate her breakfast alone, she wondered at her blithe acceptance of the encounter. She really had acted in a most wanton fashion, but the climax to the unusual escapade had not left her bemused. Instead, as she tucked into the shirred eggs and ham with a healthy appetite, she was surprised to realize Piers St. Robyns's kiss had soothed some of the feelings bruised by Harry's treatment. Shocking she knew it was to find another man's attentions so flattering, that was the result; she had to accept that she had invited his intimacies by consenting to dine with him so privately. Obviously she would not be embarrassed by any further meetings, for she had not observed him in the premises this morning. She could consider last evening as a unique experience, not to be repeated. She would not forget it, perhaps, but it should be relegated to the past, soon to be superceded by more important events.

Jenny noticed that Cornwall's capricious weather had decided to welcome her with one of its balmiest April days. As she stepped into the coach for the last brief portion of her journey, John informed her they should be in Trevarris by midafternoon, a most convenient hour for her cousin to receive her.

Jenny wondered if Amy had changed since their last meeting some years before. Jenny had been a schoolgirl, impressed with her more worldly relation who had enjoyed a Bath season and had captured a wealthy Cornish gentleman, Sir Francis Morstan. Amy and her husband had paid a brief visit to the Wiltshire vicarage en route to London a few years later, and Jenny recalled their small daughter, Barbara, with more clarity than the little girl's parents. Amy had not appeared the type to settle down contentedly in an obscure corner of the kingdom. She no doubt preferred the fashionable environs of Bath or London where she could shine, for Jenny remembered Amy had been what the wags called an Incomparable, a beauty of outstanding merit.

Well, she would have to contain her impatience at what awaited her at journey's end. With youthful optimisim she expected the best and the day rewarded her by displaying its brightest face. She watched the wild scenery from the window, finally lowering the sash to catch a whiff of salt breezes, for they were but a few miles from the sea.

They passed through Redruth, center of the tinners. Cornish miners had been streaming the ore from the nearby rockface since Roman times. Then they moved over the Hayle and across the towans, that peculiar wasteland of sand and stiff-stemmed reeds, and hence into Penzance, Cornwall's largest town.

A brisk breeze met her as she descended from the coach. Away to the west she could glimpse the Scilly Isles across a blue but turbulent sea. John escorted her into the imposing hostelry on the front where she would have luncheon. She found her appetite was ravenous. How horrid to be cooped up in a stuffy coach on such a glorious day, she reflected. Jenny longed to wander along the seafront and examine the tropical growth, for she had heard Penzance, although on first sight it seemed prosaic enough, had some imposing buildings and, hidden behind the facades of the esplanade, some notable gardens. Perhaps she could prevail upon her cousin to escort her on a lengthier visit.

After a satisfying meal, she was about to regain her coach when she was almost overset by a tall officer in his red regimentals just entering the inn. His whirlwind approach halted with effort just short of knocking her sideways and startled them both. Raising his busby he bowed in apology, saying, "So sorry, ma'am. I am a careless fellow not to see you. I hope I have caused you no harm," obviously unnerved by the encounter, although Jenny had come to no harm.

"That's quite all right, sir." Jenny accepted his excuses with a charming smile. Really, she was having the oddest meetings with handsome gentlemen. The tall officer, and she could not guess his rank, was indeed a striking figure, with a suntanned open face, kind gray eyes, and light brown hair worn *en brosse.* She realized she was staring and averted her eyes in some confusion as he made no effort to continue on his way. He appeared equally bemused by the sight of a young girl with a fetching smile and chestnut curls peeking beneath an unexceptional straw bonnet. Then, recollecting his manners, he bowed again and went on his way.

Jenny, hopping agilely into the coach and settling back as John pulled up the steps, chuckled aloud. Really, attractive men seemed to abound in Cornwall, for she had met two likely specimens within twenty-four hours. Her mother would nod sagely as if to say that her insistence on this visit would expose Jenny to various opportunities not available in Tidmouth. If by opportunities she meant matchmaking, Jenny found the obvious admiration from both her dinner companion the night before and the handsome officer flattering, but she did not echo her mother's hope that she would find a permanent mate. Now that she had left the shelter of the vicarage behind, she found herself anticipating freedom—from convention, from her established routine, from the kindly if inquisitive interest of the villagers—quite a tonic.

Cornwall was proving to be most exciting, and as the coach rolled sedately away from Penzance, she saw rising to the south the dominating moated walls of St. Michael's Mount, the former Benedictine abbey now the seat of a noble family. Certainly Wiltshire had no such romantic castles set in a sparkling sea.

However, as they passed through the small fishing

village of Mousehole, where the houses clung precariously to the hillside rising steeply from the quay, Jenny's contented mood began to darken. Apprehension deepened with every mile that drew her closer to Trevarris. Would Amy truly welcome her? Amy's letter had been enthusiastic, pleading the company of her cousin in this troubled period of her life. But she might have regretted her warm offer of hospitality. Amy might find they had little in common, and the intrusion of a stranger, even if a relative, a burden on her marriage.

And how could Jenny help her cousin? She knew nothing of childbirth, the sorry experience of losing a baby, the strains which such a tragedy could put on a happy marriage. She knew little of marriage either, except for the wholesome example of her parents, and she sensed theirs was an unusual union. She was not so innocent that she did not realize that many couples wed for other reasons than love and companionship. And how taxing to the most amiable of characters to be tied inextricably to a mate one found boring, indifferent, insensitive, even cruel. How miserable to be the lover and the unloved, she thought.

But really, there was no reason to suspect that all was not well in the Morstan household, except that she had felt unease and unhappiness in Amy's letter. Well, she must do her best to adapt to whatever she found, to take some of the strains and fatigues from her cousin's shoulder, to be a companion to six-year-old Barbara and so relieve her mother. Jenny was a firm believer that moping produced little good and that self-pity was unrewarding. She had spent enough time considering her own plight. It was now her duty to think of others. Her father would say that brought its own lightening of heart.

As the coach rolled through the hamlet of Trevarris, where several of the villagers eyed it with interest, she determined to put aside her recent personal troubles, behave in a model fashion toward her relations, and enjoy herself, too.

Pencairn House loomed before her, approached by a long drive edged with banks of rhododendrons and hydrangeas, a square gray mass in the simple Palladian style, large but not overpowering, a distinguished but not noble house. The sea was some miles distant and Jenny wondered at the choice of site, not realizing that the Cornish gentry preferred protected shelter to breathtaking views, harsh winds, and mists that swirled in from the Channel. Eager to meet Amy and Sir Francis, she hopped nimbly from the coach, relieved to have put the rigors of the journey behind her. Her arrival was hailed by a jolly couple, husband and wife, who were, she presumed, the housekeeper and butler.

"Good afternoon, miss. Delighted we are to see you, having expected you for some time now. Milady was called out and regrets not being here to welcome you, but little Babs is all agog to meet her cousin. If you will come this way," the woman indicated, then stopped suddenly. "Lawks amercy, what am I thinking, not introducing ourselves? I am Mrs. Peabody and this is my husband, housekeeper and butler to the Morstans we are. But come now, I must not keep you standing in the hall. The men will see to the cases, and Peabody," she said, addressing her husband smartly, "take the coachman around to the stables and see to his comfort and the horses."

Obviously Mrs. Peabody, with her starched petticoats and keys of office dangling from her ample waist, was the dominant force in this pair, and she looked extremely capable as well as good-humored, with her black-button eyes and graying hair caught back in a tight knob. Jenny felt welcomed although she wondered at Cousin Amy's absence. Surely she might have stayed home to greet her, but, of course, it could have been an emergency which prevented her. Jenny was no stranger to village crises.

Mrs. Peabody, conscious that her mistress had behaved with a certain lack of courtesy, was effusive in her efforts to make Jenny feel at home. Ushering her into the hall, a great square maple-paneled room with a rococo ceiling, she preceded Jenny up the fine balustraded stairs, the walls lined with what Jenny took to be family portraits. At the top was an excellent painting of Sir Francis Morstan, in the Joshua Reynolds manner, depicted in his hunting clothes with a spaniel at his feet. Jenny stopped for a moment to renew her memory, very vague, of her host. Thin features under a high brow and corn silk blond hair held a certain arrogance; his thin lips were drawn tightly together. A handsome man but not a comfortable one was her assessment.

Stopping to look at the portrait she could not resist asking, "Is there a companion portrait of my cousin, Lady Marston?" she asked, hoping to lure the housekeeper into some friendly confidences, for she sensed the lady was the garrulous type.

"Oh, yes, indeed, a lovely picture. It hangs over the

fireplace in the drawing room," Mrs. Peabody said, turning to the right at the top of the stairway. "Milady is truly worthy of any painter's brush."

"I remember her as particularly beautiful," Jenny agreed. Beautiful, but not kind, she recalled, and wondered if her cousin would patronize her. She then decided that she would not prejudge Amy just because she had not bothered to stay at home to welcome her. She smiled cheerfully at the housekeeper. Mrs. Peabody threw open a door some way down the hall and indicated that Jenny should enter. It was a large chamber, the walls painted a soft pink. A pastel Aubusson rug covered the floor and the Adam-styled furniture was covered in rose and pale green fine glazed cotton. Altogether a charming room. Crossing to the wide-sashed windows, Jenny looked south over an Italiante garden. Really, it was a most luxurious residence. Obviously Sir Francis lived in great style, although in the wilds of the country.

"Quite lovely, Mrs. Peabody. And what gorgeous flowers," Jenny approved.

"From our own hothouses, miss. I arranged them and I rather pride myself on my touch," the housekeep replied gratefully, for she did not always receive such enthusiastic thanks for her efforts. "I will send up your maid with some water and towels. No doubt you would like to rest a bit before tea. Travel is so tiring, I think. And both Sir Francis and Lady Morstan will be back for tea, I am sure," she assured Jenny anxiously.

"That will be fine, Mrs. Peabody. Thank you for all your trouble. I can see you have gone to a deal of work to prepare for me. Will you see that Polly has proper accommodation? She is from our village and a stranger to a house such as this," Jenny confided, not mentioning that she herself was rather over-awed. Even Sir Henry Ruston's manor house did not aspire to this state of stylish comfort.

Mrs. Peabody agreed to take Polly in hand, pleased that their new guest was such a considerate girl. She would give a good report of her in the servants' hall. With assurances that Jenny must ring if she needed further service, Mrs. Peabody withdrew, leaving Jenny to wonder how she would adapt to this luxurious standard. Impressed, despite her intention to take it all in a matter-of-fact manner, she wondered what this new life into which she had been casually drawn would demand of her. Her speculations were interrupted by Polly with the promised towels and hot water, trailed by a smart liveried footman with Jenny's cases.

After the man had deposited his burdens and bowed himself politely out, the abigail, round eyed and excited, bustled about assisting Jenny, who found her ministrations less than helpful, so distracted was the poor girl.

"Oh, Miss Jenny, it's ever such a grand place. There are seven servants in the hall besides those Peabodys. I've never see so fine a kitchen and so starched up are the servants you would think they were all nobs themselves. But I expect I could settle," she said ingenuously. Her intention of returning home with the coach was obviously fading under the prospect of these novel experiences.

"Well, Polly, you must do as you think best. John

will be going back to Wiltshire within the week, after the horses are rested, so you have some time to decide. No, no, I can arrange my hair myself, no need for you to bother," Jenny insisted, unused to such service.

"But miss, I am to be your maid, so I must learn to do all these things. You must tell me how to go on. I would not want to disgrace you," Polly pleaded, determined to learn her new role, a determination Jenny could not help admiring, thinking she would do well to emulate Polly's enthusiasm.

"We will just have to learn together, Polly, for I, too, am unused to such luxury. That will do for now, I think. I must meet my cousins for tea, and you can get on with the unpacking. There seems to be a great deal of space in the wardrobe for my meager store of gowns," she advised, giving a final look at her image in the cheval mirror, an elegant piece of furniture much finer than anything that graced her vicarage bedroom. She stared at herself with dissatisfaction, noting that her cream muslin frock and green spencer was far from the latest mode. Oh well, she was a country cousin and should remain so.

Jenny stood irresolute at the top of the stairs, wondering where she would find the drawing room, but before she could descend she heard a small voice asking, "Are you my Cousin Jenny, come to play with me?" Then an equally small hand tugged at her skirt.

Jenny, turning around, found herself staring at a round young face with a sprinkle of freckles across a snub nose, button brown eyes, and golden brown hair cut squarely across front and back, making the owner look more like a Dutch doll than the six year old she was.

"You must be my cousin Barbara and, yes, I have come to play with you. I hope we will be fast friends." Jenny smiled at the little one who returned her smile with a wide rather doubtful stare.

"Mama says I shouldn't bother you, as you are suffering from a disappointment in love and must not be worried. I quite understand because I have suffered from a disappointment in love, too," she confided simply, as if this were a not abnormal state of affairs and as fellow sufferers they would be bound together in mutual convalescence.

Jenny, inwardly wondering why Amy had told her small daughter such a tale, felt some disgust that she had been depicted as a swooning heroine in a gothic novel. "You will not bother me, and any disappointment I suffered has now disappeared on meeting such a delightful person as yourself. It is Barbara isn't it?" she asked gently, wondering what this little girl's disappointment in love meant.

"You may call me Babs—everyone does—although Mama thinks it's common. It's sometimes hard to please Mama. I think I am her disappointment. She wanted a son, you know, and the new baby died. But Papa doesn't seem to mind as much. Odd, really, because men should prefer sons, I think," she said with an absurd adult air of making allowances for the vagaries of parents.

"Not at all. My father prefers girls, he tells me, although he is very fond of Richard, my brother, too. Parents should not have favorites. It's very unfair," Jenny informed Babs gravely. She rather wondered at this odd conversation, so revealing and in a way so sad.

"Life is apt to be unfair I've found," Babs informed her. "When Johnny Granthum and I fell into the ornamental fish pond where we had been expressly told not to play, Mama said I was an impossible child, and said no tea that day—and it was strawberry jam day, too—and Johnny had no punishment at all. But that may be because he has no papa and his mother is a bit silly about him. She rubbed oil of camphor on his chest, though, and made him stay in bed for two days."

"I would say Johnny had the worst of it, although it is too bad you had to miss the strawberry jam," Jenny agreed, entering into the spirit of the matter. "And perhaps I will miss the strawberry jam today, if I am late for tea. Could you tell me where the drawing room is?"

"Through the double doors to the right of the stairs. I don't think this is strawberry jam day, even in the drawing room, and here comes Nurse for me. I will have horrid bread and butter and no cakes for tea. You are the fortunate one," Babs informed her readily. "See, Nursie, here is my cousin come to play with me. Tomorrow she must have tea in the nursery," Babs said, determined to brook no opposition.

"Good afternoon, miss. Miss Barbara, you must mind your manners. I am sure we will be pleased to entertain Miss Dryden at any time, but now come along and don't keep the lady waiting. Sir Francis and Lady Morstan will be wondering what has happened to her, with you holding her up with your chattering." Jenny did not really warm to this tall, spare custodian of Babs, who looked a rather strict type, not able or willing to make up the "the disappointment in love" that Babs claimed to suffer from her mama. Giving a friendly nod to this personage, who obviously stood on her dignity, Jenny bid Babs farewell, promising to see a great deal of her on the morrow.

Entering the drawing room, a vast chamber with more Adam-styled furniture and flowered damask curtains, Jenny's eyes were drawn immediately to the huge portrait over the fireplace. So entranced was she by the sight of Amy Morstan painted in a flowing white gown, holding a blue-ribboned bonnet and leaning against a Grecian pillar that she did not notice much else in the room. Indeed, if this was a faithful depiction of Amy Morstan she was a beautiful woman with an ethereal classic beauty that was so revered. Blond ringlets cascaded about a flawless high-boned face, accenting blue eyes which gazed wide-eyed above a wistfully smiling sculptured mouth. Jenny was much struck by the portrait and the sitter.

"An uncommonly good likeness. Lawrence did it soon after we were married. Impressive, what?" The man who asked the question had risen at Jenny's entrance, but she had been so taken with the portrait she had not seen him immediately. Blushing a bit at her gaucherie, she dropped a short curtsey.

"Yes, it's most striking. You must be Sir Francis. I am afraid you don't remember me but you are very kind to invite me," she rushed, aware that she sounded countrified and unversed in proper manners. The combination, however, of the portrait and Sir

Francis's sudden appearance had set her all at sixes and sevens. He was as impressive in his way as the picture of his wife, looking just like his portrait on the stairs. Before she knew what she was about Jenny blurted out, "You should have your portrait in here, too, Sir Francis. Such a handsome pair."

"I am afraid my wife would not take kindly to the notion," he replied ironically, his thin lips curling a bit. Oh, dear, Jenny thought, I have said the wrong thing, but how was I to know there are turbulent domestic undercurrents here. But before she could venture anymore injudicious remarks, Sir Francis took the initiative.

"Do sit down and let us renew our acquaintance. I cannot think what is keeping Amy. Not at all nice of her to be absent for your arrival. I take it you had a pleasant journey," he asked in that polite social tone which Jenny believed masked complete indifference to whether she had enjoyed her travels or not. Sir Francis certainly looked the role of the sophisticated man of the world, more at home in London than in the depths of Cornwall. She supposed he lived here because of the inheritance, and he certainly had made no sacrifices in the elegance of his surroundings. Before she could answer his question, the door opened and Amy Morstan glided into the room, coming up to Jenny, pressing a scented smooth cheek against hers, and begging for forgiveness.

"Most horrid of me to abandon you so, dear Jenny. But I was called down to the village by an old woman who was in service to the Morstans for a donkey's age. You remember Mary Polter, Francis? I simply had to go. I know you understand these matters, having lived in a village and being a vicar's daughter," she explained merrily.

Shrewdly Jenny decided that Amy's pretty ways smoothed her path through life very successfully. Few women and certainly only the most determined misogynist among the males could deny the charming woman whatever she requested. In the years since Jenny had last met her she had grown even more lovely, if that were possible, and certainly her manner could not be faulted. She flutterd about Jenny, ringing for tea, pressing questions about her parents and Wiltshire, and tactfully not referring to Jenny's recent "disappointment in love," as Babs had called it.

Stemming Amy's chatter, Jenny mentioned having met her daughter and how much she had enjoyed her. This comment elicted the only smile yet from Sir Francis. Certainly his greeting to his wife had lacked warmth.

"She is a minx, but I find her conversation fascinating," Sir Francis admitted, winning Jenny's approbation. Whatever his other faults, there was no doubt that he loved his daughter.

"She is such a chatterbox. You must not let her bore you with her demands, Jenny. Children of her age can be so wearying with their questions," Amy protested somewhat languidly, ignoring Sir Francis. "But we are so pleased to have you here, just what we need to relieve the doldrums in this wilderness. I do miss London," she sighed.

"You insisted that we spend the summer season here, my dear, and you know I cannot be away from my responsibilities for more than a few weeks," Sir Francis insisted gently, as if reminding his wife that their absence from London was not entirely his choice.

"Francis has to keep an eye on those ghastly mines, you see, Jenny. So tedious, we will not talk of them, but of what jollities we can arrange to make your visit more exciting. We must have a dinner party to introduce you to the local notables, not that there are a great many, but still . . ." she said vaguely, as if already bored with the idea.

"Certainly we must see that Jenny meets our neighbors," Sir Francis responded, and then added, "but I understand she likes country pursuits, and we have some lovely walks and dramatic countryside."

After a brief, uneasy silence, he asked, "Do you ride, Jenny?"

"Of course. I love it above all things," Jenny said hastily. She did hope she could enjoy some good gallops, for it appeared she would need this form of healthy escape from a household she already sensed had more than its share of trouble. She wished to offer whatever help she could, but since she did not yet understand where the problem lay she must walk warily. Perhaps the death of the longed-for son had altered realations between the Morstans, but Jenny wondered if perhaps they should be trying to comfort one another, not retreating into snideness.

Amy then suggested that they must set a date for the dinner. "We are especially fortunate that the Earl of Trevarris is in residence. Not that he will accept. He's quite aloof from the local affairs, prefers London, and when he comes here to Arthmore he usually brings a house party. But I will certainly invite him for next Saturday. Will that be acceptable to you, Francis?" she asked tentatively, eyeing her husband with a look Jenny could not interpret.

"By all means, my dear. We must entertain Jenny in a proper fashion, althought I am not sure Trevarris is quite the thing. The man has a formidable reputation with the ladies," he explained in an aside to Jenny, attempting a jocular air that gave every indication of being forced.

"Please don't go to any trouble for me. I am quite content to explore the neighborhood on my own. I am not accustomed to fashionable entertainments," she confided simply.

"Well, you should have the opportunity, Jenny," Amy insisted. "We have quite a social group: the Pencrists and her cousin, Henri d'Aubisson, Major Bosworth from Penzance and some of his junior officers, and the Herrons, brother and sister. He's our vicar, but young and eager."

And so the date was established and the talk continued on a rather restrained level about family matters, Richard's ship, her parents' parochial duties, and other mundane matters. Jenny hoped when they had settled down together in the days ahead, the Morstans would relax and treat her less as a guest and more as a member of the family.

Amy and Sir Francis treated one another with exquisite politeness and were obviously prepared to put themselves out to entertain Jenny as best they might, but she was not easy about their relationship. How difficult marriage was after the first romantic days. She was just as well out of it, for no doubt if she had married Harry, they, too, would have encountered shoals. Well, if she wished to be a peacemaker, an intermediary, she would have to go carefully. It was not a role she fancied, nor one with which she had any experience. Until now, she realized, she had led a very sheltered existence, the subtler shades of marital intimacy a mystery to her. Still, there was the fetching Barbara, who needed a friend, and here she had every confidence she would succeed.

Chapter Four

Her expectations about young Barbara were fulfilled in the days that followed. A solitary child who had few playmates in the area, she welcomed Jenny with enthusiasm and introduced her older companion to all her favorite haunts. In the morning Babs did lessons with Robert Herron, the young vicar to whom Amy had referred. Jenny found him friendly and dedicated, a rather stocky young man with a rubicund face. He possessed a somewhat scholarly air, much like several of her father's curates.

His sister, Evelyn, was not so forthcoming, expressing much of the native Cornish restraint toward strangers. Her unprepossessing appearance and astrigent nature made her rather unpopular among her brother's parishioners. Overly tall and lanky, with mousy brown hair scraped into a bun, she did nothing to improve on the rather meager store of looks nature had given her. It was her manner, however, which Jenny found puzzling, but she treated Evelyn Herron with a cheerful nonchalance which ignored her small discourtesies, thereby further exacerbating the situation.

That morning she found Miss Herron particularly exasperating when she delivered Babs for her lesson. It was a small chore she had willingly accepted and thoroughly enjoyed, for Babs had a great deal to say as she bounced along by Jenny's side on the mile or so to the village.

Jenny greeted the vicar, who was standing by the front gate, and urged Babs to abandon her efforts to win a holiday, although she could hardly blame the sprite for wanting an excuse to ignore her lessons. It was a bright April morning, mild and windless, a day to roam the fields and shore, not sit poring over sums and geography. Robert Herron agreed with her but told Babs affectionately that she must endure a little suffering to become an educated young lady. Babs received this teasing homily with an indignant sniff, but, brought up by Jenny, apologized prettily.

Jenny, leaning casually on the gate and in no hurry to resume her rambles, asked the vicar about a gravestone she had glimpsed on a previous visit to the churchyard. He eagerly expounded on his hobby, the history of the parish. Babs, content to delay her lessons as long as possible, wandered off to investigate a finch's nest in a nearby tree, leaving the adults alone.

However, Evelyn Herron, spying the tête à tête from the drawing-room window, was not about to allow this situation to continue. Jenny looked far too comely in her cream muslin frock with the cherry ribbons which accented the russet gleam in her curls that were wildly dancing in the April breeze. She hurried down the path, interrupting the two enjoying their idle chat.

"Robert, you must not dally here when Barbara is waiting for her lessons. And you have to call on Eliza Pendeen shortly. I am sure Miss Dryden, who understands the pressing nature of a vicar's calling, would not want to keep you from your duties," she admonished, implying just the opposite, giving Jenny a curt nod of greeting.

Jenny, a bit surprised at Miss Herron's brusqueness but determined not to take offense, agreed. "So sorry, Vicar, to delay you. I must plead the beauty of the day, which seduces me from businesslike concerns." Then turning to Evelyn with a friendly smile she asked, "Perhaps I could help you with the flowers in the church today. My father believes I arrange the altar displays with a certain talent, but then he is prejudiced," she claimed disarmingly. But Evelyn was not to be cajoled.

"We have a very efficient altar guild, Miss Dryden, and I would not want to offend the ladies by introducing a stranger to show them up," she replied disagreeably. But Robert Herron would have none of that.

"It is very kind of Miss Dryden to offer. Willing hands are always welcome. I am sure, Evelyn, that you will accept her assistance." He spoke pleasantly, but the look he turned on his sister was stern. Why did Evelyn behave in such a churlish fashion? he mused. Her jealousy was becoming ridiculous.

Aware that she had perhaps gone too far Evelyn temporized. "Of course. I did not want to put a burden on Miss Dryden. She seems to be enjoying her holiday and must be happy to escape from the parish cares of Wiltshire. Will you be making a long stay with your cousins, Miss Dryden?" she asked, hoping to hear Jenny was a bird of passage and would not cause her further concern.

But Jenny, usually amiable, had endured enough of Miss Herron's sly innuendos. "I have no idea. It's most unkind of you to suggest that I be off so soon. I have been here barely a week."

"I am sure you miss Wiltshire, despite your recent disappointment," Miss Herron persisted.

Jenny bit back the indignant words which trembled on her lips. Really, Evelyn Herron had a very unpleasant manner. Jenny hoped the woman's allusion to Jenny's recent trial would not be bruited about the country. Calling to Babs to return from the finch's nest, she bid the couple a brief farewell and continued on her way.

Waiting until she was out of earshot, Robert Herron, normally able to ignore his sister's vinegary manner, said to her with some asperity, "Really, Evelyn, Miss Dryden will think we are the most inhospitable of creatures if you persist in treating her so. Please try to behave in a more seemly manner when next you meet. Miss Dryden is a charming addition to our circle and deserves our friendship. And no good is done by making references to her broken engagement. The man must have been a fool." He then marshaled Babs into his study where he spent a frustrating morning trying to instill the multiplication tables into her resistant mind.

Jenny, wandering down the main street, wondered

why Evelyn Herron was so inimical, causing both Jenny and her brother deep embarrassment by her curt manner. Surely she did not see Jenny as a threat, on the catch for another man since she had lost her fiancé. Jenny found Robert forthcoming and pleasant, eager to offer friendship, unlike his sister and many of the villagers, but she had no designs upon him. Indeed, he was a welcome exception to this closed village whose inhabitants appeared to distrust foreigners.

Looking about her, Jenny conceded there was little in Trevarris to attract outlanders. The humble cottages clung precariously to the hill rising from the rock-bound shore, huddling together for protection against the elements. Most of the householders either worked in the tin mines, some distance away, or fished. She could see the small dories and nets stretched out higgledy-piggledy in the sun. Gulls and ravens swooped over the small harbor, screeching and diving, but there were few natives about. They kept to their homes.

Aside from the village shop, a respectable pub, and the blacksmith's forge, Trevarris boasted little in the way of attractions. Up the hill surrounded by its graveyard and square stone vicarage, the fifteenth-century church dominated the village, a stark, rather forbidding house of worship, sparsely attended as Robert Herron had complained to her.

Artists would no doubt find the scene evocative, crying out for paint or charcoal. Jenny had a certain talent for sketching but she did not favor the usual bucolic vistas of meadow and pond, sylvan glades and stands of wildflowers. Instead, she drew people and animals with a certain flair. She could not often be persuaded to exhibit these portraits outside the family circle because they were rarely flattering to the subject. Farmer Andrews she pictured as a bull goggling at a fetching prize heifer with a rose in his teeth. Her caricature of Hortense Mawes, the church organist and pillar of good works, depicted a rather frustrated spavined horse and was not for public display. Her mother had often warned her that her sketches would get her into trouble, but her father laughed and encouraged her.

Certainly there was a great deal to sketch in Cornwall, and most artists would be inspired, but Jenny's current porfolio held none of these natural marvels. Instead, she had drawn a wicked portrait of Piers St. Robyns looking fierce and haughty in the guise of an impatient tiger, a ferret who definitely resembled Evelyn Herron, and a harrassed woolly bear drawn in her brother's image. Only Babs had received gentle treatment, Jenny trying to capture the endearing little girl as she really was. Jenny was rather ashamed of these portraits, but could not restrain her impulse to depict her new acquaintances as she saw them. She must guard them from curious eyes. Perhaps in Cornwall her small gift could be channeled along traditional lines.

Shaking off a sudden yearning for the comfort of the vicarage, she hesitated, then walked back along the main street and turned into the general store to complete an errand for Amy, a commission which was grudgingly completed by the proprietor, a grizzled elderly man, who eyed Jenny with suspicion. The Cornish, aloof and wary of the English, were living up to their reputation. Jenny, accustomed to the friendly concern of the Tidmouth citizens whom she had known all her life, found her Trevarris reception intimidating. Turning away from the store, she decided to work off her energies and her unease with a bracing ride along the shore, and hurried back to Pencairn House.

Within the hour she had changed into her riding habit, a shabby brown velvet costume which had seen much use. She prevailed upon a groom to saddle a sprightly mare, and was on her way to explore the shoreline, a visit she had promised herself from the moment Francis had escorted her on a tour of the small estate. Sir Francis farmed some of his acres, but his wealth rested in the tin mines which his family had owned for generations, some miles from the village. Amy was apt to disparage the wheal which gave them such a fine income, but Sir Francis, if he was ashamed of the source of his wealth, showed no such reticence. Jenny had heard that the miners were a rough lot, but since the wheal was quite distant from the hamlet, she had little experience of their brutal, coarse, and dangerous life.

In deep thought, she rode toward the shore. Today Cornwall was showing its best side to her, but she had heard tales of the tinners' rebellions, the smugglers' cruel treatment of shipwrecked crews and passengers, the fierce battles during the Civil War when the county had held out for the royal Stuarts long after Cromwell had secured his hold on the rest of the land. The Cornish had long memories and no love for the English.

Too, Jenny was increasingly concerned by the

attitude of the Morstans. Amy appeared distracted and bemused. She spent a great deal of time driving in her carriage on mysterious outings, Sir Francis never accompanying her. Jenny had tried to express her sympathy over the death of their baby to Amy, but had received little response. "I don't want to talk about it, Jenny."

"Surely you could have another child," Jenny offered timidly. Being young and knowing little of these matters, she assumed it must be much like taking a severe toss on a horse. One had to mount up again immediately to show one had not been intimidated. She pondered the metaphor and wondered if it was fitting. Really, she was being callow. How could she possibly understand Amy's distraught air?

But she sensed it was not just the death of the baby which was at the root of her cousin's behavior. She could not fault the welcome which had been extended to her. Both Francis and Amy told her repeatedly how pleased they were to have her, and she and Babs had become fast friends. And most importantly, neither Amy nor her husband referred to the broken engagement, a tactful silence that Jenny much appreciated. Jenny had not yet managed to dismiss her broken engagement from her mind, nor had she been able to forgive Harry and Amelia for treating her so. Her father would continue to be disappointed in her lack of charity, but her pride, if not her heart, was still bruised from the experience.

But Cornwall, so distant from the scene of her humiliation, was working its charm, and Jenny found herself fascinated by the new drama in which she remained an onlooker as yet. Who could remain distressed on such a glorious day? she reproved herself as she galloped her skittish horse down to the beach. The mare picked her way daintily along the shoreline where the waves lapped gently upon the pebbled strand. Jenny had chanced upon a protected cove, shielded on two sides by high rocks, a charming oasis in the hostile rock-lined shore which repelled casual visitors. Here there was little wind and the sun shone diamond bright upon the water, tempting her to dabble in its inviting coolness.

She jumped from the mare and, securing the reins to a convenient tree, hitched up her skirts, tugged off her boots and stockings, then ran to the water's edge. It was cold, but refreshing, and the sun beat down on her shoulders, giving her a feeling of well-being. So absorbed was Jenny by the exercise of running back and forth playing tag with the waves she did not heed the approach of another explorer.

A tall commanding figure, his booted feet apart, stood firmly on the rise above the beach watching her. His expression was both puzzled and forbidding, as he continued to follow Jenny's antics with his hard blue eyes. There was a familiarity to the young girl who had her back turned to him which jogged his memory. Who could she be? Well, whoever she was, a stranger undoubtedly, she had no business trespassing. This was his cove, a treasured spot since boyhood, where he had escaped from the bleakness of Arthmore, and he would not countenance strange females covorting in its seclusion. Especially now, when he had affairs of great moment pending. She certainly was no village lass. He knew them all, and this girl possessed a grace and a carefree abandon which no villager owned. Could she be a gypsy? He had glimpsed them in the area yesterday, even allowed them to camp on the edge of his lands, although the local citizens distrusted and despised them.

He strode down to the cove, making an easy trek of the steep incline. Jenny, suddenly sensing she was not alone, turned and faced him, giving a gasp of surprise, for she recognized him immediately.

"What are you doing here?" she asked, conscious of her disheveled state and aware that he might have been watching her childish frolicking in the sea.

"I might ask the same of you. This is my land and you are trespassing," Piers answered sternly. He had never expected to see his companion of the inn again and yet here she was, bold as brass, demanding what he was doing on his own land!

"Your land. Why, you must be— Oh, no," she gasped.

"Quite right. I am Trevarris. Have you followed me here and now pretend surprise?" he asked scornfully, accustomed to young women seeking him out, but not truly convinced she was of that company.

"Of all the conceited boors!" Jenny came back smartly, her anger overcoming her embarrassment at meeting him again. He appeared to hold no such shame. Could he have forgotten? "I am here visiting my cousins, the Morstans, and if I had any idea this was your land I would never have put a foot on it. I thought it was part of Francis's acreage," she explained indignantly.

"A natural mistake. Our property matches just about here. You may play here as much as you choose, just don't venture around the point. It's rocky and the current is treacherous beyond this idyllic spot. Cornwall is not bounded by halcyon seas, you know. It's a very dangerous place," he said, his warning more stringent than Jenny felt warranted.

Embarrassed by this encounter, having the stiff-necked earl of Trevarris catch her barefoot and behaving like a hoyden, she nodded and walked over to where she had left her boots. Much as she would have liked to have flounced off and left him, she could not depart without her boots. But he forestalled her and picked up the offending footware.

Giving her what she thought was a most unfair and beguiling smile, he coaxed, "Come, Jenny, don't be angry with me. I am sorry if I offended you yet again. We are going to be neighbors—and friends, too, I hope. Trevarris is much too small a community for you to avoid me. In fact, I will be meeting you at your cousin's dinner party next week. Much better to have encountered one another here, and no need to tell Sir Francis and the beautiful Amy of our earlier unconventional first meeting." No need to tell her either that he had originally decided to refuse the dinner before this unexpected meeting.

"No, that would be best, I suppose," Jenny said a bit grudgingly. She did not like admitting he was in the right of it. If she had not forgotten the stranger at the inn, she had managed to dismiss him when he invaded her thoughts with the assurance that she would never see him again. If that caused her any disappointment she firmly squashed the wayward feeling.

"Let me assist you with these boots. Devilish hard to put on yourself, I think." He indicated she sit on a nearby boulder and gave her a slight nudge in the direction.

"There is no need . . ." Jenny began, a bit piqued at being treated like Babs, but seeing he would brook no argument, she subsided with a wry grimace. "Really, you know you are a most arrogant man. Spoiled in the nursery, I suppose. Do you always insist on having your own way?" she asked, aware that while wet and disheveled she could not don the dignity necessary to depress his lord-of-the-manor air.

"Not in the nursery," he replied brusquely, but offered no other explanation as he busied himself with wiping her sandy feet with his handkerchief and deftly restoring her stockings and boots. Then helping her up, he led the way to her mare, chiding her in what she considered an insufferably top-lofty tone. "You really are a most imprudent, rash young woman, tumbling into adventures. You should not be dashing about the countryside without a groom, exploring strange environs. You are asking for trouble."

"Well, if I find it, I will not ask you to extricate me from any peril into which I might tumble, sir," she answered, thoroughly irritated by his manner.

"You might not have a choice," he replied

enigmatically, unperturbed by her testiness. "You didn't on our previous encounter," he unfairly reminded her, enjoying her blush.

"And you, sir, did not behave like a gentleman," she responded tartly, not to be outdone.

"I often don't," he agreed cheerfully. "But come, Jenny, let us cry peace, You do arouse the strangest protective instincts in me, and Cornwall is not Wilshire, where the vicar's daughter is cloaked in the sanctity and propriety of her position," he explained, hoisting her up on her mare with a deft movement that spoke of long practice.

"What could happen to me in this charming village? Although I must say the inhabitants lack the friendly interest of my home. The Cornish seem to resent outsiders," she said, hoping he might explain why this should be. But he was not to be drawn.

"They have their reasons. And it is not just the locals I must caution you about. There are some gypsies camping on the outskirts of the village. They are capable of any villainy," he insisted, privately, though, admiring their way of life.

"We have gypsies in Wiltshire, too, you know. Some people think they are thieving rascals, but I rather like them—so independent and proud," she answered, surprising him yet again.

Handing her the reins as she settled her skirts across the saddle, he looked up at her, suddenly grave. "Do take care, Jenny. I would not want you to suffer any peril." Then, realizing she did not understand why he was warning her, he smiled and bowed in a courtly manner at variance with his rakish grin. "I will look forward to our next encounter, minx, when we will both have to be on our best behavior. Now, be off with you," and he gave her mare a light slap on its rump to speed the parting.

Jenny, trotting up the steep incline to the meadow above the cove, wondered what he had meant by his strange warnings. The earl of Trevarris was an unaccountable man, at times kind and understanding, at others arrogant and demanding. Still, she could not repress a small sigh of satisfaction. She was pleased that she had not seen the last of him, however their future relationship developed.

Chapter Five

Dressing for the dinner party some evenings later, Jenny wondered how the Earl of Trevarris would behave. She wanted to face him looking her best and to that end had chosen from her limited wardrobe her favorite gown, a jonquil silk robe *à l'anglaise* worn open over a white silk petticoat, part of her trousseau which she had never worn before. Probably she would be quite put in the shade by Amy, but she owed it to her hosts to dress to the nines. If she had a sneaking hope that Piers St. Robyns would think her attractive, she jeered at herself for being a ninny. He had not apologized for shabby behavior in Truro, had not even referred to that shocking episode. Probably believed it of little importance. Still, he had been friendly if not effusive when they met at the cove. Like the villagers, the earl was a man who revealed little, and perhaps with good reason.

Of course, she had heard all the tales of smuggling, prevalent even now with England at war with

France. Somehow she doubted that the natives concerned themselves much with decisions made in Whitehall, carrying on their free trading with their Breton counterparts as if no war existed between the two countries. She knew the smuggling existed, but she had heard no mention of it since arriving at Trevarris. Most of the rather apocryphal tales she had heard had not come from the Cornish, but from ill-informed gossips in Wiltshire.

Still, she had little doubt that some such activity continued. Amy, for example, wore gowns of Parisian silk, and the brandy Francis offered to guests, she suspected, had never seen an excise tax. However, it was churlish of her to criticize the customs of the country, to cast aspersions on her cousins who had taken her in. She must try to be charitable toward the local practices. Who was she to judge? Tonight she would be on her best behavior.

It had been some time since she had enjoyed a social occasion. It was at the last dinner party which she had attended as guest of honor, she remembered ruefully, where Amelia Langdon had first flirted with the susceptible Harry. Fortunately the broken engagement and Amelia's perfidy was fast fading from her mind. Obviously she was not suffering from a broken heart, but she had learned a valuable lesson in not accepting events or people without question. Cynical, no doubt, but justified in view of her experience, she concluded shrewdly, not realizing that her natural optimism and good nature made it difficult to take less than positive approach to life.

"You do look a treat, miss," Polly interrupted her

musing, reminding her that she could not stand here philsophizing or she would be late to the point of impoliteness.

"Thank you, Polly. Father would say that vanity is a sin, I guess, but one does want to look one's best when meeting a new cast of characters," Jenny confided winningly. She never stood on ceremony with Polly, for she was finding the abigail a comforting and familiar confidante, a reminder of the home which she missed at times. Polly rewarded her trust with a touching willingness to oblige in all things and a sincere admiration.

"You would never think there would be so many gentry in this neighborhood—so as to have a fancy dinner party, I mean," Polly said. She respected the elegance of the Morstan appointments, but was not yet convinced that Cornwall was fit for any but barbarians.

"I am sure the guests will be delightful," Jenny said, although not at all sure, but she was reassuring herself as well as Polly.

"There's a real earl and all, they tell me in the kitchen. We had none of them in Tidmouth," Polly continued, eager to impart such exciting news.

Unwilling to say that she had already met the "real earl," Jenny just nodded, poked at a wayward curl, and decided she could postpone her descent to the drawing room no longer. Comforted by Polly's smile she went on her way.

"Ah, there you are Jenny, and looking quite a lovely, too." Sir Francis hailed her entrance in his heartiest fashion. If this dinner party proved an antidote to the Morstans' depressed spirits, Jenny thought it would have served its purpose.

"You have preceded Amy, but she is apt to dawdle over her preparations," he complained, recalling with a frown his last glimpse of his wife.

Hastening to soothe matters Jenny protested, "But she always looks so fabulous when she does appear, the wait is well worth it, don't you think?"

"She has a faithful champion in you, at any rate, my dear," he agreed dryly, and was interrupted by the appearance of Lady Morstan. Jenny wondered fleetingly, if Amy had been further delayed, if Francis would have confided in her, at least asked her opinion of his wife's malaise.

But if Amy Morstan was suffering from any discomfort of mind or body, she did not evidence it this evening. Wearing a high-waisted pale pink satin gown embroidered in gold and silver, Lady Morstan did indeed look stunning. Her golden hair was brushed into an elegant Grecian knot and she wore an unusual necklace of gold carnelian and pearls with matching earrings and bracelet, a costume which would turn eyes in London not to mention Wiltshire, Jenny conceded.

"How stunning you look, Amy. Such a wonderful gown and jewels. Not that you need such adornments," Jenny complimented generously.

"Yes, you look quite breathtaking, my dear," Francis agreed somewhat tardily. "And just in time, too, for I hear a carriage coming up the drive."

Jenny sighed inwardly. She did hope the evening would not be marred by a spattering of barbed remarks.

The first arrivals, ushered with suitable ceremony

into the drawing room by Peabody, were introduced as Sir Austen and Lucia Pencrist, accompanied by a tall, thin, aristocratic gentleman who appeared to be a connection of Lady Pencrist's, Henri d'Aubisson.

Sir Austen, unlike his relative by marriage, had neither the manner nor mien of an aristocrat, being stocky with rather coarse features, a florid face, and a gruff voice. Only his eyes, a startling blue, redeemed him from true ugliness, for they were wide and expressive below a broad forehead. Lucia Pencrist, taller than her husband, proved a foil for Amy's blond beauty, for she was a statuesque brunette, with more than a hint of French chic in a simply cut emerald silk gown, but with a décolletage which Jenny found almost shocking. Both the Pencrists expressed their pleasure at meeting Jenny with quiet dignity, but Henri d'Aubisson was most effusive, his expressive eyes wandering with obvious admiration over her piquant face.

"*Enchanté, mademoiselle.* I am *bouleversé* to meet such a charming addition to our little circle here in the wilds of Cornwall. I do hope your visit will be an extended one," he flattered, captivating Jenny who had little experience with Gallic charm. He immediately took advantage of her obvious interest and steered her over to one side of the drawing room, intent on continuing his conquest. Jenny was not averse to hearing the adventures of this gallant émigré, who told her of his misfortunes at the hands of the Republicans and received her sympathy with appreciation.

However, M. d'Aubisson was not allowed to monopolize her for long. Within moments Francis had interrupted them to introduce several military gentlemen, among them the tall officer Jenny had seen briefly in Penzance. Major Bosworth, who towered over the Frenchman and his fellow officers, surprised Jenny by remembering their previous encounter.

"Why, I do believe, ma'am, that you are the same young lady I almost bowled over at the inn in Penzance a fortnight ago," he said, bowing over her hand with grace. "I hope you will forgive my clumsiness and not see it as an impediment to future friendship."

"No harm done, Major, and I could see you were in a hurry," Jenny responded, liking this courteous giant. He quickly introduced his fellow officers, freckled, red-haired Lieutenant Carstairs and the bold, dark-eyed Captain Anders. Jenny much preferred Christopher Carstairs to the more sophisticated Oliver Anders. She was chatting gaily with all three officers when she was interrupted by Amy.

"Come now, gentlemen. I know Jenny is a challenge to the military, but I cannot allow you to monopolize her completely. Come, Jenny, you must meet our last guest to arrive," she insisted, taking Jenny by the arm and directing her to the fireplace where Piers St. Robyns stood talking to Francis.

"Piers, I want you to meet my cousin Jennifer Dryden, who is paying us a visit from her home in Wiltshire. Jenny, Piers St. Robyns, the Earl of Trevarris and ruler of our little kingdom. We are quite overcome by his presence as he usually does not honor us," she finished a bit bitterly.

Ignoring Amy's attempt to provoke him, Piers

smiled lazily down at Jenny and, taking her hand, said warmly, "Ah, but Miss Dryden and I are already old friends." He paused and Jenny gave him a speaking look from flashing eyes. Would he reveal the story of the inn? But no, he could not be so outrageous.

"Oh, Jenny, you did not mention this encounter," Amy said sharply. She did not like the idea of Jenny sharing any intimacy with the Earl of Trevarris.

"Well, actually I forgot, Amy. You see . . ." Jenny began, hopelessly confused and embarrassed but Piers came to her rescue adroitly.

"What she means, dear Lady Morstan, is that I made such a little impression that naturally other more important people and concerns left me in the dust. Quite right, too, and depressing to my consequence, but no doubt, very salutary."

"Yes, Piers, you rarely are rebuffed, I fancy. And I would warn our innocent Jenny that she should beware of your smooth words and winning ways." She spoke lightly, but Jenny sensed both resentment and admonition underneath the careless comments.

"Really, my dear, you are harsh on Piers. I am sure he always behaves with circumspection," Sir Francis interposed quickly, not unaware of the undercurrents. "And just where did this meeting take place, may I ask?" he continued, mindful of his role as Jenny's protector.

"Down by that cove just where our property merges, Francis. I thought Miss Dryden was a trespasser and was inclined to speak harshly to her, until, of course, I learned who she was and became captivated by her charm," he explained mockingly.

Jenny did not care for his tone. "I thought the cove was on your land, Francis, or I would not have presumed to test Lord Trevarris's hospitality. I will not venture there again," she informed them with some asperity.

"Nonsense, Miss Dryden, or may I call you Jenny since we are neighbors and should not stand on ceremony. You must frolic there whenever your heart desires," he insisted in paternal tones, but before she could retort hotly, and unwisely, they were joined by the vicar and his sister.

"Ah, Lord Trevarris, I see you have met the newest addition, and a delightful one, to our little community." Robert Herron beamed on the group gathered about the fireplace. Then remembering his manners: "You remember my sister Evelyn?"

"Your servant, Miss Herron," Piers replied correctly, then, turning to Robert Herron, he said, "I know this is a gentle way of reminding me, Herron, that I have been neglecting my duties to the villagers. I will surprise you and arrive for service tomorrow and redeem my soul," he promised with a twinkle.

"And read the lesson," Robert Herron insisted, making small effort to repress his amusement at Pier's shameless effrontery.

"And read the lesson," Piers agreed. "You must come and hear me, Jenny," he said, turning to her and causing both Amy and Evelyn Herron to view her with disapproval.

The devil, he knows exactly what he's doing, Jenny thought hotly. She would liked to have given him a swift kick in the shins, but before she could be tempted to such outrageous action, Peabody made a stately entrance into the room and announced, "Dinner is served, my lady."

As the most important guest, Piers escorted Amy into the dining room and left Jenny to the mercies of Major Bosworth, which relieved her a good deal. If she had been left with the Earl of Trevarris she would have let that arrogant peer know that she did not appreciate being the object of his humorous sallies. With Major Bosworth she immediately established a rapport over the mulligatawny, and by the time the Davenport fowl had been removed and she had to turn to Francis, she felt she had made a friend.

"Has the major been seeking your sympathy, Jenny?" Francis asked.

"Whatever for? He seems a most capable officer and well able to handle whatever onerous duties he must pursue," she answered, not quite grasping Francis's meaning.

Basely deserting Evelyn Herron with whom he had valiantly been conversing to very little reward, Lieutenant Carstairs, across the table, answered for his commanding officer. "I believe Sir Francis is referring to thwarting the local past time—smuggling."

"How exciting. I know free trading, as I think I have heard it called, is illegal, but I must admit it has a certain romantic appeal. Crossing the stormy Channel on a blustery dark night, manhandling kegs of contraband into hiding places, expecting every moment the sounds of approaching Revenue men . . . It creates a thrilling picture." Jenny, her eyes sparkling, was thoroughly captivated by the idea of it all.

"I am afraid, my dear Jenny, that you have been listening to the wrong stories. Of course, Cornishmen have been free traders since Tudor times and do not consider it a crime, just cocking a snook at their English masters. But it is not all romance and daring escapades, you know. Free trading breeds greed, corruption, blackmail, brutality, even murder, not attractive results of your romantic adventuring," Sir Francis explained, a certain severity in his tone.

But Jenny would have none of his realistic morality. "Come now, Francis, you must not be so disapproving. I am sure there are few households in Cornwall which do not enjoy the fruits of smuggling—brandy, silks, whatever," she insisted.

Major Bosworth, listening with half an ear to this conversation, interrupted a bit bitterly. "A few kegs of brandy or a bolt of Lille silk is not of great matter, but we are at war with France and Fouché, Napoleon's police chief, has taken advantage of the free trading network to run in his spies, a far more harmful cargo than brandy or silk."

Jenny, perturbed at the serious turn to the conversation, immediately tendered her apologies. "I understand I have been somewhat foolish, Major, and quite agree that smuggling men is far more dangerous, not to mention unpatriotic, than brandy or silks. I stand reproved," she smiled, seeking forgiveness.

"And that is why Sir Francis believes I am asking for your sympathy, Miss Dryden, for I have neither the men nor the resources to bring these free traders to justice, whatever that may be. It is really a task for the Revenue men, but we have been seconded down here to help them. The natives are not cooperative and who could blame them? They rightly resent outsiders monitoring their affairs. It's very discouraging trying to accomplish this distasteful job in such an inhospitable climate," the major explained. Jenny sensed he would have preferred to be fighting on the Peninsula than tracking villains in Cornwall. He sounded as if he had a certain respect for his enemies here.

"It is true that the Cornish have a long history of smuggling and we are inclined to turn a blind eye to the prepetrators," Sir Francis agreed politely, "but I am sure, Major Bosworth, that none of our people in Trevarris would obstruct you in carrying out your duties." Obviously Sir Francis did not want to discuss the local smuggling any further.

Jenny, realizing that a certain coolness had descended over her dinner partners, hurried to change the conversation, expressing her enthusiasm over the natural wonder of Cornwall. Soon peace was restored. When Amy rose to gather the ladies together and leave the gentlemen to their port, the company seemed quite harmonious.

Amy, who prided herself on her accomplishments as a hostess, said in an aside to Jenny as they walked toward the drawing room, "Well, that seemed to go off rather well. Of course, having the odd number of gentlemen is a drawback, quite improper, and never tolerated in London, but we are limited as to company in this isolated spot."

"I think you have quite a few interesting neighbors. I have yet to talk to the Pencrists, but I hope to repair that omission before the evening is over," Jenny replied before they parted.

Lady Pencrist evidently found the newcomer in their midst also worthy of attention for immediately upon Jenny's settling down on the settee before the fire, she was joined by the lady.

"We must become better acquainted, Miss Dryden. I suspect you are a clever young woman, hiding several talents under that demure facade," the striking brunette insisted, leaving Jenny to make what she would of this equivocal gambit. Was the lady complimenting her or insulting her? But Lady Pencrist appeared much too langorous to be spiteful, but Jenny suspected that she was not a woman who really enjoyed the company of other women. Jenny thought Lady Pencrist resembled a luscious cat, basking in the admiration of others, but unwilling to exert any effort to attract them. Strange that she had married a man of such unprepossessing looks, when she herself was so handsome.

Ignoring the reference to her talents, Jenny asked politely, "Are you a native of Cornwall, Lady Pencrist?"

"Oh, no, my dear! Heaven forbid that I should claim kinship with these farouche people. We came here from London when Austen inherited the place, rather on a repairing lease really, as he was deep under the hatches before his uncle providentially turned up his toes and left Austen the lot," Lady Pencrist explained with what Jenny thought was an appalling breach of manners before a stranger.

Before she could make any reply to this frank disclosure, Lady Pencrist continued in her lazy drawl, "I am really a cosmopolite, with a French grandmother and many ties to the Continent. You have met Henri, my half brother, poor darling, driven from France and his estates by that wretched Napoleon, forced to seek asylum here."

"He is fortunate to have devoted relations to take him in," Jenny replied dryly, hoping to forestall Lady Pencrist's complaints about her country which she felt sure would be forthcoming.

"Well, yes, we are very glad to have him, and he seems to have settled happily. But it must be boring for the poor dear, and, of course, with his French background, he is viewed with suspicion. I am convinced that that rather stolid Major Bosworth thinks Henri is a conspirator of some sort, just because he is French," she explained, waving her fan and looking as if the effort to explain all this was exhausting.

"I think Major Bosworth is probably too astute to jump to unwarranted conclusions," Jenny replied a bit sharply, reluctant to listen to any aspersions on her new acquaintance. Was Lady Pencrist as indolent and incautious as she appeared at first meeting? Surely she did not reveal the details of her life in this casual manner to all who crossed her path. What an odd woman she was.

"When the gentlemen join us, Lucia, I do hope you will sing for us. Lady Pencrist has a beautiful voice, Jenny, and if we can prevail upon her to honor us this evening you will be charmed, I am sure," Amy said as she approached them.

"How kind of you, dear Amy. Of course I will be delighted to sing for my supper, if Henri will accompany me. I am quite hopeless at playing myself," Lady Pencrist replied in her low soft voice. "But perhaps Miss Dryden will entertain us," she suggested.

"Never. I have no musical talents, although I enjoy hearing others who have the requisite ability," Jenny assured her.

"That's settled then," Amy said with relief. She had been endeavoring to converse with Evelyn Herron while awaiting the men and found it heavy going, and she never felt completely at ease with Lucia Pencrist. She suspected the lady found her amusing and Amy did not quite know how to counter this reaction.

Before more could be said about the matter, the door opened and the gentlemen drifted into the drawing room. Henri d'Aubisson headed directly for Jenny and adroitly drew her away from his sister to look at some excellent porcelain displayed in a cabinet across the room. Jenny did not fail to notice that the Earl of Trevarris had settled into her former seat close to Lady Pencrist.

"Ah, *ma chère mademoiselle,* regard the lovely colors on these plates. What artistry and skill created these pieces. *Hélas,* my countrymen now are more interested in killing than art, and such designs are considered frivolous," he mourned, in what Jenny thought an affected manner. Henri d'Aubisson had a certain contrived charm and a sincere interest in women of all types and ages coupled with the ability to make every one of them feel they had captured his full attention, assets shared by few Englishmen. Jenny had little experience with such men, and although she sensed his appeal, she realized it was not to her taste. She responded politely to his verbal stratagems while wondering how he occupied his time in Cornwall. He would be far more at home at a London soiree than rusticating here, even in the best company the country offered. Did he have some other reason beside exile and penury for living in Trevarris with his accommodating sister?

She reproved herself for her suspicions, aroused by Major Bosworth's discussion at dinner, and responded with suitable appreciation to M. d'Aubisson's witticisms and gallantries. So involved did they become in their bantering that they did not hear Amy's approach and her rather tart interruption.

"If you can spare Henri, Jenny, we are waiting for him to accompany Lucia."

"Of course. I am sorry to have delayed you, sir," Jenny replied, conscious of the rebuke and a bit embarrassed. It would never do for Amy to think she was flirting with the dashing Frenchman. She was so maladroit. She must learn more worldly manners if she were to survive in this more sophisticated environment. There had been no one in the least like either Henri d'Aubisson and his sister, or, for that matter, the haughty Earl of Trevarris in Tidmouth.

Lucia Pencrist did not disappoint. She had a clear, melodious, well trained voice and a certain presence which enabled her to deliver a charming French ballad in liquid tones, and then followed it with a popular Mozart fugue. Jenny would have enjoyed the recital more if she had not been so aware of the Earl of

Trevarris who had taken the seat next to her on the settee. For some reason, she found the earl unsettling and believed he knew this and found it amusing. She was determined to be on her guard against this disturbing man. His charm was less obvious than that of the suave Henri d'Aubisson but all the more potent.

After the last notes of Lucia Pencrist's voice had died away and she had received the appreciative applause, the earl turned to Jenny and said, "Did you find that enjoyable, Jenny? You appeared wrapped in reverie. Did Lucia's tender sentiments evoke sad memories?"

Suspecting mockery in the earl's tone, Jenny turned to him and replied frigidly, "Not at all, sir. I would like to disabuse you of the notion that I am languishing away like some rejected spinster. My mistake was in telling you anything of my history in Truro."

"Believing that you would never see the recipient of those confidences again. But life plays monstrous tricks upon us, Jenny. Come now, don't be angry with me. You appear the soul of affability to Bosworth and that French mountebank. I do not see what I have done to earn your displeasure, aside from listening to your tale. My own opinion is you are well rid of your childhood playmate, and that he deserves all he will probably get from the designing hussy who captured him. I do not believe your heart was broken at all," he mocked, expecting an outburst and being rather surprised when all she replied was, "You must think what you will, Lord Trevarris."

Stung by her indifference, not the treatment he

usually experienced from young women, he grasped her hand and, looking with irony into her shuttered face, begged her pardon. "Jenny, if I have offended you, it was unintentional. You are such a prickly young thing I can see I must tread gently on your sensibilities. After all, I only accepted this invitation tonight to make my peace with you."

"I cannot believe that, sir, so please do not try to cozen me with your idle flattery. I may be a country miss, but I am not so foolish as to believe that you care a farthing for my feelings," she said sharply. "And I object to being gulled."

"Alas, Jenny, you wrong me, and if you continue to speak to me in that chilling tone I will be cast into the boughs. Now say you forgive my transgressions and promise to ride with me tomorrow. I want to show you the countryside." Jenny had the feeling he would be gravely disappointed if she refused. And she was not proof against his beguiling manner.

"All right, Piers, but only if you behave and treat me with due circumspection," she agreed, laughing at his rueful expression.

"Well, I will try, but you will tax my powers to the utmost, Jenny. Believe me when I say I have no ulterior motives but the enjoyment of your company," he insisted.

"As an antidote to boredom or because you have rarely met such an innocent? I wonder," Jenny mused, causing Piers to raise his eyebrows in acknowledgement of her hit.

"Unfair, unfair. But we must postpone our duel until tomorrow morning, about eleven, if that meets with your approval?"

"That will be acceptable, unless Amy wants me for some commission."

"I will secure her cooperation. Until tomorrow then." He rose upon the words and was soon making his farewells to the company, leaving behind a rather confused young woman. She doubted very much that the Earl of Trevarris was romantically interested in her. She was neither so conceited nor so foolish as to entertain those thoughts, she decided stoutly. But he wanted something from her. What could it be?

Chapter Six

If Jenny was puzzled by the Earl of Trevarris's interest in her, Piers himself wondered why he found the girl so intriguing. Women had always had a negligible place in his life. He had availed himself of their services often enough, even had the requisite mistress in keeping when he was in London, but he neither trusted them nor found them essential outside of the bedroom.

His father had married late with no other motivation than to provide himself with an heir. When he had accomplished this he paid little attention to his young wife, who had fallen deeply in love with her arrogant, indifferent husband. Piers had few memories of his mother, a fragile invalid, who had died when he was barely out of leading strings, as much from neglect as any real malady. His father had trained him to care for his vast estates, to hunt, shoot, and ride as befitted a gentleman, and to treat women casually. Of course, someday he would marry and provide a heir, but at twenty-eight he had not felt any matrimonial urgency. Affection had not played a role in Piers's life. He and his father had shared a respect and a responsibility for the land and their tenants, but little else.

Piers had gone straight from Eton into the Navy where he had served with distinction throughout the wars with the French. Upon his father's death he had given up his naval career reluctantly. A wound suffered during the battle of Trafalgar had meant a long convalescence and then he was forced to take up the reins of his estate and the other properties which made the Earl of Trevarris a man of considerable wealth and position. He missed the camaraderie of his fellow officers and the adventurous freewheeling navy life. Under his facade of cynicism lay deep feelings of duty and honor, although he would be loath to profess them.

When Admiral Coniston had requested his assistance, Piers did not feel he could deny his former commander. The admiral had confessed that both the Foreign Office and the War Department were baffled. They had pinpointed the location but not the culprit. Somewhere in Piers' neighborhood was a master traitor, responsible for a network which had inflicted grave damage on the English war effort. Whitehall had few illusions about the patriotism of Cornishmen, those mystic and stubborn Celts who had been subdued but never really conquered. The Cornish disliked and distrusted all foreigners. They felt more kinship with their fellow Celts, the Normans and Bretons, than with the Anglo-Saxons east of the Tamar River. Piers had a certain sympathy with this parochial attitude, but none at all with traitors when his country was besieged.

Now that Napoleon had secured the Continent with his victories over Italy, Austria, and Russia, England stood virtually alone against the Corsican tyrant, her only shield the Royal Navy. French troops occupied Portugal and this past spring Napoleon had forced Charles IV to renounce the Spanish throne in favor of his own brother, Joseph. The Peninsular War to reverse these disasters was not marching well. And Napoleon had instituted a paper blockade against his chief enemy, closing the entire European coastline to British ships and trade.

Now, in April of 1808, England awaited the first invasion of her shores since the Armada attempt. The French were preparing for their landing by infiltrating spies into the coastal area. Their task was simplified by the company of émigrés, aristocrats who had fled the terrors of the Revolution and received refuge in England. Aware of Napoleon's success and dominant position in Europe, many of them were having second thoughts, consenting to cooperate with the emperor in hopes of regaining their estates. If that cooperation entailed betraying their hosts, some among them had little compunction in doing so.

Piers did not really suspect Jennifer Dryden of any nefarious actions. She was so obviously what she claimed to be, a country vicar's daughter recovering from a broken engagement by escaping to her relatives in Cornwall. He had behaved with insensitive carelessness in kissing her in that first meeting at the inn. He tried to put the blame on the intimacy of their surroundings, too much wine, her provocative appeal, but he knew he had behaved badly. He told himself that she really did not interest him except in a casual way. He had never expected to see her again. He believed he was taking an objective view. Any stranger in the area warranted investigation and Jennifer's arrival could prove to be a catalyst. He would keep an eye on her, and if she was foolish enough to read more into his attentions than casual friendship, that was not his fault.

His chief suspect at the moment was the obvious one, Henri d'Aubisson. While inquiries were being made in France as to the truth of Henri's story, Piers had come to Cornwall to seek the evidence convicting d'Aubisson. He had his doubts, for the fellow possessed neither the sharp intelligence nor the energy for such a role.

Jenny's arrival at this critical time could be a complication. If she were innocent, he could discount her, both as a traitor and as a factor in his life, but she must be protected against her own recklessness. If Jenny were a different type he might have enjoyed dallying with her, but now he had neither the time nor the inclination, he told himself. She would prove no distraction and she might even serve as a screen to his investigations. What he must establish and soon was the role of the smugglers in the treachery.

Piers was inclined to ignore the illegal free trading which had been a tradition along the Cornish coast for centuries. He rather applauded the ingenuity and courage of the natives who added to their slender incomes from fishing and mining by importing luxuries illegally.

But, if the smugglers were bringing in human cargo, they must be stopped. Napoleon's men were infiltrating the country from Dover to Land's End. Whitehall had become seriously alarmed by the increase in this traffic, which the government believed was a precurser to an invasion. Both the Army and Navy were hard-pressed to fill their quotas. Forces for the Revenue service were just not available. Piers had been told to call upon Major Bosworth if he needed assistance, but he was reminded that even Revenuers and the Army were not immune from bribery. The smugglers, swollen with success, managed to corrupt many of those sent to apprehend them. All in all it was a desperate situation and Piers was determined to put an end to it.

When Jenny mentioned to Amy her projected ride with Piers, she was a bit taken aback by her cousin's frown of disapproval. The two were chatting over morning chocolate, discussing the previous evening's dinner party. Jenny, already dressed in her riding costume, was not prepared for her cousin's objections.

"I don't quite know how to say this, Jenny. I would not want you to think I am being prissy or unduly censorious, but Piers St. Robyns is not a proper companion for you," Amy said, her wide blue eyes dropping beneath Jenny's candid questioning ones.

"What do you mean? Is he too worldly, too much of a womanizer?" Jenny asked, a bit amused.

"Exactly. And his motives in inviting you to spend time in his company puzzle me. He has never been interested in young girls, or for that matter serious about any woman. I fear he is flirting with you because he is bored. He never stays here long. His real life is in London. And you would be unwise to read any lasting interest in his attentions," Amy explained a bit tartly. Then feeling she must step warily, she continued, "You have just been through a trying time. Harry Ruston's rejection must have left you vulnerable to the next halfway attractive man you meet. But Piers is not the one to soothe your depressed spirits. If you are looking for a suitable escort you would do much better with Robert Herron, whom I can see already admires you excessively."

"Robert Herron is a dear man, although I cannot say that his sister is exactly winsome. Do not worry, Amy, I am not likely to be swept off my feet by Piers St. Robyns. Even in the depths of Wiltshire we have some experience of his type. I admit he is much too sophisticated for a country vicar's daughter, and I am not stupid enough to believe that he has taken a *tendre* for me. He is probably at loose ends, and the idea of flirting with a gullible girl just a passing fancy. I will not take his attentions seriously, but I will enjoy his introduction to the countryside. Of course, I must be guided by your concern. If you would rather I not see any more of him, I will obey your strictures." Jenny assured her cousin, although she thought Amy's warning unjustified.

"We have so few amusements here I would not be so mean to deny you the few available. I would not like you to be hurt again, that's all," Amy said, smiling at Jenny, having made her point.

"You are trying to spare me another 'disappointment in love,' as Babs would say. Never fear, Amy, I have had a surfeit of deceiving men for the moment. I hope you do not think I am impressed by his title or wealth. Father taught me to understand the danger of material ambition, you know. But I find him entertaining and his interest is flattering to my self-esteem. He's quite soothing to my consequence," she teased, rather touched by Amy's care for her.

"Well, I have done by duty," Amy sighed, realizing that short of actually forbidding Jenny to leave the house in the earl's company, she had done all she could. She did not take the responsibility of chaperoning Jenny too seriously. After all, the girl was not a fool. And Amy would not want to antagonize Jenny. Her presence in the household was too convenient for several reasons. Francis liked her and Babs positively doted upon her. Amy would not quarrel with Jenny over Piers St. Robyns. Amy was honest enough to feel a little regret that the earl had not tried his wiles upon her.

But she had more than she could handle right now in the clandestine relationship upon which she had embarked, more from ennui than any pressing interest. If Francis could only understand how much she disliked Cornwall, if he were not so involved with his mine, and if she had not lost the baby, her attitude toward him might not be so indifferent. Amy had not been in love with Francis when she married him, but she had come to accept her marriage which had rescued her from a dull Cheltenham existence.

She had enjoyed several flirtations and received several offers before she had met Francis at a country house party. His address, his obvious wealth, and his devotion had persuaded her. She liked being Lady Morstan. She had two younger sisters, a father who had wasted his slender resources on gambling, and a complaining mother. Francis had rescued her from that unhappy situation and she was grateful. But after the birth of Babs he appeared to accept their marriage complaisantly, and his earlier fervor had disappeared. Amy needed admiration and gallantry. If Francis would not supply it she must look elsewhere, she considered. After all, husbands and wives should not live in one another's pockets—too tedious for words.

So she rationalized her current affair, for Amy was basically a shallow and rather conceited woman, with little domestic talent. She refused to become a brood mare, content to bear dozens of children and moulder in the country. If Francis would not take her to London, the only suitable arena for her beauty, he must bear the consequences. If Jenny would not listen to her advice, then, she, too, must suffer the consequences. Amy's concern for her fellows did not extend further than tepid sympathy. Her own affairs were paramount, and as quickly as she had spoken her unease to Jenny, as quickly she forgot it.

However, Jenny did not. Amy's suspicions about Piers's motives matched her own. She had not forgotten that assault upon her senses at the Truro inn. Well, she was in no danger of succumbing to the earl's casual caresses again. Foolishly she had told him about Harry's rejection. He must have felt she was ripe for a dalliance. He could not be more mistaken and if he tried to repeat that experience he would be rudely rebuffed. Jenny's trust in men's nobility had been severely shaken.

When Piers arrived to escort her on the promised ride, she had worked herself into a bad humor. She greeted him absently, as if she had only just remembered the engagement, and busied herself fastening her gloves.

Sensitive to the atmosphere, Piers did not press her, assisting her to mount her horse without further conversation. She drew back from his helping hand as if burned. What had happened to make her shrink from him? Had Amy Morstan been filling her head with a lot of rubbish?

Only slightly in jest Piers asked Jenny as they trotted down the drive, "I am surprised you consented to accompany me on this ride today. It appears you view me with some suspicion."

Jenny gave him a startled look, but recovered and answered impudently, "Well, I have been warned that you are not a proper companion for me, but after due consideration, I thought I would risk it. It might improve my standing with the villagers if they see me in the company of the lord of the manor, being so wary of foreigners as they are."

"The devil you say. And who has been giving you these dire warnings?" Piers asked, although he was certain he knew the source of the cautionary words. Amy Morstan. For some time now a wary truce had existed between Amy and Piers. She had wanted more admiration and attention than he was willing to give. Not that he was averse to initiating a liaison with a lovely agreeable lady, but an affair with a neighbor was not the thing in this tight little community. Besides, he quite liked Francis Morstan and had no intention of cuckolding him. He had rejected the lady's advances with as much tact as he could, but he was convinced she had not forgiven him, and hence the warning to her cousin.

Jenny, knowing nothing of this past relationship, nevertheless had some inkling that Amy found the earl attractive. Who could blame her? He was a man whom most women would find intriguing. In other circumstances Jenny might have found his attentions flattering, but past experience had taught her a harsh lesson.

Suddenly aware that an embarrassing silence had stretched between them, she gave him a toss of her head and a careless smile. "I will not reveal my sources, sir, and anyway, it is too nice a day to worry about gossip. Shall we let our horses out?"

"Of course, my dear. We will trot through the village to show off your conquest as you requested," Piers answered, vaguely disappointed that she should have such a shabby view of him, and cursing Amy for her bitter words.

However, the brisk ride through the village dispelled some of the constraint on both their parts, especially as Jenny could not help an endearing giggle escape as she saw the gruff storekeeper and one of his companions eyeing them with surprise.

"You see, Lord Trevarris, already my stock has risen," Jenny pointed out as they clattered down the final yards of the main street toward the wharves. He could not help but return her grin and indicated the fishing boats on the horizon. Reining their horses to a stop they watched the scene with enjoyment. The sea was incredibly calm under an even sky, only a few clouds scudding across the horizon, and a gentle breeze tugging at the nets laid out to dry.

"You are seeing Trevarris in a benign mood. Cornwall climate can be capricious, and rarely do we have such fine weather. But the tide is rising now and before long when the white mist drifts in you will not recognize this bay."

"It is idyllic. What are the fishermen catching?" she asked.

"Mostly pilchards, some sole, plaice, and mackerel, and the men put out lobster traps. But fishing is not what it was, unfortunately. That's why so many have to go into the mines." Piers grimaced for he disliked the stannaries, driving the men from the open seas and fields into the dank and dangerous earth.

"You mean like Francis's wheal?" Jenny asked, frowning. She did not like the idea of the tin mines either, but was loath to criticize her host.

"Yes," Piers said sharply, then, perhaps feeling he had been too abrupt, "Francis inherited the mine and as owner he has been just and careful, initiating safety standards where he could, but still . . ."

"I have not seen the mines and I don't think I want to," Jenny confessed and then, changing the subject, asked, "Is that why so many Cornishmen are smugglers, because the fish are disappearing and mining is so hard and brutalizing?"

Piers hesitated. What did she know of smuggling and what really lay behind her questions? "Of course, and then you ladies would be most grieved not to have your silks and laces, which would cost many more guineas if Whitehall had its way. And during the war no furbelows at all since the most elegant fashions come from Paris," he mocked.

"And you gentlemen would be denied your brandy and wine, probably a vast improvement to your health," Jenny came back smartly.

"Touché, Jenny. But let us be on our way. I want to show you more of the countryside," Piers said, touching his crop to his horse's neck, and Jenny perforce had to follow after him.

Absorbed in their conversation she had not noticed a dark, sullen fisherman, a giant of a man, lounging against a bulwark, watching them all the while as they surveyed the harbor.

He spat at their backs and growled menacingly at his companion. "I see Lord High And Mighty has another female in tow."

"Visitin' Sir Francis and his lady she is. A likely looking wench, eh, Jack?" his confederate joked slyly. "But not for the likes of us."

"A milk and water miss is no use to me. Give me a saucy buxom lass with no hoity-toity airs and graces," he returned, grinning lewdly. "But they all want gold, the greedy bitches, never satisfied."

"You gots that, Jack, and know where to get more," his companion returned serviley.

"That's right, Bert. And no cursed lord or maggoty Revenuer is going to stop me. Now keep your lip buttoned. No more loose talk," he commanded, giving Bert a fierce look which caused the man to cringe.

Black Jack Morton was a man of towering height, rough strength, of dark visage and eye, who imposed his leadership of his band by a force which few cared to challenge. He respected neither God's law nor man's and went his own way. He had a bad reputation in the village, but such was his brutality he had so far eluded trouble. He lived alone in a fisherman's cottage at the end of the village, kept his secrets, and with low cunning had escaped any retribution for his various dark deeds. He kept his followers in line by talent as well as by strength, for his was the hand that managed all the smugglers.

Without his leadership, and his contacts across the Channel, the Trevarris free traders would not have escaped justice for as long as they had. And now, with war straining the government's resources, they had almost a free hand in running illicit cargoes. Black Jack laughed at his pursuers' futile efforts to catch him with the evidence, which further raised his stock with his band of villains, a score of rough angry men as rebellious of authority as he was himself. The Earl of Trevarris might own the village, land and cottages, but Black Jack Morton held the real power, and through respect or fear, the villagers paid him a certain allegiance.

If Jenny had not noticed Black Jack, Piers had been more observant. For some time he had been aware that the man was a leader in Trevarris and Piers knew, too, that any illegal activity in the area could be traced to Black Jack's authority. Piers was inclined to ignore the free trading as long as the contraband imported did not include French spies. But since his arrival in Cornwall on this visit, he had more than a suspicion that Black Jack, who feared neither the Revenuers nor the local magistrate, might be involved in traitorous activity. He intended to investigate just what Black Jack was up to, knowing full well the man represented a threat.

As Piers and Jenny trotted up the steep hill that led from the village, he thought it wise to warn her about untoward interest in the activities of the wharf area.

"You may not have noticed, Jenny, but among the fishermen lounging about the wharves was one great surly brute, our local villain, one Black Jack Morton."

"Well, I didn't notice particularly, but every village has such a one. In Tidmouth, our village in Wiltshire, Angus Miller, a notorious poacher, is my father's despair," Jenny informed him.

"Somehow I feel your Angus is not quite so fearsome as our Black Jack. He's a nasty character if crossed, and fears no one," Piers continued, determined to alert Jenny to the danger of poking her delightful little nose into affairs which did not concern her. He had the idea she was more than curious about the village and had sensed the secretive, sullen attitude of the villagers.

"I cannot believe he does not have the proper respect for the lord of the manor," Jenny mocked. "If so, he is to be congratulated on his daring."

"Black Jack and I have wisely avoided one another, but if I am forced into a confrontation with the man, I have no doubt that I can survive his challenge," Piers replied wryly. "I do not like his influence on

Trevarris and have allowed him quite enough leeway. I will take the matter in hand."

"Poor Black Jack, I fear his days are numbered," she replied, unwilling to take Piers seriously.

"Perhaps, but what I am trying to impress upon you is that he is a dangerous man and I think not above brutal retaliation against anyone who interferes with him."

"Well, I doubt very much if I will have any reason to tangle with this villainous rogue, but I will remember your words and step carefully if the occasion arises," she promised, tilting her head and giving him a provocative grin.

"Somehow I have the feeling that your very presence is disturbing. I know you disturb me," Piers answered, only half in jest.

But Jenny, who did not enjoy this type of flirtation, quickly depressed any ideas Piers might have of indulging himself in this manner. "You need not play your London games with me, sir. I am not an object for your false gallantries. Shall we let the horses out and have a good gallop?" Without waiting for his assent, she spurred her horse ahead and lengthened the distance between them so that further conversation was impossible.

Piers, grinning at her attempt at a set-down, followed and soon passed her on his fleet stallion, but he promised himself that prickly Jenny Dryden would not dismiss him so easily. He had not finished with her yet.

Chapter Seven

Jenny had thoroughly enjoyed her morning ride with the Earl of Trevarris and acquitted him of any devious design in tendering the invitation. Despite Amy's fears, he had made no further attempts to engage her in a flirtation after her stern warning that she was not available for such pursuits. In fact, he had behaved much like an elder brother, pointing out the interesting aspects of the countryside, including a distant view of his own house, the impressive Arthmore, but not suggesting a closer inspection.

He explained that Arthmore in Cornish meant "high place" and that there had been a castle of some sort on the point since Roman days. His great-grandfather, disgusted with the uncomfortable drafty medieval structure which had housed the Trevarris clan since Norman days, had pulled down the building and erected a spare graceful manor house in the Queen Anne mode. What Jenny had glimpsed of this smooth gray stone facade with its wide sashed windows and imposing long drive had looked attractive, but a bit cold—rather like its master, she concluded naughtily.

Resolutely she turned her mind away from the enigmatic Earl of Trevarris and concentrated on entertaining Babs and acquiescing to whatever plans her cousins initiated for her visit. With Babs and her father she found no difficulty in establishing an easy relationship, but Amy proved elusive, and her attitude did not encourage intimacy. On the surface she was all that was polite, concerned for Jenny's entertainment and comfort. But beneath the mask of the charming hostess Jenny sensed impatience and unhappiness.

Determined to discover what lay behind all these undercurrents in the Morstan household, Jenny hid her concern and accepted the distraction that Babs offered while she decided what to do. Caught up in the drama of this new experience of secrecy and suspicion, she had almost forgotten Harry's rejection.

She was quite surprised one May morning upon reading a letter from her mother to realize that she had not given her former betrothed a thought in some days. Her mother, however, appeared to think of little else. She wrote with some satisfaction that Amelia had managed already to annoy most of the villagers and thoroughly irritate Sir Henry with her la-di-da manners. Even Harry was disillusioned by her carping about the boredom of village life and her insistence that he take her to London, or at least Bath, where she could parade her new expensive wardrobe and flaunt her title. Harry had never cared for town life and was reluctant to accompany her on such a visit, pleading that his presence on the estate was necessary.

Indeed, Mrs. Dryden insisted, Sir Henry appeared irritable and tired. Certainly all was not well in the Ruston household and Mrs. Dryden could only put the blame where she felt it belonged, on the encroaching Amelia. Jenny, smiling at her mother's doughty championship, wondered why her budget of news evoked so little concern. The happenings in Wiltshire seemed distant and of little moment to her now. In that her mother had been correct, her journey to Cornwall had proved a distraction from her own troubles.

Folding the letter away, she looked up as Babs burst into the dining room. Sir Francis had left for the mine and Amy rarely appeared in the dining room for breakfast. She preferred a solitary meal in her bedroom.

"I have no lessons today, Jenny. It's Saturday, thank goodness. What can we do which will be exciting?" Babs pleaded, eager for a respite from her studies. Babs was intelligent if not dutiful, and if she desired could have been an exemplary scholar, Robert Herron confided, but her impatience and a certain lack of discipline prevented her from working to her capacity. The young girl missed the competition provided by Johnny Granthum, her companion of the fish pond escapade, who had recently returned to Sussex with his widowed mother. A sturdy, self-confident child, reluctant to admit that she suffered from her mother's indifference and her father's distraction, she went her solitary way with an endearing stoicism Jenny much admired.

"Well, let me see. Didn't Mr. Herron set you a

passage in the Bible to commit to memory before your next session?" she said, attempting to adopt a serious reproving expression, but was forced to grin at Babs's downcast face.

"Oh, Jenny, it's such a lovely day, who would want to brood over some dreary parables? You cannot be so mean as to suggest I give up my holiday to learn lines," she wailed, her button-bright eyes darkening at the horrid thought.

Jenny could not repress a laugh. "I was just funning, moppet. I quite agree it's much too fine to stay indoors. What do you say to a picnic down by the cove? The earl of Trevarris has given permission for us to trespass there if we behave. Not that I am sure you will heed his admonitions," she suggested.

"Oh, Jenny, that would be grand. And I will behave and do just as I should. Can we have strawberry tarts, do you think, if I ask Mrs. Peabody prettily?"

"You have an inordinate passion for strawberries, Babs," Jenny sighed. "I only hope they don't give you spots."

"Of course they won't. I eat quarts every summer. You are mean to even suggest such a nasty idea. And what does *inordinate* mean? You see, I am extending my education by learning a large vocabulary," she concluded smugly.

"You have an inordinate desire to have the last word, too, Babs," Jenny insisted with mock severity, then seeing her small companion's uncertainty took pity on her. "*Inordinate* means exceeding reasonable limits, and sometimes can mean disorderly or unregulated, all of which occasionally describe you. But that's acceptable. How dull it would be if we were all reasonable, moderate, orderly people."

"Like Miss Herron," Babs agreed with a wicked grin and every intention of having the last word.

Although Jenny was inclined to agree with Babs's assessment of the vicar's sister, she felt she must offer a reproof. "That's unkind, Babs. Miss Herron is a very worthwhile person and a great help to her brother in the parish."

"Yes, of course, Jenny, but he would much rather have you," Babs concluded with a saucy smile and danced off to plead for the strawberry tarts before Jenny could remonstrate further.

Sometimes Babs's perception startled her. For a six year old she understood far more than was healthy, Jenny believed, as was so often the case with an only, lonely child. She was too sensitive to the moods of her elders and Jenny hoped that Babs had not observed the estrangement between her father and mother. As for her reference to Robert Herron's interest in Jenny, she could only hope that the dear man would postpone any avowal if indeed he had such intentions. Jenny did not want to hurt Robert Herron, but she knew she could never return his devotion.

Shaking off a sense that events were marching rapidly beyond her control, she hurried after Babs to request the picnic lunch, with or without the strawberry tarts.

The pair set off on their expedition, their spirits in accord and happy with the day that presented itself for their enjoyment, althought Mrs. Peabody had warned them that she felt an early mist hovering and they had best be home in good time.

"Mrs. P. always thinks we will come to harm when we are out rambling," Babs confided as they rode down the drive. She looked a forthright solid little figure on her piebald pony, Winky, her chubby legs astride his fat rump. Jenny, riding her usual mare, reined her horse to walk beside the plodding Winky, who did not take cheerfully to spirited canters.

Within a half an hour they had come upon the cove, carefully hitching Babs's pony and Jenny's mare to a tree before climbing down the steep slope to the shore. Babs, who loved to explore and rarely had the opportunity for such an adventure under supervision, her mother not inclined to such outings, squealed with delight as she wandered along the beach.

While Babs explored, searching for shells and driftwood, Jenny busied herself with her sketchbook, trying to capture a true likeness of the little girl. After a moment shc abandoned her pad in disgust. Her latest attempt at a real portrait appeared stiff and wooden. Alas, she was not a true artist, nothing but a caricaturist. Almost without volition her fingers designed a frolicking inquisitive otter with Babs's distinctive features, the squared golden brown hair and button-bright eyes, the study stance and playful nose for adventure.

Jenny smiled at Babs's enthusiasm. She had certainly enjoyed her picnic lunch. Now she was telling Jenny, through bites of strawberry tart, that she knew there was treasure in the secret cove.

"Father would never allow me to explore it, since it is really not part of his land. And then, until this summer, I was too young, you know. But now that I am six, almost seven, I can accomplish more incredible feats," she boasted, giving Jenny an admonitory glance as if to frustrate any challenge to her statements.

"Of course, Babs, you are a great age, and capable of astonishing deeds," Jenny agreed, peeping from under her lashes to see if Babs took her teasing in good heart.

"Well, I know about the treasure, because Johnny Granthum heard all about it from his nurse, who is a cousin of Black Jack Morton, and I bet you don't know about him. He's a fearsome villain," Babs explained, eager to tell what she knew of the legend.

Unwilling to spoil her small companion's pleasure in revealing the secrets of Black Jack, Jenny forbeared from telling her she had already learned of the local ogre. Babs, wiping off her mouth with a careless hand, and disdaining the napkin Jenny tendered, rushed on with her tale.

"He's head of the smugglers, you know, a great giant of a man and strong beyond anything. He can fell a man with a blow and terrorizes his band of followers. And he's so clever that he laughs at the Revenue men. They will never catch him." Babs spoke with a certain cachet of the Cornish village which was her home. Jenny felt, as her father's daughter, she must point out to Babs the folly of admiring a lawless brutal varlet, who broke the King's law and caused misery to many.

"Black Jack is not an admirable man, Babs. He is engaged in illegal activities, endangers the village, and causes misery to many. Smugglers are not gallant knights, you know, but rough violent men, who have no notions of decency and honor." Jenny felt as the words left her mouth she sounded prosy and straight-laced. How much she had detested that kind of advice when she was Babs's age. In fact she usually reacted exactly the opposite to what her moralists intended and found the forbidden adventure all the more enticing. Still, she could not allow Babs to romanticize a man like Black Jack Morton.

"Oh, pooh, Jenny. I had not thought you were like most adults, all stiff and disapproving. I think smugglers are exciting, eluding the revenuers to bring in barrels of brandy and bolts of silk from France. And they face all kinds of dangers, too," Babs argued as if that sealed the matter.

"And cause danger, too, Babs. It's not just silks and brandy, but often other more dangerous cargo, sometimes even Frenchmen, and we are at war with Napoleon, you know."

"When I am a bit older, stronger, you know, I shall ask Black Jack to take me on one of his voyages," Babs insisted boldly. She was not impressed with Jenny's arguments and Jenny realized that lectures on the subject would avail little.

"Very well, I can see you are determined. But now let us forget the smugglers and the fearsome Black Jack and make a sand castle. This is a great treat for me, for you know, I did not grow up by the sea as you have, and I greatly envy you all this. I am sure you have made many sand castles and can instruct me in the art," she indicated with a wave of her hand.

Jenny was too astute to continue her strictures against the smugglers, and instead hoped Babs would be distracted by her appeal for instruction in the art of sand castles, as she was. And the two set about constructing a moated structure worthy of King Arthur. So diligently were they occupied with their task, they did not heed the shift in the wind and the insidious creeping mist which drifted in from the sea, borne by the quickening breezes.

Jenny, feeling the dampness wetting her skin, looked up from their work to see the tide creeping in, nibbling at the edges of the fine roadway they had built to the entrance of their castle.

"Oh, my goodness, Babs, I fear we must abandon this magnificent work and be on our way before we are cut off by the tide," she said, trying to keep the concern from her voice. Already the white mist was obscuring the cliff above them and she could hear the whinnying of her mare, as if in warning of their danger.

Babs, undeterred by the threat of the weather, protested, "Oh, Jenny, I want to see the water fill the moat."

"Sorry, pet, but I think we should leave." Jenny could not believe how suddenly the weather had shifted, the cloudless sunny day now shrouded by the enveloping heavy white clouds which hid the sun. Even as she spoke, she noticed the mist obscuring their path which led to the horses above.

Deaf to Babs' protests, she gathered up their luncheon hamper, and Babs' shoes and stockings, prepared to scurry up the path. As they made their way with some difficulty toward the rocky crag, the water lapped at their heels. Determined to show no fright, Jenny turned to chivvy Babs along with bright assurance.

But the water continued to chase them, and she could no longer see the path. Concealing her real apprehension, she grasped Babs hand, and swerved to one side. The water had now reached her ankles, and Babs' knees. How stupid to be caught like a mackerel by this quickening tide. She had been warned and she could not forgive herself for exposing Babs to danger.

The little girl, now aware of their peril, set her chin over quivering lips. She was beginning to be scared, but equally determined not to howl like a baby, after all her boasting of being grown up. What a brave little soldier she was, Jenny thought.

The path had now disappeared, and Jenny guided Babs in what she thought was the right direction only to come against the stark face of a shielding rock. She edged around it, not realizing they had left the shelter of the cove and wandered onto the spit of land beyond their sheltered inlet. This stone outcropping lashed by waves, seemed even more perilous, but just as Jenny was about to despair, Babs shouted to her, "Look, Jenny, in here, a cave. We can shelter here." Before Jenny could demur she dragged her toward the rift between the rocks and into a relatively dry haven.

"See, we will be safe here until the tide turns, or the mist lifts. Sometimes it passes very quickly," Babs explained bravely, and Jenny was grateful for the small girl's attempt to put a good face on their predicament. Indeed the cave, in which she could stand upright, seemed secure, leading back from the threatening water for some distance. Perhaps Babs was right. They must stay here for some time, hoping their horses were safe, or that someone would come upon the animals and realize their plight.

"It really was very stupid of us to be caught so by the tide and mist. Mrs. Peabody warned us," Jenny apologized as she deposited her burdens on the damp floor of the cave, realizing that they could easily have been swamped by the tide and mist. Even now, she thought, they were not out of danger, but she turned a cheerful face to Babs.

"Come, let me help you with your shoes. I fear this cave is full of stones and I would not want you to injure yourself," she insisted, wiping off Babs' small feet with her skirt and hurrying her into the stockings and shoes she carried.

"It's an adventure, isn't it, Jenny?" Babs asked valiantly.

"A great one, and you are a brave girl not to cry and moan because I have taken such poor care of you," Jenny said admiringly. In fact she was more than inpressed with Babs' stoic acceptance of their danger, and admired the girl's ability to meet this contretemps with fortitude. "Come, let us venture a little further into the cave. Perhaps there is an exit of some sort," she insisted with little hope of finding such relief.

They walked warily forward, the darkness now pervasive and not at all comforting. No beckoning vestige of light hinted that the cave might have another opening, so Jenny decided that they would be wiser to halt their exploring and just wait out the tide.

"Here, Jenny, I am a bit tired. Let us rest on these boxes," Babs suggested, having glimpsed some water-stained crates piled carelessly along the side of the cave, but far enough within the shelter to be protected from any encroaching water.

"All right, pet. I do hope we are not causing too much worry to your mother and father. They will be concerned that we are gone so long. It must be past tea time." Jenny did not want to alarm Babs more than necessary, but she knew that their absence was bound to be troubling. And how would any of their searchers discover them here?

Her immediate problem was to keep Babs from panicking. But that stalwart young girl was far more interested in exploring their surroundings than in brooding over their rescue. Jumping up from the crates, she poked at them with an insatiable curiosity.

"Look, Jenny. I do believe these are some of the smugglers' loot. Wouldn't it be capital if we discovered their cargoes, possibly even treasure," she asked tugging at the lids of the crates. Jenny, considering they had best leave well enough alone, was about to protest, when Babs with a mighty heave, pried open the lid of the crate upon which she had been sitting.

"Oh, dear. How disappointing. Nothing. I wonder what was in it," she mused, her bobbed blond head disappearing into the empty crate and sniffing with all the enthusiasm of a terrier. "Ugh, I believe it was spirits. How nasty," she complained, thoroughly disgusted.

"Quite possibly. But it is really no concern of ours, Babs," Jenny reproved, wondering if this discovery could lead to trouble. She must do her best to make Babs see it would not do to noise her discovery abroad. "I really think we would be wise not to mention this to anyone, except perhaps, your father." She was torn between the feeling she should not encourage Babs to have secrets from her parents and a certain prudence which she felt might serve them both far better than revealing what they had inadvertently found.

"Oh, Jenny, secrets. How lovely," Babs crowed, wide eyed with delight. She saw nothing but an adventure in this discovery, not sensing any danger. And Jenny did not want to disabuse her, but she felt uneasy at the knowledge that Babs' excited chatter might lead into dangerous byroads.

"Not secrets exactly, Babs," Jenny said solemnly, determined to make her small companion see the seriousness of the position. "I am sure most of the villagers know that smuggling is prevalent here, but no good can be served by informing all and sundry that we know one of the caches of the smugglers. From the state of these crates I believe whatever they held has been long removed. No doubt, other less obvious hiding places have now replaced this one, for it does not appear anyone has visited this cave for some time. It would be best to keep this to ourselves, except you must tell your father and be advised by what he says," Jenny explained.

"What we should be thinking about now is how to get away from here. It is not a comfortable position," she said wryly with a small shiver. The damp was pervading the cave, and she did not relish having to spend many hours waiting for the tide to ebb, knowing that Babs' household would be frantic. Certainly Amy and Francis would have some severe words for her, leading their small daughter into this sorry situation, and Jenny would not blame them.

Babs gave a long mournful sigh. "I do wish we could have found some treasure, or at least seen some of the smugglers at work. Black Jack even. How exciting that would be," bright eyes round with the thought. "A real adventure."

That Black Jack Morton might not view it so, crossed Jenny's mind, but she turned resolutely away from such a thought. "Are you cold, Babs? Perhaps if you come here we can huddle together for warmth." Suddenly she knew she needed the comfort of that small body to keep her mind from the troubling and nebulous fears which insisted on obtruding despite her best efforts. But Babs evidently entertained no such concerns.

"Of course, Jenny, if you are cold, I will warm you," she said stoutly, nestling up to her side. "I am never cold, having what mother calls, a stout constitution," she informed Jenny proudly, while wrapping her arms around her cousin.

"Good for you, Babs. That's what we need now, two stout constitutions and brave hearts. Shall I tell you a story of an adventure Richard and I had when we were young, to pass the time?" she asked, forcing a cheerful note into her voice.

Thank Heavens, Babs did not sense the aura of evil she did in this dark depressing cave. Most children would be wailing for their mothers, in a near hysterical state at their dilemma. But, of course, Jenny concluded, Babs had little experience of a comforting mother who soothed childish cares and aches. She had learned to be self contained and stalwart, facing her problems with an engaging independence. It was a quality Jenny much admired, and although she was quite unaware of it, possessed more than her own share of such resolute self-sufficiency.

She launched into a tale of one of the more hair-raising escapades involving Harry, Richard, herself and Farmer Andrews's prize bull. Babs enjoyed it, especially Jenny's role as the saviour of her two companions at some risk to her own safety.

Jenny was wracking her brains for another tale to distract Babs, when she heard a faint halloo, coming from the entrance of the cave. Hoping her ears had not deceived her, she hushed Babs, and taking her by the hand, edged her way to the opening, sloshing through the rising water. Dimly, she saw a shape looming beyond the rolling waters. A boat, she thought with a sigh of relief.

"Jenny, are you in there?" came an exasperated voice. Jenny had no doubt of its owner. Oh dear, if they had to be rescued why did it have to be by the arrogant Piers St. Robyns? Then, realizing how foolish she was to complain now that they appeared to be spared more uncomfortable hours in this wretched cave, she shook off her irritation and hailed him with suitable gratitude.

"Yes, we are here, marooned by the tide," she called, wading further into the water, now swirling about her calves, still clutching Babs who was in danger of being submerged.

"Stay there. I will bring the boat in and pick you up," he ordered. And Jenny, realizing the sense of this, obeyed. Within moments he had unceremoniously hauled both Babs and Jenny into the boat, leaving the piloting of the small craft to the burly seaman who sat in the bow. Wrapping them in waterproofs, he directed the man to make all speed for home, meanwhile castigating Jenny for allowing herself to be trapped and involving Babs in her stupidity. Meekly Jenny allowed his wrath to break over her head, although she would dearly have liked to answer him in kind, but withstood the temptation since she was grateful for the rescue.

"How did you know we were marooned?" she asked, when he ceased his fulminations.

"I stopped by to take you riding and learned from Mrs. Peabody that you and Babs had gone on your picnic. Knowing your preference for this cove I thought perhaps you had come to some misadventure when the mist rolled up. I did warn you it was dangerous to poke about beyond the safety of that inlet. But, of course, you were too stubborn to heed my advice," he complained bitterly.

Unwilling to brangle before Babs and the fisherman, Jenny bit back the explanations she wanted to make. Really, he was impossible and any gratitude she felt for their timely rescue was fast dissipating under his caustic manner. She was an adult, not Babs, to be treated in such a fashion. And it was Babs who made the explanations.

"It was not really Jenny's fault, sir. We did not intend to explore the cave, but lost the path to the top of the cove where we left the horses in the mist. I do hope Winky and the mare are all right," Babs said through teeth which however valiantly she tried to hold steady were beginning to chatter.

"You are a brave little poppet, and yes, your horses came home safely, but without their riders, which did raise the alarm, but since we have you safe now, I will say no more. Best get you both into hot baths as soon as possible." Piers soothed the little girl, but turned a dark eye on Jenny, and she knew she had not heard the last of the affair.

Chapter Eight

Fortunately, neither Babs nor Jenny suffered any ill effects from their escapade. Although Jenny felt a deal of responsibility for her careless action in allowing Babs to fall into possible danger, neither Francis nor Amy had much to say about the outing. Amy had seemed annoyed that it had been Piers St. Robyns who rescued them, and her annoyance was all out of proportion considering she should have been grateful to any Good Samaritan in the circumstances. Jenny apologized meekly for her heedless actions and Sir Francis accepted her excuses kindly, telling her not to worry. Now that she had experienced the vagaries of their Cornish climate she would take care in the future he knew.

All in all she felt she had brushed through the matter well, although she still felt a measure of guilt for Babs' danger. However, the little girl assured her father that she had found the whole thing exciting, and then had blurted out the matter of the decaying crates. He did not appear to take the smugglers' cache, if that was what it was, too seriously.

"No doubt, you did discover some ancient hiding place of the smugglers. There have been free traders operating along these shores for centuries. But I doubt if that cave is used by any of the group pursued by Major Bosworth and the Customs Men. It's too exposed, too well known. I would not worry about it. Of course, I will inform the authorities and they can do what they wish about investigating it. I am only happy that neither of you suffered any indisposition from your wetting. Jenny tells me you were a brave girl, Babs, and I am proud of you," Sir Francis said, giving his daughter a comforting hug.

Jenny was always pleased and surprised at watching the aloof Sir Francis with Babs, when he seemed to lose all his stiffness. He really loved and cherished his daughter, although he was strict in his standards and in no way could be thought indulgent.

"Thank you, Poppa," Babs replied, burrowing her sturdy body against him. "Jenny thought we must not keep the secret but share it with you. You will know what to do," she said with assurance.

"Thank you for your confidence, Babs, and you have behaved most properly. Now I must turn you out, for I have a deal of work to get through," he said and patting his daughter on the head, watched with a smile as she skipped out of the room. Jenny lingered for she felt she had not expressed her deep regret for the incident as well as she might.

"You are most forebearing, Francis, but I really feel most abject, and would not wonder if you thought me an unfit companion for Babs after what has happened. I promise to be more careful on any future outings, I promise."

"Nonsense, Jenny. Babs adores you and it is wonderful for her that you are content to spend so much time with her. I fear we are imposing on you, as an unpaid governess, and no one could doubt your care and concern for her. Let us say no more of it, except that I thank you for championing Babs and giving her real affection. I am afraid she does not get what she deserves from her parents," he concluded bitterly. And then as if regretting exposing his unhappiness to Jenny he turned away toward the window.

Jenny sensing his embarrassment at the sad admission withdrew. But she sorrowed not for the first time at the rifts in this small family who seemed so beset with problems when they had so much which promised happiness. She dearly wanted to help them toward some resolution of this mystifying estrangement but could not see her way clear to effect it.

Abandoning her fruitless thoughts she went to chivy Babs into her bonnet for they would be late for church if they did not hurry. The carriage came around in good time, and both Jenny and Babs were waiting at the entrance when Francis and Amy appeared, the latter insisting on riding to church, although it was less than a mile to the village. Amy believed her consequence might suffer if she were seen afoot and not ensconced in state behind her husband's fine grays. Really Amy was a most beautiful woman and could not be faulted for insisting on the homage that beauty required. She was wearing a cerulean blue walking dress styled in the redincote manner and set off by a very fetching straw bonnet which threw into relief her lovely blue eyes and golden hair.

Jenny sighed for the worldly wish that she could look so ravishing. She knew her father would reprove her, but walking up the aisle of the church a few moments later in Amy's wake, she did indeed feel like a dowdy poor relation in her simple cherry merino frock and chip straw hat which had to serve for many occasions. Babs, trudging by her side, looked sturdy and well scrubbed, her pinafore for once clean and her hair brushed, if her usually sunny face was a bit solemn.

Settled in the Morstan pew Babs could not resist peeking around to see who was in the congregation, earning a whispered reproof from her mother. "Stop fidgeting, Babs."

Robert Herron, who knew his congregation, did not linger over his brief simple sermon. True to his promise, Piers St. Robyns read the lesson, in a strong beautiful voice which made the time-hallowed words of Jeremiah: 26: 12 "Now therefore amend your ways and your doings, and obey the voice of the Lord your God, and the Lord will repent of the evil which he has pronounced against you," resound in the church. Jenny could not help but wonder if the lesson had been chosen as a warning to the smugglers or other miscreants, but Robert Herron's sermons stressed the advantages of repentence before a merciful God and said little about vengeance and retribution.

The Earl of Trevarris looked his usual imperturbable self, unaware of the interest his presence had aroused in the congregation, which saw the earl but rarely. And why was he remaining so long in

Cornwall, absent from his London haunts? Amy had implied he found Trevarris boring and of little interest beyond the revenues it supplied, but somehow Jenny did not accept that assessment. The earl might be haughty, overbearing and determined on having his own way, but Jenny did not believe he was insensitive to the problems of the villagers, nor unconcerned with their poverty and lawlessness in trying to relieve it.

Jenny was convinced he had some deep reason for lingering so long in their midst. She did not want to believe his stay involved a liaison with one of his neighbors' wives. She knew he had paid only the most cursory attentions to Amy, although Jenny suspected her cousin would have welcomed a warmer attachment. So that left the luscious Lucia Pencrist, who certainly had a generous supply of the attractions a sophisticated man would find appealing. Or perhaps, Piers St. Robyns was involved with a village girl, exercising his droit de seigneur.

Jenny repressed an unseemly giggle. How wicked she was thinking these uncharitable and carnal thoughts in church, but unfortunately she often found the most unsuitable ideas invading her mind when she should be praying for forgiveness of her sins and the welfare of others. She had once confessed her wayward behavior to her father, who had smiled and admitted that even he sometimes found his prayers disturbed by vagrant fancies that had little to do with piety.

After the service, Jenny joined her cousins in greeting their rector and exchanging parish news with the other members of the gentry.

Piers St. Robyns earned Babs's approval by inquiring with every evidence of sincere concern about her health and welfare and commending her bravery.

She thanked him politely, and then, unable to suppress her excitement, explained, "It was a great adventure, and, of course, I have a stout constitution, not apt to get vapors and megrims and childish ills." Her wise little air appeared to amuse Piers although he agreed gravely that she was most fortunate. Jenny applauded his manner with the girl, for it lacked any of the condescension she might have expected.

"And I can see, that you, too, Jenny, suffered little from your ill-fated expedition," he said suavely, turning to her.

"Like Babs, I, too, have a stout constitution, Piers. I am greatly in your debt for rescuing us. No doubt we would have had an uncomfortable stay in that dreary cave until the tide receded and the mist lifted so that we could see our way to the path." Jenny was grateful to Piers, but she would not fawn all over him for the unexpected kindness.

"I have no doubt you would have contrived. You are such a resourceful girl," Piers agreed sardonically. Jenny did not like his tone and would have taken him up on his implication if they had not been interrupted by Lady Pencrist who glided up and greeted them in her indolent fashion, looking ravishing in a high-waisted crimson silk spencer over an embroidered cream shift.

"We heard you would read the lesson, today, Piers, and I was determined not to miss such a treat. You see, Miss Dryden, he so rarely honors us by joining in our simple pleasures that we must take every advantage when the opportunity offers." Her words were prosaic, but her expression and tone were suggestive.

"How kind of you, Lucia, to notice my comings and goings so acutely," Piers returned, with equal equivocation, reinforcing Jenny's suspicions that there was an intimate relationship between the two.

She was about to make her excuses when Piers said to Lucia with a question in his voice, "I do not see the ubiquitous Henri today."

"You must know, Piers, that Henri is a Catholic and does not worship with us."

"Ah, yes, of course." His tone was bland.

"At any rate, Henri is away for a few days, visiting some émigré friends in Penzance," Lucia offered smoothly.

Jenny, irritated by the nuances she did not grasp, hastened to take her leave. "I see Francis and Amy are becoming impatient. Come, Babs," she said, turning to the little girl, who, bored with the adults' conversation, was scuffing her new shoes on the path.

However, Piers, sensing her perplexity at the cryptic conversation, would have none of that. He had made his point, learned what he wanted to know, and so had no reason to linger. "Come, let me escort you, Jenny. I have a few words to say to Amy and Francis. A pleasure always, Lucia," he concluded, bowing with an ironic smile. Lady Pencrist rewarded him with a knowing look. Whatever the duel between the two, Jenny could not decide who had come off the winner, or even what their passage had meant, but she was soon to glimpse some of Piers's purpose.

He greeted the Morstans cordially and said mockingly, "Now, don't you two tell me what a treat it was to hear me read the lesson. I am beginning to feel that I have been notorious in my neglect of Trevarris. And I will try to pay more diligent attention to my responsibilities if this is the reaction I inspire. I know Jenny feels I am the veriest reprobate—untrustworthy, worldly, and thoroughly beyond redemption—but I hope for a more charitable view from you, Amy."

"You do not have a reputation for devotion to the parish, Piers," Amy replied a bit sharply. She was not quite certain if Piers was amusing himself, and the sense of being the butt of some private joke of his did not please her. She never knew quite what to expect from him.

"Nonsense, my dear. Piers is quite diligent. Don't you agree, Robert?" Francis insisted, turning to the vicar who had joined him after greeting many of his humble parishioners.

"I am most grateful to you, Lord Trevarris, and I think you are responsible for a greater turnout this Sunday than usual. The villagers were intent on seeing their landlord read the lesson," Robert soothed. "Not that their curiosity speaks well for my own efforts."

"They do not deserve such a diligent parson," Piers said graciously. Then turning to Jenny he asked, "Don't you agree, Jenny, that Trevarris is most fortunate in its spiritual leader?"

"Mr. Herron is both devoted and sincere," Jenny

answered shortly, not liking Piers's irony. To dutifully lead a flock of such indifferent, if not actually surly, sheep would try the most Christian of men, she thought, although she did not voice her opinion.

"Robert, perhaps you will join us for luncheon, and you too, Piers, if you are available," Amy interrupted, having heard enough. And then tardily remembering, "And Evelyn, too, of course." The stern Miss Herron was not an addition the Morstans welcomed, but they had no choice but to include her.

"Alas, Lady Morstan, I must ride out to Poker's farm. His mother is dying and I should be on hand," Robert explained. "Thank you for the invitation and I hope I may crave your indulgence at another more propitious time." Regret framed his words.

Although she had come to admire Robert Herron, Jenny often wished he were not so obseqious toward her cousins. Surely the living was the gift of Piers, not the Morstans, but since the lord of the manor was so rarely in the area, perhaps Robert Herron thought he must stay in well with the resident gentry. Ashamed of herself for such unkind thoughts, Jenny gave the vicar a blinding smile and said softly, "We will miss you."

"But you will have me as a substitute," Piers offered, earning a dark look from Jenny, who suspected he was teasing her again. Turning to Sir Francis, he accepted the invitation and added, "I have several matters I want to discuss with you, Francis, so this will suit admirably." With mutual assurances of goodwill the party separated, Jenny taking Babs's hand and following the Morstans to their carriage. No more was said about Evelyn

Herron joining them, for which Jenny could only be grateful. She had made a valiant attempt to become friends with the Vicar's sister, but she found herself up against a wall of hostility which could not be breached.

The addition of Piers St. Robyns to the Morstan Sunday board alleviated much of the constraint Jenny had experienced when dining with her cousins lately. They were both too well-bred and experienced socially to allow any disharmony between them to affect their duties as hosts. Often, Jenny had wished for Babs's engaging presence at the table, for when the child was about, it was difficult to stand on ceremony. However, Babs was relegated to dinner in the nursery, much to her disgust, and Jenny could only be grateful for Piers as an antidote to the usual cheerless mood of the Morstan table.

For his part Piers made every effort to entertain, giving the eager Amy all the latest London *on-dits*, but not ignoring Jenny who had no notion of the society of which he was an integral part.

"I know you must miss the Season, Amy. You should add your charms to what promises to be an unusually dull one, and perhaps take Jenny with you. She would enjoy seeing the sights and tilting her lance at those beaux and bucks who are always anxious for a new conquest," Piers chaffed.

Jenny refused to rise to his jesting, and only smiled as if at the antics of a mischievous child, which caused Piers to raise a wry eyebrow as if acknowledging her hit. She wouldn't play the role of a naive innocent or lovelorn spinster. She smiled cheerily, neither agreeing nor demurring, while thinking what an aggravating opponent Piers was. True, he had unfairly more than his share of good looks, charm, and presence, but he had badly mistaken her if he believed he could toy with her as a distraction from the boredom of the country. He could be kind, understanding even, but Piers St. Robyns was too aware of his consequence and definitely not interested in settling down into tame domesticity. Of that Jenny was convinced. She knew how to guard her heart now, she decided bitterly.

Amy signified that she and Jenny would retire to leave the men to their port and whatever confidences they wished to exchange. The ladies left the room, Piers politely standing and holding the door for them, giving Jenny a wicked wink as she sailed through as if he had quite easily read her mind and found her amusing. Provoking man. In the hall Jenny excused herself to seek out Babs, whose company she found preferable to the adults. Amy nodded her acquiescence languidly.

In the dining room, Francis passed the port and waited for what Piers had to say. He was not expecting the curt question which followed.

"What do you know about Henri d'Aubisson, Francis?"

Francis frowned. He was not about to confide to Piers that he suspected the suave Frenchman was his wife's lover.

"Not a great deal. He claims to be an émigré, and has found a comfortable niche with the Pencrists. I understand Lucia is some sort of relation, a half sister or cousin. He seems pleasant enough but with little bottom. What is your interest in him?"

"I think he's a spy. There are too many of these blasted émigrés wandering around the countryside. They play the role of Napoleon's persecuted victims, but most of them would endorse the Corsican in a trice if they could regain their titles and land through such a ploy. I intend to invite a few of my own pet émigrés down here and try to discover if the wily Henri is all that he seems," Piers explained.

"Well, good luck to you. But I really don't think Henri has the energy or the brains to conspire even if he could regain his fortune by such maneuvers. I don't particularly like the fellow, but I doubt he is a spy." Then, realization hitting him, Francis added, "Of course, that is why you are making such an extended sojourn down here. Normally you only make a flying visit."

"Yes, and I think that has been a mistake. I should keep a closer eye on what is happening at Trevarris. There are dark deeds abroad. Black Jack Morton, for one, needs to be watched. He is a menace, and not just because of a little casual smuggling," Piers replied, toying with his wine glass.

Francis hesitated, unwilling to say what he feared. "That's reassuring. I am happy to learn the real reason for your long visit. I was afraid you were flirting with Jenny, and that would be unkind. She's a dear girl, but not up to your touch, Piers, and I would be negligent in my role as her temporary guardian if I did not warn you that I will not stand idly by while you toy with her affections."

"For shame, Francis. You must acquit me of such fell designs. I think you underestimate Miss Dryden. She doesn't really like me or trust me. Her recent experience has given her a justified caution of rakes, which is what she thinks of me. But you are wise to keep an eye on her. She is apt to rush into situations which could cause her grievous harm. A real catalyst, that girl. And I, too, would not want her to suffer the consequences of her heedless actions. I find her quite refreshing, but you mistake my interest in her," Piers insisted, wondering if he were being entirely honest with his host. Jenny had a fresh innocent appeal he found surprisingly attractive and he had a strange desire to change her opinion of him. If he had known he would be meeting her again he would not have behaved as he had during their encounter in Truro.

"My house party will be arriving in a few days and I will be giving a few dinners and other entertainments for them. I want my friends to see Henri in a relaxed convivial setting, off guard, so to speak. I can tell you frankly there are some odd doings in this corner of Cornwall and I am determined to get to the bottom of them. We are in a perilous position vis-à-vis Napoleon, with few allies and the expectation of an invasion. If Henri is our miscreant I must see he does no further harm," Piers said with decision.

Francis was slightly taken aback by the earl's grim expression. Francis had obviously misjudged Piers, believing him to be somewhat of a Corinthian, intent on pleasure and the sophisticated life of a London man about town. Francis prided himself on reading men's motives and assessing their worth. He should have remembered Piers's brilliant naval career and his reputation in Whitehall. Now he appeared to have accepted another assignment and was prepared to see it through with equal skill and determination.

Francis could only applaud the man's dedication.

"Of course, Piers, you can rely on me for any cooperation if Henri is your man. I can tell you from my own experience that Black Jack Morton is a troublemaker. He's cowed the villagers, even causes rebellion at the mine. There are several men there who take orders from him, I know, and I don't like it," Francis confided.

"Thank you, Francis. I was sure I could count on you; I need all the help I can get. Of course, there is Bosworth and his troop, but they are in Penzance. I am thinking of requesting Bosworth to detail a squad to Trevarris. With soldiers on the spot it may serve as a warning, but I am not too sure of the men's loyalty. You know full well that in the past Revenue officers, even the army, have been bribed to turn a deaf ear to smugglers' activity. I have a sneaking admiration for the traditional free trading, and we both benefit from the cargo, but I believe Black Jack is involved in more dangerous contraband, perhaps with d'Aubisson's aid. I intend to get to the bottom of it, I promise you. And I do hope the inquisitive Miss Dryden will not impede my efforts," he concluded with a rueful grin.

Francis could not deny the force of Piers's arguments. "I quite agree with you about Jenny's penchant for dangerous escapades. My small daughter is her accomplice and the combination gives me some anxious moments. Which reminds me, Piers, I have not fully thanked you for their rescue from the inlet yesterday, an example of what I mean. They have both confessed to me that they found some empty crates in the cave where they were marooned before you found them so fortuitously. It does indicate that the smugglers at one time have used that cove for depositing contraband goods. I just hope that Black Jack has not learned of their discovery, that he does not consider them impediments to his activities," Francis concluded with a worried frown.

"Jenny will need to be watched. She does not trust me for a variety of reasons, some my own fault, I admit. I half suspect she thinks I might be in league with the smugglers," Piers agreed lightly.

They said no more of the affair and drifted into conversation about the war and certain news of common London acquaintances.

Francis was within an ace of confiding in Piers about Henri d'Aubisson's dalliance with his wife, more evidence of the man's untrustworthiness, but he was too ashamed of his suspicions, and he owed Amy his loyalty. By nature he was a reserved man and he loathed the idea of casting doubts on his wife's fidelity. He could not expose her to gossip. Not that Piers woud betray his confidence, but he loved his wife and had too much pride to imply that she might be deceiving him, and with d'Aubisson.

Francis and Piers had known each other since boyhood, had shared a great deal, but even so Francis could not confess his fears. Both men had secrets they held closely. Neither wished to embarrass the other by emotional revelations. They had been bred in the tradition that it was bad ton to discuss such matters and even in extremity could not discuss intimate details. Francis remembered with some embarrassment that he had thought at one time that Amy might encourage overtures from Piers. He should have known better.

Chapter Nine

If Black Jack Morton suspected that his activities were under investigation he would have sneered at the prospect of paying the price for his various crimes. He had too much contempt for authority, gained over years of immunity and an insolent faith in his own power to evade the law. Success had deepened his defiance and intensified his belief that he would never pay the penalty for his deeds. Like his fellow Cornishmen, he did not consider his free trading an offense against the realm, but a practice hallowed by centuries of tradition. The fact that his country was at war with France and that any concourse with the enemy hinted at treason, he paid little heed. What had he to do with English notions of war and peace? His responsibilities were entirely personal. Any opportunity to improve his fortunes would receive a hearing. Morality did not enter into his dealings.

On a particularly dark Sunday evening he was expecting not only the usual shipment of brandy and silks from across the Channel, but a passenger whose destination and business was no concern of his. The agent had paid well for his assistance and Black Jack considered that of primary importance. If he had known how much money the man was carrying, he would have had no compunction about murdering him and pocketing the coins, but he valued his contacts on the Continent too much to take that chance, although he had often been tempted. But he dare not risk disturbing the prosperous chain which he had taken such pains to establish.

It was well after midnight when Black Jack and his cohorts met outside the village and stealthily crept down to the beach. Long practice had insured that the rendezvous with their Breton counterparts would go easily. In order to protect the cargo from curious eyes, only about half of the contraband was unloaded directly onto the shore. The rest of the kegs were moored to buoys in the bay, concealed under seaweed, where they would be picked up by the smugglers during their fishing runs at some later date. This maneuver insured that if the landed cargo was intercepted and commandeered by the law, half would still be safely concealed and could be dispatched in safety to the distribution point. That way some profit would accrue whatever happened.

Tonight the smugglers moved quickly about their business, hauling the kegs ashore in dinghies and trundling the contraband into the wagons hidden nearby, not an easy chore because of the rocky shale to be crossed and the heaviness of the barrels. There was a deal of cursing and muttering as the shadowy figures bent to their task. Black Jack took no part in this donkey work. Standing booted feet apart, a pistol in his waistband, he looked a formidable figure to the agent who stepped ashore with the first shipment. Black Jack's villainous crew took no notice of the meeting between their chief and the cloaked figure, having learned to ignore what did not involve their immediate profit. As for the stranger, he was hustled into the shadows where he delivered his bona fides to Black Jack and then sped on his way.

With the disappearance of the mysterious passenger and the final off-loading of the crates and barrels, the men relaxed with several swigs of liquor, their voices rising in dispute. Believing themselves safe from any observation after years of carrying out their secret trade without interference, they had become flagrantly defiant. They knew Black Jack had intimidated the villagers, keeping them deaf to the smugglers' coming and goings on these Sunday evenings.

The people who were not actually involved in the smuggling activity had a certain sympathy for the lawbreakers. And if not participating themselves, most of the villagers had a relative who did, or else they benefitted in some way by the trade. The few who had the temerity to challenge Black Jack had been silenced ruthlessly, and few would now defy the chief. So the smugglers had little to fear. Only the occasional Revenue man posed a threat, and the Custom officers were severely taxed to cover all the suspected caches. Moreover, there was always plenty of warning of the government officers' arrival.

At last wagons rolled from the shore through the village toward the disreputable inn some miles distant from which middlemen would collect the goods for distribution. Much of the brandy and fine wine, the silks and velvets, found their way to London to grace the tables and the wardrobes of the Ton who saw no impropriety in enjoying French goods while at war with the purveyors of such luxuries. As the wagons lumbered over the cobblestones and into the shrouded darkness beyond the village, none appeared to watch their progress. It was well after midnight now, and if questioned the villagers would have insisted that all law-abiding folk were long abed and asleep.

But this Sunday evening the smugglers' operation had been observed. Piers St. Robyns had watched the whole business from behind a convenient crag jutting over the very cove where Jenny and Babs had enjoyed their picnic the day before. He had learned from rumors in the village the infamous crew might attempt a landing, and had decided to watch, hoping to learn more of the smugglers' methods. He had been annoyed and then amused at the effrontery of the smugglers, using his land as the rendezvous. Of course, he had seen smugglers plying their trade in the past. But that had been years ago, before Black Jack had begun to organize the trade and tyrannize the village. Then smuggling had been a far more casual affair, just a matter of adding a few guineas to their pockets by accepting the odd barrel or so. Now under Black Jack's hard fist smuggling had corrupted the whole of Trevarris and Piers would no longer tolerate it.

What was even more invidious, the arrival of the mysterious passenger, another in the deepening chain of French agents landing on their shores, convinced Piers that he must act with decision before more harm was done. He had no doubt that the stranger had delivered some message which Black Jack would forward to the proper quarters. Piers was in a dilemma. Should he follow Black Jack or the stranger? Whatever message the man had brought had already been delivered, which meant Black Jack would now hurry to turn over the documents to his contact. But, if that was his destination, he appeared in no rush to meet the appointment.

Piers, following at a discreet distance, watched Black Jack ride carelessly after the wagons, but turn off before they reached their rendezvous. Convinced that Black Jack was on his way to meet the man he hoped to capture, Piers felt a rush of satisfaction. If he could catch the villain in the act of receiving treasonable papers then he would have his man and this whole conspiracy might be aborted. To his disappointment Black Jack whistled merrily, indifferent to any pursuit and turned off onto the lane where his cottage lay. Here he stabled his horse, swaggered into his house, and Piers could see him lighting a candle before closing the shutters and hiding his subsequent actions from the watcher in the shadows.

Damn, Piers cursed. He wondered if the mysterious contact was awaiting Black Jack in his cottage, or if the smugglers' chief was merely retiring, with no intention of meeting the traitor that evening. Of course, he might be preparing for the arrival of the person whom Piers so eagerly sought, and if that were the case, Piers had no option but to wait here for this visitation. But it was damn uncomfortable, a slight drizzle had deepened now into a steadier rain and a stiff wind was lifting up from the harbor.

No stranger to inclement weather, Piers was prepared to persevere in the hopes that more would be revealed to him, but just as he had dismounted, secured his horse, and stationed himself behind a tree to watch events, he noticed the light went out. Black Jack might be prepared to receive his visitor in darkness, but Piers doubted it. The beggar was going to sleep. He had no intentions of meeting any master spy this evening.

Piers sighed. Well, he might have expected no less. This was no amateur operation to be unveiled by one evening's detection. Obviously provisions had been made for delivery of papers, and orders given and received in some way which might be very difficult to determine. Piers decided to call it a night after a fruitless wait of another hour and he made his way wearily back to Arthmore.

Really, he had learned little. He had known about Black Jack for some time now, and he had guessed the location of the smugglers' cache when Francis had mentioned Jenny's discovery. But it would not be that simple, he thought. Tonight Black Jack had used the cove as the rendezvous, but next time (and when would that be?) he could decide on another stretch of beach. Surely the man had not become so brazen he did not take elementary precautions when planning the delivery of contraband cargo.

Piers had discovered by judicious investigation that Sunday was most likely the day of the week designated for a landing, but that would depend on the tide, so not every Sunday would see the smugglers out and about. Piers had struck lucky this time, but would he have to watch every Sunday when the tide was favorable? And where would he watch? Tonight the cove had been the landing place, next week it might be on the other side of the village. Piers suspected the smugglers had decided to use his beach for he was rarely in residence, and any signs of their activity would be long gone when he arrived in their neighborhood. Black Jack now knew he was at Arthmore and would plan more carefully in the future. Piers sighed. He would have to challenge the rogue before long, but he doubted Black Jack would be very forthcoming. Of course, he could swear out a warrant for him and the local magistrate, Sir Francis, would have him taken up and tried, but that would hardly serve Piers's purpose or the ends of his Whitehall friends. Far better to let Black Jack continue his illegal dealings and perhaps Piers might have better fortune next time and discover the man's contact.

Somehow Piers was convinced that the organization of this ring had been the work of a mind far more acute than Black Jack's. The local bully had a certain shrewd knowledge of smugglers' methods, some Continental contacts, a brutal, violent streak which impressed his followers and frightened off any who might betray him, but he certainly had neither the brains nor the resources to plan the traitorous chain which was flooding the county with Napoleon's men. Not that Black Jack had much patriotic feeling, Piers conceded, but he would never have thought of this increased source of income on his own. Someone had enlisted his aid, and as such would be vulnerable to blackmail, for Piers believed Black Jack was capable of any villainy which would enhance his coffers. Somehow, Piers must prevail upon him, one way or the other, to betray his principal.

As he slogged home over the wet rutted path, Piers, despite the miserable weather and the trickle of rain down his neck beneath his coat, felt immensely cheered by his night's vigil.

On the Monday following the rescue from the cave, Jenny, as usual, walked Babs down to the vicarage for her lessons. After a stormy night, the day promised well, clear and glistening from the rain, the wind abated to a gentle breeze. After a few words with Robert Herron she wandered into the church, intending to take a closer look at the memorials. Off the nave was a small chapel holding the tomb of a Crusader, one of Piers St. Robyns ancestors. Jenny deciphered the Latin inscription with little trouble. He had also been a Piers, and his effigy, in full mail, with his hands crossed, shared the stern features and impressive stature of his descendant. No wonder Piers took such a proprietary interest in the happenings of the village. The Trevarris family had been lords of the manor for generations, accustomed to ruling this small kingdom without interference.

Only now was Jenny coming to terms with the difference between Cornish and Wiltshire ways. In some ways it was maddening, even frightening, and pervasive. Francis for all his practical good sense, shared some of the characteristics of his fellow Cornishmen. Only the Pencrists and the Herrons, of course, foreigners as she was, were the exception. As for the enigmatic earl of Trevarris, worldly, arrogant, and thoroughly annoying, Jenny refused to categorize him.

Leaning against his ancestor's tomb she thought of the noble lord with some acerbity. He never behaved as she expected. Yesterday he had been a savior, comforting Babs but raking her with caustic words. For some reason she seemed to annoy him, and certainly he raised her hackles whenever they met, yet he could be kind. Why was her reaction so fierce and why was his so mocking? No doubt he considered her a naive foolish girl, prone to falling into scrapes and possessing none of the sophisticated manners he had come to expect from the ladies he usually honored with his attention. Well, she was hardly in that category, Jenny admitted. Even in the depths of Cornwall there were women—Lucia Pencrist, Amy—who behaved in the assured, experienced way he obviously preferred. Well, she did not care. The Earl of Trevarris need not think he could lure her into his circle of adoring admirers.

Jenny, deep in her musing, was startled to hear the harsh voice of Evelyn Herron at her shoulder. "What are you doing here, Miss Dryden? Communing with the spirits?"

Jenny, determined not to take umbrage, turned and greeted her questioner. "Yes, actually, I was. Silly of me, I suspect. But it is an interesting tomb, a fascinating church, too. You are fortunate."

"It has nothing to do with me. I care little for

pretentious ecclesiastical architecture. And it's much too imposing for this little village, rarely filled with worshippers, despite Robert's best efforts," she complained.

"Yesterday's service appeared well attended," Jenny offered with a smile. She would not let Evelyn Herron depress her.

"Yes, well, the villagers usually turn out when Lord Trevarris is in residence. This is a terribly feudal community, as you may have noticed, unfriendly to strangers but quite in awe of their own lord," Evelyn sneered as if such loyalty disgusted her. "But he is never here for long, finds Trevarris dull and insipid compared to his London life."

Although Jenny had come to the same conclusion about Piers, somehow she did not want to agree or discuss him with this waspish dour woman. She wondered fleetingly why Evelyn was so bitter.

"Have you and Robert been here long?" she asked brightly.

"Eight years. We came from a Sussex parish, near Brighton. I was glad to get away," she replied, a stark look in her eyes. She then recollected herself. "But it matters little where we are, if Robert is comfortable."

"He seems very settled here, but then, I suspect he has the happy facility of adapting to whatever circumstances he finds himself. You are fortunate to possess such an amiable brother," Jenny concluded kindly, hoping she could soon leave for she found Evelyn a dispiriting companion, try as she might to find a common ground.

"Too amiable for his own good and easily taken advantage of by ambitious females," she warned, giving Jenny a baleful look. Short of assuring Miss Herron that she had no designs on her brother, which would make her feel the veriest ninny, Jenny had no reply. Still, she wondered again why Miss Herron was so disagreeable. Her father would say it was because she was unhappy, and should be pitied and helped, but then her father had a great deal more tolerance and Christian charity than Jenny could ever hope to achieve.

"Well, I must not linger any longer. Amy will be expecting me." Somehow Evelyn Herron had taken much of her delight in the morning away, and Jenny yearned to leave the damp confines of this church and restore her spirits.

"Oh, I am sure Lady Morstan has much to occupy her. You need not worry," Evelyn said mysteriously. Jenny could not fathom her meaning. Really, this woman was a trial.

"Still, I must be on my way, unless you need some assistance with the flowers or other business," Jenny asked, determined to be helpful, despite her instincts to flee.

"Not at all. And, Miss Dryden, lonely vigils beside the Trevarris tomb are not healthy. I would not repeat the experience," Miss Herron advised with the whisper of menace in her tone.

"I quite like tombs and churches, Miss Herron, so we will have to disagree on that. Good morning," Jenny replied, unwilling to give quarter. But as she walked slowly down the aisle of the church she felt Evelyn Herron's inimical eyes boring into her back and with some effort repressed a shudder. Really, the woman was quite unhinged. Poor Robert, Jenny concluded as the heavy nail-studded oak door of the church clanged shut behind her and she walked briskly down the path through the graveyard on her way home.

Gratefully she turned her face toward the sun, relieved to bask in the blessings of nature after her strange interview. She must take care not to be alone with Evelyn Herron again. If she, or any woman, seriously considered Robert Herron as a husband, they would certainly be deterred by such a sister-in-law. No right-thinking girl would entertain the idea of living in the same house with the vicar's sister for a moment, and Jenny feared Robert was too kind and too under Evelyn's thumb to turn his sister away. Still, it was none of her business.

As Jenny stepped cheerfully along toward the manor she realized, watching a skein of curlews flying in perfect formation through the azure sky, that she had put Harry Ruston completely from her mind. She felt content to be enjoying this delightful May morning, with no worries or unhappy thoughts for company, and that was evidence of her parents' sense in sending her to Cornwall. She was to look back on this morning later and wonder how she could have been so unperceptive.

Chapter Ten

Lucia Pencrist, like Francis Morstan, had noticed her half brother's interest in the fair Amy. Indolent by nature and disinclined to interfere with others' pleasures, she had watched his pursuit with a certain cynical amusement. She thought she recognized in Amy just such an *amoureuse* as she believed herself to be. That her neighbor could be reacting from the death of her baby never crossed her mind, for Lucia had little interest in children. She wondered lazily how far the affair marched and decided she would do a little injudicous meddling.

She greeted Henri with an indulgent smile as he entered the dining room for luncheon. She herself had only recently descended from her chamber, always breakfasting in bed, spending the morning on her toilette.

"We will be lunching alone, *cher*, as Austen has ridden off on some pursuit of his own," Lucia informed her brother as he held her chair politely for her.

"I do wonder what Austen finds to occupy himself

down here in this *farouche* environment. He's always so energetic, riding about hither and yon," Henri replied, eyeing his sister with appreciation. Really, she was a most beautiful woman, with a certain feline air that had a potent attraction. She must find it damnably dull immured here after her successes in London. Not for a moment did Henri believe she found her husband so enthralling that she enjoyed life in this isolated corner of England in his company.

Lucia responded with a careless shrug. "Who knows, Henri, perhaps he is having a liaison with some fisherman's daughter or even dabbling in the smugglers' trade." At times Lucia Pencrist appeared surprisingly shrewd, more aware of people and events than most would credit her.

"If you really believe he is dallying with some rural beauty you don't seem at all disturbed, but then I doubt very much if Austen is capable of a *grande* or even a *petite passion,*" Henri replied. Considering that his brother-in-law had supplied him with a bolt-hole when he was sorely tried to find a haven, his sneering remarks to Sir Austen's wife were in doubtful taste. But Lucia did not take them amiss. Her mind was following an entirely different track.

"You are so skilled in affairs of the heart, dear Henri. Is your current interest marching well?" she asked slyly, intent on stirring up some reaction from her urbane brother.

"Well, as you know, *chérie,* these things take time and patience. I am sure eventually the object of my pursuit will reward my devotion," he assured her with a certain complacency.

"You have little competition. Of course, now that

the formidable Trevarris has appeared on the scene, who knows what will happen. A fascinating man, that, and one who guards his secrets well," Lucia purred.

"You find him so?" Henri said silkily, not liking to admit that any man could rival him as a chevalier.

"Of course, and so does the lovely Amy. But I do not *il en est épris?* No. If the distinguished Piers has any romantic interest in the neighborhood it is not the wife of Sir Francis," Lucia informed him with a mysterious smile.

"Who can you mean but some gypsy maid or local lass, and he is a bit too high nosed and discriminating for that kind of crude amour," Henri insisted, but relieved that his sister did not think the earl's attention had strayed toward Henri's own target.

"I think he is spending an inordinate amount of time with the innocent Wiltshire visitor, Miss Dryden. So often men who have been pursued so diligently on the Marriage Mart and in London's most sophisticated drawing rooms fall suddenly for a naive schoolgirl. Yes, I think the engaging Miss Dryden interests our noble lord," Lucia offered with a knowing smile.

And before her brother could either agree or protest, she continued, "And that is just as well for you, Henri. For if he is distracted by an amour he will lose interest in your activities. He is quite suspicious of you, you know. He thinks you may be involved in some devilish conspiracy and yearns to discover you in the very act of betraying your friends and neighbors." She paused for effect, then continued. "Why do you think he is spending so much time down here in the depths of Cornwall at the height of the Season? He is searching for the rogues who are smuggling Frenchmen onto our coast. You know, the Whitehall cabbage-heads are shaking in their shoes over the possibility of Napoleon invading their sacred shores."

Henri looked at his sister with respect. Really, she was a shrewd one. She might appear bored with her surroundings, caring only for fashions and her comfort, but she understood far more than most people realized. If she thought Lord Trevarris was intent on trapping him she was probably right.

"Thank you for the warning, *ma belle*. I will be vigilant and not let Trevarris find me in any evil deeds," Henri said lightly, but his eyes looked hard and wary.

Although neither Lucia nor Henri appeared unduly concerned about the activities of Austen Pencrist, they might both have been startled by his meeting that morning with Black Jack Morton. Sir Austen made no effort to hide the encounter, and, as a matter of fact, it took place in full view of any loiterers at the harbor.

Among those watching the meeting between Black Jack and Sir Austen was Jenny Dryden. After delivering Babs to the vicarage, she had wandered down to the harbor with the idea of sketching the view to send to her mother who had asked for a description of Trevarris.

Settling herself on a convenient bollard, Jenny looked out on an idyllic scene, for southern Cornwall was showing its best face this morning. The sea was calm, lapping against the harbor in benign waves, the sun sparkled across the water, and in the distance a sloop, its sails extended to take full advantage of the slight breeze, tacked across the bay.

Lounging at some distance from her perch Jenny saw several fishermen gathered around what she suspected was the notorious Black Jack. Really, he was a fearsome-looking character and Jenny had no difficulty in believing that he exerted his power over his followers by his mere presence, so menacing and dark was his posture and expression. Distracted, she watched the men, apparently taking orders from their leader, and wondered if they were being instructed in their next free trading assignment. They were an unprepossessing lot, scruffy, rough, and at the same time servile before their leader. She drew their figures without much detail, concentrating on the outlines of wharf and shore. For once she thought in drawing a traditional sketch she was capturing the essence of the scene.

Abruptly the men about Black Jack scattered, interrupted by the arrival of Sir Austen Pencrist. Jenny's eyes narrowed. What could the austere and grim Sir Austen want with Black Jack? They held a hurried colloquy, Black Jack arguing and Sir Austen insisting. Surely if he was in league with the smugglers he would not meet with their leader in such a public place. As Jenny watched the two, she saw Sir Austen hand over some notes to the smuggler and then turn suddenly on his heel and walk away. He must have been aware of the distant spectator, for he veered in her direction and, to her confusion and embarrassment, approached her.

"Good morning, Miss Dryden. Lovely day, what? I

see you are taking advantage of our gentle weather to do some sketching. May I see?" he asked in a conciliatory tone.

Wordlessly, Jenny handed over the drawing, relieved that it followed the traditional lines acceptable for a lady's amateur portfolio. How dreadful if she had captured Sir Austen in some unflattering pose and it was highly possible, for he resembled to her artist's eye, a squat, lumbering hippopotamus, not that she really knew much about those African quadrupeds. Her imagination could supply damning details. However, Sir Austen could not criticize this bland depiction of the harbor.

"Very nice, Miss Dryden," he said after a perfunctory look. "But you know it really is not the thing for you to wander down here by yourself. Some very rough types frequent the quay. I am sure Sir Francis and Lady Morstan would not approve," he admonished her.

"I am waiting to collect young Barbara from her vicarage lessons. Surely there is no harm in my doing some idle sketching to pass the time," she answered a bit sharply, taking back the drawing and slipping it into her tablet. Really, the man had a very brusque way of going about things or was he truly warning her? She could scarcely believe that he was in league with the smugglers. But what did she really know about Sir Austen and his Francophilic wife?

"Not at all, my dear, but the villagers about here are a suspicious lot. They do not take kindly to strangers and dislike any inordinate meddling in their affairs." Evidently he thought she was much too interested in the daily life of Trevarris. How ridiculous, Jenny thought, while at the same time aware that Sir Austen meant to convey more than casual concern. If so, she would not be intimidated.

"Naturally, Sir Austen, I am interested in the life of the village. I have never visited Cornwall before and find the activities of the fishermen and miners fascinating," she explained dulcetly, while inwardly thinking that Sir Austen was taking too much upon himself. It was not for him to criticize her behavior.

"Now I have offended you. You mistake me, Miss Dryden. But I thought it only prudent to tell you that the Cornish are a peculiar breed and not at all what you might expect. I apologize if I have annoyed you," Sir Austen said with a grin, changing his whole aspect. He really was not such a bad sort, and Jenny wondered if his manners could be blamed on shyness. How sad, and she immediately felt ashamed and acquitted him of anything but a laborious effort toward politeness.

"Thank you, Sir Austen. I will heed your words. I cannot help but be impressed by your knowledge of Trevarris, although I believe, you are not a native?" She gave him a wide-eyed speculative look.

"I was born here, but lived most of my life until recently in London. But come, I am wasting your time, and I must be off. Charming to see you again and I hope you enjoy the rest of your visit," he said hurriedly, bowing and walking off jerkily, obviously regretting that he had stopped to talk to her.

What a strange man, Jenny thought as she watched him stride up the quay toward his horse and carriage waiting on the main street. Was he just what he seemed, a gruff exile from London who had returned to live out his days in some comfort while pining for the pleasures of the metropolis? Somehow she thought there was more to Sir Austen than that. And his lovely wife was also an enigma. Really, Trevarris abounded with exotic types.

Jenny returned to her inspection of the harbor, noticing that Black Jack, lounging against one of the boats drawn up on the shingle, was now, in his turn, watching her. He straightened, as if coming to a decision, and she believed he was about to accost her. But if that was his intention, he was thwarted.

The woman appeared very suddenly, running from behind the boats. She was a tempestuous beauty, dressed in a colorful red skirt, a collection of gold bangles, and trailing scarves. Her feet were bare and brown. There was no mistaking that dark hair, flashing black eyes, and the dusky complexion. She was a gypsy. Jenny recalled that Piers had mentioned a Romany tribe camping in his fields.

Whatever her business with Black Jack she would brook no denial. Standing arms akimbo she screamed at him, the breeze carrying off her words, but Jenny was in no doubt that the gypsy was attacking the smuggler chief for some slight, either justified or imagined. He listened with grim amusement to the shrill tirade, but finally, tiring of the sport, turned his back on her with a shrug and began to walk away. She would have none of that and grabbed Black Jack by the arm, intent on finishing her recriminations.

Jenny applauded the girl's courage in facing such a formidable man, for the gypsy showed no fear. She danced before him in a rage, her words indistinguishable, but Jenny kept hearing the name "Janos" over and over again. Then, when she wondered how the gypsy could continue in the face of such stoic indifference, Black Jack, suddenly losing his temper, turned and gave the girl a mighty cuff across her face which felled her to her knees.

Jenny, appalled at his brutality, could not stand by and do nothing. Without a thought for her own safety, she ran up to the pair and bent over the girl. "Are you all right?" she asked, bending down to offer what help she could.

Shaking off Jenny's proferred hand, the girl rose unsteadily to her feet, her eyes flashing, and she turned to renew the battle.

"'Tis not blows will hurt me. I want my due and Janos's, you dirty bastard," she spat at the dark man, the bruise purpling on her cheek.

Jenny, not shocked by the language, but furious at Black Jack's violence, turned on him, prepared to add her objections to his vicious reaction.

"How dare you strike this woman," she protested fearlessly, although she should have been wary of the man, knowing his reputation for barbarous behavior.

"Ho, what's this, a fine lady interfering in this trull's affair? Pay no attention to her rantings, missy. It's none of your business," he growled.

"It's the business of any right-thinking person to prevent cruelty. You have no cause to strike this woman, no matter what your differences," Jenny replied heatedly, realizing that she was foolhardy to challenge him. Then, turning her back on him, she said kindly to the gypsy, "Can I help you in any way?"

"Just be on your way. I can deal with the vermin," the gypsy said ungraciously. "And I can protect myself from the likes of him. He will pay for his false promises," she insisted and, to Jenny's horror, drew from her bodice a wicked-looking knife.

"As for you, you devil, you will give me the coin I asked or t'will be the worse for you," she stormed, brandishing the weapon and looking as if she would, without compunction, bury it in his chest.

Black Jack only laughed and grappled with her, trying to wrest the knife from her grasp, but she resisted with surprising strength and ended by biting the hand that tried to force her.

"You little spitfire, stop this nonsense. Why should I pay for your brat? You say it's mine, but you gypsies will try any dodge to wing a few coins from any fool. You'll not get a penny from me, my doxy, so forget it and clear out or it will be the worse for you," he threatened, raising his hand to strike her again.

Jenny grabbed his sleeve. "Stop it. You must not strike her. I will take you before the magistrate, you villain."

Black Jack looked at her in disbelief, more amused than deterred by her threats. He sneered at the picture of this very proper miss taking him to task, but Jenny met his eyes with scorn. She was not afraid of him.

"You are a bold one. I could crush you in a minute and I will give you a bit of what I gave Maritza here, if you don't slope off. 'Tis none of your affair and I want none of your plaguey high falutin' airs about here. Be off with you or you will rue the day," he menaced, raising his arm as if to give her the blow he had promised.

"I think not, Black Jack. Assaulting women will

certainly get you up before the beak, if your other lawless activities can't bring you to book," drawled Piers St. Robyns, who had come up on the scene without the knowledge of the combatants. Then, ignoring the smuggler, he turned to Jenny. "Really, Jenny, you are a trial. I am constantly rescuing you from dangerous predicaments into which you rush with careless abandon. It will not do, my girl," he reproved, causing her to blush with mortification.

"Ah, my lord, make him pay up. He promised to give me gold for my boy. 'Tis Black Jack who is Janos's father. Now that he has had his way with me, he throws me out. My people scorn me for taking him as my man and will only allow me back in my caravan if I pay much gold. Damn him, I say, but I wants my due," Maritza complained, giving Piers the full effect of her flashing eyes.

"Is this true, Jack, that you promised Maritza here to pay for your pleasure and are now welshing on your promise?" Piers asked sternly.

"She's nothing but a dirty gypsy whore and she was eager enough. But since Your Honor insists . . ." And then, as if eager to be quit of the business, he threw two sovereigns at the gypsy's feet. She scooped them up quickly and turned to Piers. "Thank you, my lord. You are a true gentleman." She smiled at him provocatively, offering more than gratitude, if Jenny's surmises were correct.

"On your way now, baggage, back to your caravan, and steer clear of this brute in the future. I will see you and the boy are provided for," Piers smiled in return. Maritza, her aim accomplished, was quick to obey, paying no attention to Jenny, but, flashing

Piers yet another grateful look, she rushed off. Black Jack growled under his breath some dreadful curse, but was relieved to be out of the wretched business without further trouble. However, Piers had not finished with him.

"I have several matters to take up with you, Jack. But now is not the time. And let me warn you to watch your language and your actions around your betters. If you had laid a finger on Miss Dryden I would have had no compunction on seeing you transported. Probably the fate in store for you anyway, unless you mend your ways. Now get out of here before I lose my temper."

Black Jack glowered at him and Jenny feared he would test Piers's mettle, but after a moment he, realizing the futility of challenging the earl, shuffled off, not hurrying at all. At least he had not won this round.

Piers, taking Jenny by her arm, steered her away from the wharf and toward a more secluded section of the beach.

"Now, my girl, tell me what you thought you were doing, interfering between Black Jack and Maritza? You could have suffered some hurt, for neither of those characters is the least bit civilized and in the passion of the moment would not have considered your status or your innocence." He held onto her arm with a strong grip, forcing Jenny to run in undignified skips by his side.

Irritated at his criticism she stormed, "I hope I never learn to ignore injustice or people in trouble. True, I do not have the power of the great Lord of Trevarris, but if I had not protested, that miserable brute would have attacked the poor girl and really injured her."

"And if I hadn't come along, you might have suffered the same fate. I don't think Black Jack would have hesitated. Serve you right, too," he added callously.

"I would do it again and no doubt I would have contrived even if you had not come dashing to the rescue in your usual high-handed manner." Actually, she had been most grateful for Piers' arrival, not that she would admit it to the aggravating man.

"And what would Sir Francis say, knowing you had been embroiled in a scuffle on the town wharf with a villain and his doxy? And such language, which I must say did not appear to shock you. Any properly bred female would have fainted dead away at hearing such coarse words," he chided, but some of his earlier irritation began to dissipate. Jenny would always get into trouble. Her warm heart and courage lured her into all sorts of situations most girls of her age and class would ignore like the plague.

"Pooh, I have heard worse when Will Siddons is in his cups. He knocks his wife around, too, and I have dealt with him, I will have you know," she boasted, then bit her tongue, a bit ashamed of her admission.

"I am sure you have, but let me assure you your Will Siddons is a bleating lamb compared to Black Jack Morton. And you have made a bad enemy there, Jenny. He will not forget that you interfered, nor that you saw him back down before a superior force," Piers warned. "What in the world were you doing anyway, idling along the wharf?"

"Just admiring the view, doing a bit of sketching, while I waited for Babs to finish her lessons at the vicarage. And I must collect her now. She will be waiting," Jenny said, anxious to get away from his censorious upbraiding. The arrogance of it, too, criticizing her, then crowing over his defeat of Black Jack. The trouble with Piers was that she became resentful around him and behaved in a way she knew was unladylike and impolite. Well, he must bear some of the burden for her attitude. He needed a sharp lesson. And she had several questions she wanted answered, but she was not lingering here for another set-down.

Shaking herself free, she ran off calling, "I must meet Babs. Good-bye and thank you, Lord Trevarris," knowing that designation would annoy Piers, but feeling she had scored, if ever so slightly, in their ongoing duel.

Chapter Eleven

In London, matters had reached a crisis stage. Adm. William Coniston, Gen. Lucien Valentine and Lord Sterling-Hicks, of the Foreign Office were closeted in secret conference to discuss the latest threat of an invasion from Napoleon's forces. All three men were veterans, accustomed to dealing with the French at sea, on the battlefield, and in diplomatic drawing rooms. They had no illusions about the peril in which England stood.

"If your sources are correct, Lucien, we can expect the Corsican's ships on the horizon within weeks," Sterling-Hicks said gloomily. He was a tall thin man with a jutting chin and cold blue eyes. A long time servant of the Crown who had survived dozens of political shifts of power but managed to maintain his own, he was an adroit and clever manipulator, although none could deny his patriotism nor his service to England.

"Yes, our man in Normandy seemed quite certain and there is no denying that ships, supplies, and men are congregating at Brest. It appears the invasion could be aimed at Plymouth or Falmouth, but, of course, we must consider other ports, too. Unfortunately we have heard nothing but that vague report. I greatly fear the man has been apprehended by Fouché. Pity, for he was invaluable," General Valentine reported tersely. His was the unenviable job of securing intelligence for the Army. He would have preferred to be leading troops, which he had done in past Continental wars, but his superiors felt his experience at running an espionage network and ferreting out spies on the home front made him irreplaceable. A handsome man, dark haired, with compelling dark eyes and a rather stern expression, he cut quite an intimidating figure. To everyone's surprise he had married a vivacious American, who had presented him with two lively children. His intimates claimed that he enjoyed a rare domestic felicity not owned by many. However relaxed he might be in his family circle, he was a formidable opponent to French conspirators and a worthy rival to Napoleon's Chief of Secret Police, Joseph Fouché.

Admiral Coniston, the eldest by far of the trio, a white-haired, blue-eyed retired officer who spent a good part of his life at sea and missed active duty acutely, now added his bit to the discussion.

"I have every hope that young St. Robyns will be able to supply us with the landing site before too long. He is down in Cornwall now, on his estates near Penzance, where I believe a troubling network of spies are preparing the ground. The Cornish are very hospitable to smugglers, you know, and by nature secretive and not too fond of Anglo-Saxons," the admiral explained.

"Damn Celts. They have never accepted that they

are part of Great Britain. The Scots, the Irish, the Welsh, the Cornish—all troublesome, testy characters," Sterling-Hicks complained, tugging at his lower lip in frustration. "But we have not much time. Beacon fires have been laid all along the coast from Land's End to Dover. Every citizen knows what to expect. The weather will be a factor, for Napoleon will not chance the autumn gales. What do you think, Coniston?"

"Yes, I believe he cannot delay past mid-September at the outset. It is now early June. We must have more information. What's the likelihood of your contacts in France coming up with a definite plan?" he asked Valentine.

"I hope for more news soon, but security about the Channel ports is tight. Napoleon knows we are expecting an invasion. His chief weapon will be surprise, to keep us off guard as to the place and time, by mounting diversionary tactics," Valentine said, frowning. "Why do you think St. Robyns will have better luck than our people in France?"

The admiral, never one to rush into inconsidered speech, hesitated. "Of course, I know this will be kept within these walls, and nothing committed to paper, but we have reason to believe the ring which is preparing the ground for Napoleon is headquartered in Cornwall and in that area near St. Robyns's estate. It would not be the obvious choice, too far from London, a rugged shoreline, but Cornwall has some advantages. The people themselves, as you have mentioned, are less willing to rise to the defense of the English, many of them kin to the Bretons and Normans with whom they have traded illegally for centuries. And we would have difficulty getting troops down there in a hurry. No, Cornwall might be a canny choice for the Corsican," he concluded with a sigh.

"Well, your informant had better produce the goods soon," Sterling-Hicks replied grumpily. The Foreign Office was notorious for its dislike of espionage and intelligence activities, trusting instead to the tortuous diplomatic exchanges at which its minions were skilled. Men of Sterling-Hicks' class and position felt that spying was not a gentleman's business.

"I have every faith in Piers, sir," Admiral Coniston, who generally found the Foreign Office stupid and shortsighted, replied curtly.

"He's a good man, St. Robyns." Valentine joined the Admiral in praise. "He will discover what we need to know, but in any case, I have not completely exhausted other avenues."

"Well, perhaps it would not go amiss if you reminded St. Robyns, Coniston, that the fate of England may rest in his hands," Sterling-Hicks insisted, and took his leave without more ado.

Valentine and Coniston, career military men, looked at each other with amusement. "Dramatic johnnies, these Foreign Office types. Like to get them on a quarter deck with the grape falling and see how they react," Coniston muttered, half to himself.

"Yes, they can be annoying, not wanting to dirty their hands with spying, but eager to use the results of some poor fellow's bravery. I have lost too many good men to Fouché's nasty methods not to have every respect for a man who woud fight his battle behind the scene and get little credit for it," Valentine agreed.

"Well, I will post a dispatch to Piers at once and ask him for progress. He's a clever fellow, will not be easily taken in by his neighbors, even if the ringleader of this conspiracy is one of the most noble in the duchy. He will do the trick for us," the admiral assured Valentine.

"If he needs help, perhaps another troop of soldiers. Let me know, and I will wring them out of the War Office. Keep in touch, sir," Valentine said as the two men parted.

Piers was in no need of nudging from Admiral Coniston. He had been at Arthmore several weeks now, and although he was convinced that a highly placed traitor dwelt in the neighborhood, he was not as certain as he had been that the culprit was Henri d'Aubisson. True, there were d'Aubisson's unexplained visits to Penzance and the midnight landing handled by Black Jack, who had spirited a stranger away to some concealed place before Piers could discover the destination or the contact. Piers would have to exert pressure on the smuggling chief and threaten him with dire reprisals if he was to learn what he wanted to know. Perhaps Maritza could help. She obviously knew Black Jack well, although Piers doubted she would have learned any vital facts from the smuggler.

He sighed with frustration. It was a dirty business, investigating his neighbors, viewing them with suspicion. And he had not resolved Jenny Dryden's presence in Trevarris. It might have been unwise to have confided in Sir Francis Morstan. He appeared safe, a magistrate, landowner, and proprietor of the mine. Surely, he would not risk all that security to aid the French. But his wife Amy was another story. Her interest in Henri d'Aubisson might produce some information. But his first task was to question Black Jack.

Piers finally tracked the rogue down in a disreputable pub on the edge of town, where he believed some of the smugglers' cargo was often hidden. Still, Piers cared little for that. It was Morstan's connection with French spies he must discover, and that would not be easy.

The Bull's Head was an unprepossessing tavern of weathered stone and wood, crumbling and dirty both within and without. The host was a burly man with a lame leg, suffered in an accident aboard a fishing schooner, irascible and taciturn. Most of the respectable folk of Trevarris frequented the Blue Anchor on the main street of the hamlet, whose chief attraction was Molly Portlock, the owner's buxom cheery wife. The Bull's Head offered no such amenities, the barmaid and pot boy as uncommunicative and sullen as their employer. But Piers was not deterred by either the pub's help nor its proprietor. He was taking a chance to invade this thieves' den, even in daylight, but he could delay no longer, and he did not want any witnesses to his talk with Morton.

As he expected, the smuggler was sprawled at a rickety table scarred by countless tankards and rarely scrubbed. Although it was barely past noon, Black Jack had imbibed more than a few mugs of the pub's contraband brandy. If his wits were not befuddled, he was not completely sober either. When not actually engaged in his wicked trade he was more often than not half-cast. In this state he could be argumentative and brutal, but he had too much sense to treat Piers as he did his cowed followers.

"Black Jack, I want to talk to you," Piers said, flicking his crop and looking about the almost empty inn with distaste. The pub's owner, Hobbity Pete, recognizing the lord of the manor, had made himself scarce, and two of Black Jack's crew, on seeing Piers, had mumbled their excuses and retreated, leaving the two men alone.

"'Tis an honor, governor. But what can you be thinking of to put your fine foot into Hobbity Pete's den?" Black Jack asked mockingly, but his expression was wary. He wanted no truck with the earl of Trevarris, who had rarely interfered with him before this. Could he be on to something? Or might the lord be willing to take Maritza off his hands? That plaguey gypsy had served her purpose and he would be well shot of her.

Piers settled down opposite Black Jack and eyed him severely. "I want some information from you, Jack, and if I don't get it, you could end up in Broadmoor or worse. You won't get fine brandy there or enjoy the charms of willing doxies, either," Piers promised in quiet yet menacing tones.

Unused to challenge and unwilling to admit any fear, Black Jack blustered, "What's it to you, Your Honor, that I like my brandy and wenches? That's not a crime and I wager you have an eye on that dirty gypsy. Well, you are welcome to her, but she's a load of trouble, that one. You would be well to keep your distance. Not worth it, for the Romany tribe are dirty thieving bastards, the lot of them."

"Maritza is not the issue, as you well know. I want to know about your contacts over the water, and I don't mean the scurvy devils who arrange for your brandy, tobacco, and silk. You bring other cargo on your trips across the Channel. Who are they and what happens to these Frenchmen when they land in Trevarris?" Piers tensed for opposition, for he had no illusions that Black Jack would meekly reveal his sources abroad.

"Now, governor, is that fair? You likes your brandy and other trifles as well as the next man. Are you trying to stop the trade? Other men have tried that and suffered for it," Black Jack glowered. He would not be threatened by this dandy, even if the earl owned the whole countryside.

"Don't be a fool, Jack. I have known of your free trading for years and care little for a few kegs of brandy eluding the customs. It may have escaped your notice, but we are at war with France and smuggling spies could get you hanged," Piers returned calmly, noting the uneasy shiftiness in Black Jack's manner. The aristocrat had hit near the bone and the smuggler was not the type to risk his own neck despite the hefty profits he had earned with his illicit business.

"You have no proof, nor witnesses, either. No one in this pawky place would betray Black Jack," the smuggler boasted.

"I saw you bring in a cargo last week and also a passenger. I want to know what happened to him."

"Well, you can whistle for that news, my lord. Even if I knew I wouldn't tell," Black Jack sneered.

"Oh, I think you will eventually, but I haven't the time to bargain with you. How much will it cost me for the name of your leader? You will not be the principal in this plot, I vow." But as the words left his mouth he realized he had made a mistake. Black Jack did not like the implication he owed allegiance to any master.

"Now, my fine lord, I don't know what you mean. And would I betray a comrade? No man gives Black Jack orders and that's the truth. Take me up before the beak and you'll see I will be back here in the Bull's Head before you know it. I'm in charge here," he growled in fury.

"Not for long, my man. The Customs are on to you and are bringing in the Army. Your every move will be watched from now on. I am warning you. If you tell me what I want to know, I might intercede for you, but if you keep quiet it will go the worse for you," Piers challenged, but feeling impotent, as he knew that Black Jack was right. He could bear witness to the smuggling but Piers had no proof that Black Jack was in league with a spy ring. Damn it, he had handled this interview with less than his usual adroitness.

"A few maggoty soldiers are no threat to Black Jack. They have tried to catch me before and much use it did them, the stupid coves," Black Jack sneered, but he looked away, unwilling to meet Piers's measured stare. The smuggler did not want the redcoats meddling into his business. It upset the men.

"This time they will be more alert. And when you are captured, don't look to me for any assistance. You will be getting what you deserve and the village will be well rid of you. I will not countenance treachery. Remember that. If you cooperate I might continue to turn a blind eye to your free trading. But make no mistake, if you are conspiring with our country's enemies, you will suffer for it," Piers promised and rose before Black Jack could offer any more threats or excuses. The man must have been paid a great deal to insure his silence and Piers saw the futility of any more conversation. Either gold or fear had guaranteed the smuggler's silence, and obviously he considered Piers's offer not sufficient to betray his principal. Piers doubted it was fear for Black Jack boasted often enough he feared no man.

"Give some thought to what I have said, Jack. If you change your mind, I might make it worth your while, but believe me, one way or another, this nasty affair will be resolved in my favor. Watch your step," Piers warned and strode from the inn.

Black Jack cursed and glowered at the fine lord's back, filled with uneasiness. The Earl of Trevarris was not a man to forget or forgive, and he could cause a deal of trouble, but Black Jack had gone his ruthless way for too long to be cowed by any fancy London lord. The earl would soon get tired of ferreting about and return to town, leaving Jack to go his own way. He laughed harshly and called Hobbity Pete. Brandy would settle whatever qualms he had, and if the pesky lord threatened him again, Black Jack would settle with him permanently. He ran this village, not some London high stickler.

Nodding his head with satisfaction, flushed with his power, Black Jack threw off his slight worry with a deep draught of liquor and, damning all maggoty earls and body snatchers, decided on his next move.

Piers, thoroughly disgruntled at the results, or lack of them, of his interview with Black Jack, rode off from the Bull's Head in a dark mood. He disliked being balked and Black Jack had successfully thwarted him. Now he had to decide how he could bring that miscreant to book. Before this maddening encounter with the smuggler, Piers had felt a certain admiration for the chief villain, but recent events had altered that conception. His treatment of Maritza and his connivance with the French conspirators disgusted Piers. Black Jack had roamed free long enough.

The obvious step was to call in the troops, take Bosworth into his confidence, and catch Black Jack in the act of conveying a Frenchman onto the shore with incriminating documents. That would be fine, but Piers doubted that the apprehension of the agent would be that simple, and, as he had learned, the identity of the real culprit, the organizer of this illegal trade in men and secrets, would still be a mystery.

As he trotted along, Piers reviewed in his mind the possible suspects if he discounted Henri d'Aubisson. Was Sir Austen Pencrist a possibility? Certainly he was in need of money, but did he have the ability to launch such an intricate conspiracy? Piers doubted it, although his wife might be more apt to plan such a course. She loved luxury and yearned to return to London. Her patriotism was feeble, he thought. Was

Sir Francis Morstan all he seemed? he wondered, not for the first time. It was difficult to trust anyone. Neither the Army nor the Customs officers themselves had proved incorruptible in the past. If Piers pushed for a more vigorous chase of the smugglers and brought in the Army, would the ringleader postpone his action? Could he afford to with the invasion imminent? Or would he just move his activities to another coast?

Piers, normally of a decisive nature, disliked not being in control. This business of chasing spies was tortuous, not at all like a straightforward command at sea, where one knew his enemy. He wished that he had never agreed to Admiral Coniston's request, but now that he had undertaken the job, he could not turn back. As he rode by the gypsy camp, he decided to put the troublesome options which faced him from his mind. He would call on Maritza and see how she fared. She might have some information on Black Jack and could be persuaded to reveal it in her anger with her former lover.

As he neared the straggling collection of caravans, he was astounded and furious to see Jenny sitting on the steps of Maritza's caravan, holding a baby on her lap. Dismounting from his horse, he approached her, ready to vent his anger, his frustration over his interview with Black Jack fueling his irritation with the folly of Jenny's presence where she should not be.

"What in the world are you doing here, Jenny?" he asked, barely able to control himself, slapping his crop against his boot in anger. Jenny felt his fury and wondered whimsically if he would prefer to use the crop on her.

"Oh, hello, Piers," she greeted him airily. "As you can see, I am trying to soothe this baby. He appears to have contracted some fever, not at all surprising in these far from sanitary conditions. Maritza is quite worried about him," Jenny informed him, turning back to the baby and crooning to him.

"Really, Jenny, have you not a modicum of sense, riding into the gypsy camp as casually as if it were an expedition to Hyde Park? Gypsies are not noted for their hospitality to foreigners. Outsiders like you have been assaulted, robbed—even worse!—when they consort with the Romany. And Maritza is hardly the type of woman your parents would approve of you meeting," he added, his anger fading a bit. Few women of his acquaintance would bother over the fate of a gypsy and her brat. He could applaud her charitable heart while cursing her indifference to personal danger.

"Really, Lord Trevarris, you are making too much of a simple call on Maritza to see if she needed any assistance. At first, I admit, the gypsies were not especially welcoming, but when I offered to see what I could do for little Janos here, she was most appreciative and the tribe's hostility vanished. I believe the poor little tyke has a serious infection, but I have bathed him in a saline solution and I think he is somewhat relieved. I have told her that she must keep his dishes and clothing clean. The gypsies have little idea of hygiene, I fear," she informed him severely, but smiled down at the baby who was responding to her care.

Before he could remonstrate further and order her to leave the camp forthwith, Maritza herself appeared in the door of the caravan and greeted him.

"Latcho dives, my lord," she smiled beguilingly, giving him the Romany salute. "You see the kind lady is helping my Janos. She is indeed an angel, and you must not be cross. What brings you here? Have you come to drive us from your land?" she asked, joining Jenny on the steps and taking the baby from her.

"Of course not, Maritza. I came to see how you were faring," he said curtly.

Jenny stood up, prepared to take her leave. He could remain here and get on with his business without her interference. Then, remembering the reason for her visit, she reminded Maritza of her duty to little Janos. "You must take better care of your baby, Maritza. He will recover from this indisposition if you follow my instructions and do not dose him with some wretched evil-smelling concoction. He needs good milk and cleanliness," she said, ignoring Piers.

"I will escort you home, Jenny," Piers insisted in his high-handed manner, annoyed by her indifference. "Or perhaps you will come with me to Arthmore and take some luncheon. My aunt has arrived and you will be properly chaperoned," he mocked, wondering why he should mention the proprieties when it was obvious that Jenny cared little for such matters or she would never have visited the gypsy camp. He wanted to dress her down, but this was hardly the place or the moment. But once he had her at Arthmore she should feel his displeasure.

Jenny, who had some idea of his intent, paid him no heed and walked to her mare tethered nearby. She did not like Piers's attitude and was in no mood to listen to his strictures. It was no business of his what she did, although she guiltily realized that he might be right about the gypsies, recalling the leader's sullen greeting when she had first arrived and the dark menacing faces of the tribe who had clustered around her horse. If Maritza had not welcomed her she wondered if she might have endured some indignity at the gypsies' hands, but as it happened they had turned away once Maritza had explained her presence.

Maritza's caravan was some distance from the general camp. The woman had explained that her tribe scorned her for her alliance with Black Jack. Only because she was the headman's niece had she been able to remain with them after the birth of the child, for Romany people prized chastity and Maritza had behaved offensively. Her life since Janos's birth had not been easy and she would have left if Black Jack would have taken her in, but he, too, had deserted her.

"If you need more money or any assistance in dealing with Morton, let me know, Maritza, but you would be wiser to keep your distance from the fellow. He's of no use to you now," Piers advised the woman before following Jenny and, before she could resist, tossing her up on her mare. Then, raising a hand in farewell, he trotted after Jenny, who was riding from the camp in haste. He would have to postpone questioning Maritza, for he did not want Jenny to learn of his investigation and this interruption in his plans did nothing to mitigate his irritation with the vicar's daughter. Damn the girl. He would have it out with her. She had no idea what was at stake or the danger she might be inviting. As they neared the path to Arthmore, away from her route to the Morstans, he grabbed her bridle and forced her mare to a stop.

"Please accept my invitation, Jenny," he urged, noticing her shuttered face and realizing she was not going to be persuaded easily. "Do come. I want to show you my house and I promise to behave and not scold you anymore." He augmented his considerable charm with a blinding smile. Why he wanted her in his home he could not fathom, but he felt it was of the utmost importance she give in to his demands.

Jenny, as quick to forgive as to rise to an injustice, hesitated, then relented. "All right, Piers. I must confess I love prying in strange houses. I will enjoy meeting your aunt and seeing Arthmore, but not if you continue to act in your usual top-lofty way."

They trotted off companionably toward the great stone house, exchanging no more words. Jenny, however, doubted that he would honor his promise and sensed that he would not allow her defiance, nor her visit to the gypsy camp be forgotten or forgiven.

Chapter Twelve

Jenny had only had a brief glimpse of Arthmore on one of her earlier explorations of the countryside, hesitant to appear curious by riding too close and gawking like an impressed traveler. Now, as she rode up the long driveway escorted by the house's master, she could gaze her fill at the gray Palladian facade with its wide-paned windows facing the sea above the craggy cliffs. Not overwhelming in the Tudor or Elizabethan manner with soaring Gothic arches, Arthmore lacked the romantic atmosphere of ancient castles and moated manor houses. Yet there was a graceful classical line to the symmetrical three-storied house which attracted her.

Piers had told her that his ancestors had held this land since Norman days and the present house was relatively new to the site, a mere century old. The St. Robyns, unlike many of the Cornish nobility, were Protestants and so had not suffered from the persecution and devastation as had families such as the Arundells, the Edgecumbes, and the Courtenays. They had held for the king during the Civil War, but had trimmed their sails to the Cromwellian triumph and had escaped punishment. When Charles II was restored to the throne, the St. Robyns's had been court favorites. Piers confessed a bit cynically that his ancestors had always managed to choose the right side in disputes, holding and increasing their assets in the manner of the avaricious merchants whose daughters they so often married. Jenny, determined not to be awed by the splendor of Piers's home, responded tartly that he had been blessed by his forebears' foresight.

"In some ways, yes. But the St. Robyns have not been blessed with domestic felicity. Neither my father or my grandfather married for love and they suffered accordingly," he said as they walked up the low stone steps leading to the plain oak door decorated with the simplest of pediments. Two grooms had appeared suddenly to take charge of their horses with respectful bobs of the head at Piers's arrival.

"Perhaps theirs was the fault," Jenny responded.

"No doubt," Piers answered, refusing to be drawn. "Now come and meet my aunt before we eat. And you will want to tidy up. Someone will show you a room," he invited casually, crossing the wide marble floor of the entrance hall and indicating that Jenny should precede him into what must be the drawing room.

As they entered, an elderly woman of severe aspect and a mass of gray hair arranged in an old-fashioned style from a side part rose from an embroidery frame near the tall sashed windows.

"Ah, Piers, so you are back. I did not know when to expect you."

"Aunt Vivian, I have brought back a guest. This is

Miss Dryden, from Wiltshire, who is visiting her cousins, the Morstans. I ran across her on my ride and persuaded her to join us for luncheon," Piers informed his aunt smoothly. "Jenny, this is Lady Lashford."

Jenny made a brief curtsey feeling a bit overwhelmed by the lady and aware that she was in a rather grubby state to be visiting such an august personage and establishment.

"How do you do, Lady Lashford. I do hope I am not causing inconvenience." She was rewarded with a smile which altered her hostess's expression and dispelled some of Jenny's nervousness.

"Not at all, my dear. I was thoroughly bored and you are a welcome relief. I do not share Piers's love of country pursuits and find time hangs heavily here at Arthmore, although Piers does his best to keep me amused," she said with a twinkle, regarding her nephew with a fond eye.

"Aunt Vivian lives at Tunbridge Wells and enjoys all the dubious pursuits of that antiquated watering hole," Piers teased affectionately.

Jenny was quite surprised at his attitude toward his aunt, never thinking that the arrogant Lord Trevarris cared much for family responsibilities or affections. It was reassuring, but did not alter her opinion of the nobleman. Probably his aunt served as his hostess and with her in residence, he could not entertain the raucous house party Jenny suspected was his usual style. In that she was misjudging Piers, but he continually threw her off balance.

"Perhaps you would take Jenny to a chamber where she could freshen up before we lunch," Piers suggested, crossing the room and ringing a bell.

"Yes, of course," Lady Lashford agreed, all amiability.

After washing her hands and subduing her hair, which had suffered from the brisk ride, Jenny joined Lady Lashford and Piers for luncheon in the small morning room. Walking down the imposing stairs, she glimpsed several portraits in which she could see a resemblance to the current master of the house. Piers promised her a tour of the establishment after luncheon and she looked forward to seeing some of the treasures. Despite its size and imposing aspect, Arthmore was not the grim pile she had expected. Furnished in the Queen Anne style which suited the design of the house, it was obviously the residence of a bachelor, but for all that lovingly kept.

During luncheon Piers and his aunt did their best to make Jenny feel comfortable, and the cozy, sunlit room induced intimacy with its small round mahogany table and soft pink draperies. They dined on a simple repast of roast chicken with vegetables followed by a peach crumble, and then Piers indicated he would escort Jenny around the house.

The downstairs rooms were large and airy, suitable for large gatherings but not overpowering. Only when he showed her the long gallery did she get some idea of his heritage. Stretching the length of the house on the ground floor, the room looked magnificent enough to entertain the largest company. Indeed, Piers mentioned that in the past balls had often been held in the gallery during his grandfather's day.

"My father was not much given to entertaining, but I have held a few revels here," he explained. "And here is my august grandfather and his wife," he added, stopping before two portraits.

The gentleman looked very much like Piers except for his powdered hair, having the same height and determined expression, his dark blue eyes under string eyebrows gleaming fiercely. Not a man to cross, Jenny decided. His wife was a surprise, not the sweet retiring figure Jenny had expected would be the choice of such a dominant lord, but a glowing beauty with a winsome figure, a mass of curling chestnut hair and a knowing look in her luminous blue eyes. Her mouth had a sensuous curl which hinted at secret delights.

"She looks a bit like you, I think," Piers offered, surprising Jenny with his comment as he stared at his grandmother's likeness. "She led him a merry dance, but he pursued her, built the house for her, and surprisingly she enjoyed Cornwall, preferring it to the pleasures of London, where she had reigned as a belle before her marriage," he confided.

"Not at all like me," Jenny responded, gazing at Lady Trevarris with admiration.

"Oh, I don't know. Under certain circumstances I imagine you could be quite as provocative," Piers answered mysteriously, guiding her toward one of the convenient bow back chairs lining the gallery. "Come, let us rest from this exhausting inspection, and you can tell me why you take such an interest in Maritza," he said in a tone that brooked no denial.

Jenny sighed, realizing he would neither forgive nor forget her expedition to the gypsy camp. Gazing at him as he sat, his long legs sprawled before him, she thought, not for the first time, that he was a man who, once set upon a course, could not be deterred and she wondered why he took such an interest in her activities.

"Well, I was brought up to offer aid to those in trouble. And certainly Maritza seems to be just such a one," she explained primly, folding her hand tightly in her lap and wondering why this man's presence caused her heart to beat uncomfortably fast and her body to tingle with unaccustomed feelings. Certainly she had never experienced these uneasy emotions before meeting Piers. She neither understood him, nor trusted him, but she could not deny he interested her and that she spent entirely too much time thinking about him.

"Black Jack appears to frighten the villagers and I think he is capable of really dreadful deeds," she confided in some confusion. "He is a brutal type and used her shamefully."

"True, and for that reason and many others you should avoid raising his anger. He is not a man who suffers questions or interference," Piers agreed.

"Like you, sir," Jenny riposted, not willing to concede that she could be warned off such a violent type. "I marvel that you allow him to go his way, unrestrained." Her tone was admonitory and she wondered at her boldness in challenging Piers.

"I have my reasons. And until lately Black Jack did not much concern me, but now he does. And I will not have you meddling in events which you do not understand," Piers answered shortly, not liking her rebuke.

"You condone smuggling," Jenny reproved, not happy with his assumption that she was a troublesome chit lacking common sense.

"It has been the Cornish habit for centuries, but I

dislike traitors, and I greatly fear Black Jack has undertaken some treasonous assignments. He must be, and will be, brought to account. And I will not be thwarted bya vicar's daughter from Wiltshire," Piers warned, suddenly serious. "You have no idea what is going on and I don't propose to tell you, but you must be careful. You have a tendency to stir up matters best left to those who know how to cope with the results."

Jenny rose, her reaction one of hurt and anger. How dare he treat her as if she were some stupid fool. She would not stand by and ignore danger. That was not her habit nor her intent, no matter what Piers insisted.

"You are much too arrogant, Lord Trevarris," she said, her cheeks reddening at her audicity. "I will do what I think fit. And who knows, I might just be of some help."

"Listen to me, Jenny. You could come to grief with your willful ways. You need a man to tame you, bring you to a realization of your role," Piers answered, angered in turn by her resistance.

"But you are not that man," Jenny protested, equally annoyed.

"I might be," he answered shortly. And before she knew what he was about, he had taken her in his arms, muttering, "There is only one way to deal with such a defiant, managing female," he pressed a hard kiss on her startled lips. The kiss which began as a warning and punishment, turned slowly into a seductive caress, his hands roaming down her slight form and evoking a response she could not repress. She found her arms curling about his shoulders as a warm glow began spreading throughout her body and causing delightful sensations she had felt before in his arms. As his kisses became more demanding and Jenny answered them with complete abandon which would later give her the deepest shame, they were rapidly reaching a point of complete forgetfulness of what had begun so carelessly. But before Jenny could surrender to all thought, they were interrupted by Lady Lashford.

"I am so sorry, Piers, to disturb you, but a messenger has arrived from London with what he insists are most important documents for you," she said calmly, ignoring the astonishing scene which greeted her.

Jenny gasped, blushed, and tore herself from Piers's arms, mortified to have been seen in this compromising situation. What must Lady Lashford think? That she was a wanton with no conception of proper behavior.

But Piers, turning to his aunt, showed no evidence of the passionate interlude his aunt had interrupted. He obviously was well experienced in such situations, Jenny concluded miserably.

"Well, I suppose I must see him," he answered with aplomb. "If you will join Aunt Vivian in the drawing room, Jenny, as soon as my business is finished, I will escort you home. Sir Francis and Amy must be wondering what has happened to you."

"That will not be necessary. I can take myself home," she protested, and, turning to Lady Lashford, made her excuses. Before Piers could utter any objection she flounced from the room, trailed by the amused Lady Lashford and an irritated Piers, who nevertheless managed to behave as if his aunt had not surprised them at an embarrassing moment.

Ignoring him, she almost ran down the stairs. Then realizing she must request her horse and thank her hostess for luncheon, Jenny turned and faced them in the hall. Not meeting Piers's glance, she made her farewells to Lady Lashford and asked, "If someone could bring my horse around, please?"

"I do wish you'd wait, Jenny. This should not take long," Piers pleaded almost humbly. But seeing she was adamant and would not acknowledge him, bit back a curse and left the two in the hall, stalking off to his library where the messenger awaited him.

Within moments Jenny was galloping as if demons were after her down the long drive, eager to reach the sanctuary of Pencairn, and wondering how she had ever allowed herself to get into such a coil.

Fortunately, both Amy and Francis were away from home when Jenny arrived, and Babs had gone to spend the afternoon with her friend Johnny Granthum, who had just returned from his visit to Sussex. So there was no one to notice that she had missed luncheon. Mrs. Peabody did offer a remark that it was a shame she had missed her midday meal, but Jenny did not satisfy the kind woman's curiosity.

Stretched out on the window seat in her bedroom, with her sketchbook at hand, she looked out upon the parkland, so rigorously carved from the barren Cornish heath, and tried to bring some order to her jumbled thoughts. Resolutely she banished the image of Piers and that shameful scene in the gallery. Shameful because it meant nothing to Piers but a moment of dalliance. After all, this was not the first time he had treated her so cavalierly and showed that he had no great opinion of her. Jenny was inclined to agree with him, for she had behaved disgracefully, responding like some demirep. The next thing she knew he would be offering her carte blanche, a fine position for a gently bred vicar's daughter, she scoffed, ignoring the niggling thought that perhaps demireps might have a more exciting time of it than well-chaperoned girls of respectable reputation.

Well, she must not allow herself to think that because Piers St. Robyns had kissed her a few times he had honorable intentions—or even dishonorable ones for that matter. She was not that much of an innocent. Probably he was bored until his house party arrived and wanted to try his amatory skills on the handiest target. And then he had been quite angry with her for the visit to the gypsy camp. She admitted now it had not been the most judicious of ideas, to wander alone into what Amy had called "a nest of thieves and rogues."

But it had been exciting, and Jenny's pencil made a record of the impressions she had absorbed from that impulsive visit. Caravans, tumbling babies about the campfire, the dark closed faces of the wary tribesmen, the flowing skirts of the women flew from her pencil, creating a tempestuous scene of gypsy life. She drew without caricature, the camp having made too vivid a picture for parody. Perhaps at last she was becoming a true artist, more traditional in her approach, now that new experiences had stirred a talent not challenged by the familiar vignettes of her past. So some good had come from her Cornwall visit, if not precisely what her mother had hoped.

Turning away from these thoughts, she recalled her meeting with Black Jack.

Obviously Piers believed Black Jack was in league with his country's enemies. Jenny could only agree that the smugglers' chief had neither the intelligence nor the contacts to manage a conspiracy of the sort Piers imagined without direction from some more sophisticated source. Certainly there were undercurrents in Trevarris she failed to understand, even if she was aware of them. The village was far from the idyllic seaside hamlet she had first envisaged, but was it the center for an elaborate spy ring, a possible target for a French invasion? Even though all of southern England was expecting an invasion and Cornwall appeared a likely target, she found this difficult to comprehend.

She smiled to herself. She knew that Piers had even suspected her initially, thinking she might have some ties to this mythical network. But she doubted that he now suspected her of being anything more than a gullible female, easily influenced by his skilled lovemaking, if she could call it that. She would not allow herself to think that passionate interlude was any more than a brief experiment, a distraction from his real business. He was certainly determined to uncover more than the smuggling of a few brandy kegs and was rightly suspicious of any unusual activity in the area. The insular, isolated situation and prejudices of Trevarris made it unlikely that any stranger could operate unnoticed, so Piers must suspect one of the neighboring gentry.

Jenny, intrigued, wanted to share in this search. Her romantic conceptions had been thoroughly dampened, but her patriotism was aroused. How dare an Englishman conspire with their country's enemies! Well, she would keep her eyes open, eyes not clouded with preconceived notions. She would show Piers St. Robyns she was not to be cowed by his orders or, for that matter, bemused by his caresses. Just how she was to contrive this stirring stratagem in which she unmasked the traitors and discomfited Piers she could not at present imagine. However, she would take every opportunity to study her surroundings and the cast of characters. She would like to score off Piers, an ignoble wish, but not to be denied.

But who among their apparently blameless neighbors could be conspiring to bring England to her knees? Certainly Francis was all he appeared to be. But there were other possibilities. Sir Austen Pencrist for one. She had, after all, seen his transaction with Black Jack on the quay. And, of course, there was the obvious suspect, Henri d'Aubisson, that Gallic flirt and ne'er-do-well. Well, she would watch and study the Morstan neighbors. As she was a stranger she could view them without the blinders long association had engendered. Feeling much comforted she rose from her window seat.

Really, she must confine her wild suppositions and behave with circumspection. If she did discover some damaging fact, she should inform the authorities, not attempt, like the heroine of a gothic novel, to solve the problem which baffled sager heads, to challenge the villain herself. Still, the idea was a provocative one, and Jenny, who never refused a dare, was determined to try her hand at exposing the master spy.

From the window she saw Babs trudging up the driveway from the village in the company of the Granthums' servant. It must be time for tea and the little girl would want to tell her of her afternoon adventures with Johnny. For the moment she would dismiss all these vague surmises from her mind and dismiss too the nagging memories of her distressing encounter with Piers. However, she would not allow him such liberties again. He disturbed her peace of mind and, if she took his attentions seriously, could cause her more misery than Harry had caused. Strange how distant and unimportant that broken engagement seemed. For that, she might thank Piers, although gratitude was not a feeling she usually associated with that enigmatic lord.

Chapter Thirteen

For the next few days Jenny clung to her resolution to avoid Piers. He made a courtesy call to enquire for her, but Jenny discounted his concern. His real purpose was to invite the Morstans and Jenny, of course, to a dinner for his London guests who had finally arrived. Jenny could not avoid the party, but she decided she would treat their host with chilling aloofness. Unable to repress a certain wry amusement at herself, she acknowledged that he probably would not even notice her disapproval. Still, it would be enjoyable to observe this group of London high flyers and Amy would accept no excuse for a refusal even if she had been tempted to offer one.

Amy was quite in alts over the party, chattering about the guests, in a dither over her gown, and recalling idle bits of scandal from her London triumphs. Whatever had kept her presence from the house for the past few weeks had evidently ceased, and she remained close to Pitcairn, appearing almost content for the first time since Jenny's arrival.

For a fleeting moment Jenny wondered if Amy could have formed a damaging connection with one of their neighbors. She had certainly seemed more than interested in Henri d'Aubisson, but Jenny dismissed that idea. Surely Amy, no matter how bored or unhappy, would not be so foolish as to take that mountebank as a lover right under her husband's nose. And if Henri was the organizer of the spy ring, he could not avoid raising some suspicion in Amy's mind if they were intimately involved. Nor would Amy, feckless and shallow as she might be, condone treason. No, Jenny decided, she must look elsewhere.

Jenny, chiding herself for suspecting her beautiful cousin of treachery or even infidelity, listened patiently to Amy's chatter about the Trevarris house party and entered into all of the woman's plans for returning Piers's hospitality with enthusiasm. Francis, seeing his wife in a more receptive and equable mood, smiled encouragingly at her transports, agreeing that it made a delightful change to welcome London society into their midst. The atmosphere of the Morstan household, which had worried Jenny, vastly improved.

On the day of the anticipated dinner, Jenny escaped from the house and the final fitting of the new gown Amy had insisted on providing for her cousin, to wander in the churchyard, which she always found fascinating. Babs was on a holiday from her studies, and was accompanying her father on a ride about the estate. Jenny had been asked to join them, but, thinking that Babs would prefer having her father to herself, had declined, pleading a need for some solitude to sketch, a ladylike pastime scorned by Babs but approved by Francis and Amy.

After a long perusal of the gravestones in the churchyard she decided to inspect the small chapel which held the tomb of Piers's crusading ancestor. The drama and pathos of the tombstone inscriptions had depressed her. "Tabitha Polten, beloved wife of Josiah"—dead at nineteen in childbirth. Joseph Tolgarth, died at sea, aged sixteen. Lt. Anthony Pencrist, no doubt a relative of Sir Austen's, felled in America with his regiment during the War of Colonial Independence. But there were also records of long full lives: Maria Cambourne, aged eighty-six, esteemed wife, mother, grandmother, remembered by her grateful family, and Abel Bond, ninety-four, "sexton of this church for fifty years and cherished by God." How reassuring it all was. Having been brought up in a vicar's household, Jenny was accustomed to the progression of life and death in a village, but had never found it depressing, only a symbol of life's renewal and a reminder that one must make the most of the time alotted to one.

Passing into the cool darkness of the church, she wondered about the stories of the departed she had briefly glimpsed. What of their fears and hopes, their loves and sorrows? It was a sobering but not unhappy thought, and she felt strongly the universality of it all, whether in Wiltshire or Cornwall. But the churchyard visit had reminded her of home and she felt a pang of longing for the comforting vine-covered vicarage, her mother's brisk, managing air and her father's homey kindliness. Really, she was becoming too introspective of late and felt she must make an effort to throw off her vague misgivings, the feeling of looming danger.

To distract her mind, she settled down by the side of the Crusader's tomb in the small chapel off the narthex and began idly to sketch the statue of the outstretched knight. Her mother would be interested in his story and a description of the magnificent catafalque. They had no such noble relic in her father's simple church. She drew deliberately and slowly, her mind troubled by her recent experiences, her head aching with a jumble of impressions. Slowly her eyes drooped with exhaustion and she rested her head for a moment against the railings of the Crusader's tomb.

Drowsing, neither asleep nor awake, she drifted into a dreamy state, where impressions of a visored, mailed Piers tilted at a shrouded enemy, and she prayed for his safety at a dim altar rail, gowned in wimple and robe. Bemused she at first was only vaguely aware of voices breaking in on her reverie from the depths of the church. She crouched behind the tomb, for some reason loath to announce her presence.

The timbre of one of the voices was menacing. "You will do as I say," Jenny heard the unknown speaker threaten and Jenny shivered at the words. She did not think it was a casual warning. She would dearly like to know who was responsible for those words, but somehow she could not bring herself to inch forward and peer into the body of the church.

Just as well, for a few minutes later she heard Black Jack Morton growl, "One of these days you'll go too far. I'm warning you, the earl is poking his long nose into our affairs and he's a dangerous man. He could blow the gaff on the whole show. There's talk that he's bringing in the troops from Penzance."

"I can handle the Trevarris. He'll soon be bored at playing the hero and go back to London. But enough of that. I want to be sure you understand the rendezvous for tonight," the low voice insisted. Jenny was now convinced the leader of the spy ring was conniving with Black Jack. She wished she could take the chance to get closer, to identify the speaker, but caution restrained her. She held her breath, waiting for the next words, but all she heard was a muttered agreement and then, the clang of the church door. One of the conspirators was leaving, but the other still remained.

Jenny faded into a corner of the chapel. It would be disastrous if she were discovered. She strained her ears but heard nothing. What could the mysterious person be doing? Could she risk a peek? Edging stealthily toward the entrance of the chapel, she peered out, her eyes scanning the long aisle and the pews. She could not see all of the altar rail or pulpit from her refuge and she dared not venture farther into the church. Then, her heart beating so hard she was sure the sound echoed from the thick stone walls, she heard a soft movement, felt a slight draft and the quick snap of the side door which led to the churchyard. Evidently the stranger was leaving from the entrance which led directly across the churchyard to the back of the vicarage. Did he not fear being observed by Robert Herron or Evelyn? Or could it have been the vicar himself? No, unthinkable. She would have recognized the round hearty voice of Robert Herron. Whoever the villain was his voice was unknown to her, although Jenny wondered if perhaps the voice and the person might have been disguised.

She tiptoed uneasily through the narthex and waited, hesitant to move from her hiding place until she was convinced no chance of discovery was possible. Knowledge of her presence by the traitors certainly would mean trouble for her. She might want to solve the mystery of the smuggled spy,. but was not so foolhardy as to rush pell-mell into danger. She knew that Black Jack would be running some kind of contraband tonight. Should she try to find out where he was delivering his cargo and his passenger, if indeed such an agent was expected? Then she remembered the dinner party. She could not avoid that engagement. But perhaps if she pleaded illness. Would Amy accept such an excuse? And she had no idea what arrangements Black Jack had made. Suddenly she remembered the cove and the evidence of a past rendezvous for contraband cargo. Would the smuggling chief be brazen enough to use that site again? Her mind jumbled with impressions and plans.

Jenny walked out of the church, intending to call upon the vicarage and ask Evelyn or Robert if they had seen any strangers about the church. On second thought, she saw the pitfalls of this approach. She wandered about the churchyard in a quandary. She must do something, but what? The possibility of enlisting Piers in her plan to apprehend the smugglers crossed her mind briefly, then she dismissed it. He would either laugh at her suspicions or relegate her to the drawing room and take over the whole business himself, denying her any role. She would not allow that. No, she would only inform Piers when she had some definite information to offer him.

Frowning blackly she paced back and forth, nimbly avoiding headstones, impervious to the unsuitability of tramping heedlessly about the churchyard. So distracted was she by her thoughts she did not hear Evelyn Herron approaching through the heavy grass. With Miss Herron was Major Bosworth, conversing politely with the vicar's sister.

"This is well met, Miss Dryden. I was just about to call at Pencairn." Major Bosworth hailed her with every evidence of pleasure, an emotion not evident in his companion's greeting.

"Ah, Miss Dryden, poking about the churchyard again. You have rather a morbid fascination with the dead, I think," Miss Herron said. Then, with some suspicion in her tone, "Have you been here long? Your young charge has a holiday from her studies, I believe."

"Yes, she has. Perhaps, Major Bosworth, you would like to come back to Pencairn now, if you have finished your business at the vicarage, of course." She had quite exhausted her charity toward Robert's sister.

"Delighted," the major responded, aware of

malicious undercurrents, but hoping not to get involved. "It's a nice day for a stroll and you can show me the sights of the town." He smiled at Jenny, somewhat relieved to being able to escape. Women were the devil when they took a dislike to one another. Not that the charming Miss Dryden seemed the type to take umbrage easily, but Miss Herron was heavy going, no doubt about that. Still, he made his farewells politely, adding that he would be seeing more of the Herrons now that he and his troop were posted in Trevarris.

"If you are not too occupied elsewhere, Major," Evelyn replied caustically and, nodding briefly in Jenny's direction, strode down the path to the church.

"Sorry about that, Major," Jenny apologized as they strolled down the street, "but I fear Miss Herron does not enjoy my company. She took an instant dislike to me and, try as I might, I cannot rid her of her first impression. So I have stopped trying, awkward really, because I find her brother a very likeable man." Her curiosity piqued at the news that Bosworth had been relocated with his men, she said, "It is quite a surprise to have you posted here. I thought Penzance was a permanent billet. Is there trouble of some sort expected in Trevarris?" she asked innocently, peeping up at the major with a delightful smile. "Or are you on some secret mission whose purpose you cannot confide to me?" she quizzed, not entirely in fun.

The major, long skilled at turning away awkward questions, was not completely impervious to Jenny's artless manner. "Not at all, Miss Dryden, but some of my superiors believe invasion is on the horizon and we might see French sails on the horizon at any moment. Cornwall in general is receiving a lot of attention lately."

Jenny almost snorted in amusement. He must think her a ninny to be fobbed off with such a fatuous explanation, but she could not fault him for keeping his own confidence. She would have little respect for an officer who could be lured into indiscretion by a little flirting.

"Well, whatever the reason for your arrival, I think it is capital. We are in need of some additions to our company. Did your officers, Lieutenant Carstairs and Captain Anders, come with you?"

"Oh, yes, the full complement, but you will make me jealous if you prefer their company to mine," the major replied gallantly, smiling down at her from his great height. And it was in this intimate pose that Piers glimpsed the pair as he rode down the main street toward the quay. He reined in his horse and greeted them a trifle shortly.

"There you are, Bosworth. I was looking for you at your lodgings. Have you and the troop settled in comfortably? Sorry I could not put you up at Arthmore, but I have a house party from London at present. You will meet them tonight at dinner if it is convenient for you to accept on this short notice. Perhaps Miss Dryden can persuade you," he said in what Jenny thought was a most disagreeable way. He behaved as if he were more than annoyed to find her walking along with Major Bosworth, exchanging a few courtesies. Really, Lord Trevarris could be taught a lesson in manners, for all his London polish. Whatever vague intention she had of confiding the strange conversation she had overheard quickly dissipated under Piers's aloof enigmatic gaze.

"Oh, yes, I do hope you will accept Lord Trevarris's invitation, Major Bosworth. You would add a great deal to the evening," she urged, hoping that Piers would grasp the implication that she preferred the major's company to his. It was rather meanspirited of her, but then she was still in a veritable rage against this haughty lord who believed he could have everything his own way, that he knew best for everyone within his purview.

"I see I am still in your bad graces, Jenny. I will have to see what I can do to mend matters this evening, but for now, I must not keep you from your walk. Good day, Major." Piers rode off with the easy assurance which made Jenny long to see him come a cropper. Little hope of that, she concluded silently. He always appeared to have the upper hand.

"Quite friendly for a peer, St. Robyns," the major commented cheerily, lowering Jenny's good opinion of his perspicacity. Determined not to let the meeting with Piers cast a blight on her day, she chatted brightly with Major Bosworth, giving that officer and gentleman an entirely mistaken idea of her interest in him. They parted with mutual assurances of goodwill and, on the major's part, anticipation for the evening ahead.

* * *

Jenny had abandoned her idea of pleading illness to escape Piers's party as a cowardly ploy, especially since he had seen her in blooming health just a few hours previously. But she was determined to somehow watch what she was convinced was a vital rendezvous of the smugglers later in the evening. Surely they would not dare be abroad before midnight. With Major Bosworth and his soldiers in the neighborhood, even Black Jack must see the wisdom of a little prudence as he went about his illegal activities.

As she dressed for the evening, Jenny felt a rising tide of excitement, refusing to accept the thought that a prospective exchange with Piers could be responsible for her elation. No, she was all agog at the notion that somehow she might discover the leader of the spy ring and incidentally show the annoying Trevarris that she was not the simple rustic he evidently assumed.

Whatever Amy's defects of character, no one could fault her fashion sense. Jenny had allowed her to choose the material and style of the gown which she had insisted on providing, and now, pirouetting before the mirror, could only applaud Amy's taste.

Disdaining the vapid white usual for maidens, Amy had insisted on a *eau de nile* silk, the greenish blue complementing Jenny's hair and eyes. Jenny had no doubt the silk was smuggled from France where the material and color were reputed to be the Empress Josephine's favorites. The high-waisted and décolleté gown was cut plainly, open over a white silk underdress, the sleeves slight and puffed, and the only decoration an intricate embroidery of gold thread outlining the bodice and the hem. Jenny could only be grateful to Amy, her talented seamstress, and the Lyons silk weavers. She had never had such a stunning gown.

Polly added her touches and arranged Jenny's wayward curls in a simple Psyche knot. Jenny admitted wryly that if some tresses escaped, as was their wont, the coiffure would not suffer unduly as a more elaborate style might. Altogether she was quite pleased with herself as she completed her costume with a string of modest pearls, white gloves, and a beaded white and silver reticule.

"Will you need your shawl, miss?" Polly asked, gazing with satisfying admiration at the creation before her.

"I don't believe so, Polly, as it is such a warm night," Jenny said, then thanked her for her assistance.

"You do look a treat, miss. I wish that wicked Amelia could see you now, and that false husband of hers. They would think again," Polly decided with a certain smugness.

Jenny protested, but then marveled that she had not given the pair a thought for some time. Actually, Amelia had probably done her a favor. She would be meanspirited to carry a grudge for what had turned out to be a blessing. That the appearance of Piers St. Robyns in her life had altered her whole conception of the sorry affair did not occur to her, and if it had she would have denied it vehemently.

She turned toward the door, anticipating an exciting evening. She might lay it down to the prospect of meeting stylish London visitors or her plan for a late-night surveillance, but not for a moment did she admit she wanted Piers to see her in all her finery. She scoffed at the idea that she could outshine such gazetted beauties as Amy and the fashionable London Incomparables she no doubt was about to meet. But all the same she felt she looked her best, always reassuring for a female about to embark on a hazardous mission.

Chapter Fourteen

As the carriage carried them toward Arthmore, Jenny found her mind was troubled by conflicting suspicions. Amy looked lovely in her azure blue silk and gauze with the silver dragonee trim, and Jenny noticed that Francis and Amy seemed in unusual accord which did hearten her.

However, the strange episode in the church that afternoon haunted her. Who had been speaking to Black Jack? If only she had been more alert, not bemused by her fancies, she would have identified the conspirator. Surely the mysterious speaker, arranging the rendezvous with Black Jack, would have shown no mercy if Jenny had been discovered listening to their secrets. Still, she now had definite proof that a conspiracy existed. But, no, did she? All she really knew was that smuggling went on—that was accepted by all the residents of Trevarris. How many of them knew that some of the cargo consisted of French spies?

She wished she could confide her doubts and fears in some trustworthy person, but her recent experiences had made her wary of everyone, including Francis. Of course, there was Piers, but she was so at odds with him, she would not choose him as a confidant. Pride insisted she get the better of him in this matter, foolish perhaps, but she was disgusted at his treatment of her and determined to show him she was a capable adult who could manage her life without criticism of her behavior from a man who was no better than he should be. Not the most polite opinion to hold of one's host, she conceded, as the carriage neared Arthmore. But, then, her feelings toward Piers were far from polite.

Whatever Piers's deficiencies as a confidant and in other ways, Jenny had to admit as a host he was all affability.

"Jenny, you do look most fetching this evening. A new gown in honor of the occasion and most attractive, too," he said, coming into the hall to welcome the arrivals from Pencairn.

"Thank you, sir," Jenny replied austerely, but she could not prevent the blush which reddened her cheeks under his admiring gaze.

"Stop using your wiles on Jenny, Piers. She is not used to London manners," Amy said sharply. She was most disturbed by Piers's attentions to Jenny, whether from pique or her tardy remembrance as a chaperone for her cousin it was hard to fathom.

Piers took the reproof in good part, only raising his eyebrows sardonically as if he knew exactly what Amy was thinking and found it amusing. He shepherded his guests into the large drawing room where his house party was assembled and punctiliously made the introductions to the strangers. There were only a half a dozen guests unknown to Jenny, who curtsied to Piers's aunt and was received kindly before meeting the newcomers. An elderly émigré couple, Mme. and Monsieur La Soutaine acknowledged the introduction rigidly. Jenny suspected that they found their exile painful and considered English protocol lax and informal, for they looked her over with hauteur but received the introduction with exquisite courtesy.

An old count whose intricate title Jenny did not catch was much more obliging, eyeing Jenny and Amy with appreciation and the practiced eye of an experienced roué. Despite his haggard looks and embonpoint Jenny thought him quite congenial. Evidently he was not married for no countess was produced. Jenny suspected the count had never entertained giving up his amatory pursuits for the constricting bonds of matrimony. The other couple were far different, the Marquess and Marchionese de Lisle. He was a dark handsome man, many years older than his gamine wife. The marquess seemed a formidable yet still approachable man, who found the foibles of his fellows amusing. Melissa de Lisle, his wife, a petite blond with a bewitching smile charmed Jenny from the beginning. No doubt keeping her sophisticated husband in line was a challenging task but she seemed quite able to cope, and Jenny suspected theirs was indeed a love match, not one of those arranged marriages so prevalent in

London society. Having met all these polished members of a world in which she felt alien, Jenny turned with some relief to Major Bosworth, leaving Amy to exercise her social skills on the visitors.

"Oh, Major Bosworth, it is so nice to see a friendly face. I must admit I am in awe of such distinguished visitors, not accustomed to meeting these tulips of the Ton," Jenny confided artlessly as she and Major Bosworth wandered over to the large French windows which were opened to catch the warm night breeze.

"Nonsense, Miss Dryden, you would be an ornament in any company," he replied a bit heavy-handedly. Obviously the major was not up to the clever bantering which Jenny suspected was the rule in this artificial world.

"Well, since I grew up in the country, I've had little experience with worldly people. My most exciting venture was to the Bath assemblies, which these exquisites would consider too tame for words," she mocked, hoping to get some reaction from the stolid officer. Really, he was much too serious, but dependable she was sure. Or was he? Jenny, chatting idly with the major, remembered his sudden appearance in the churchyard that morning. Could he possibly be in league with the smugglers? What a dreadful idea. She decided she must test the possibility.

"You were kind to call on Miss Herron upon your arrival in Trevarris. I find her very difficult and unfriendly, but perhaps she is kinder to gentlemen," Jenny probed.

The Major seemed to agree. "She is a crabby thwarted old maid. I feel quite sorry for Herron, who is such a good chap."

"I quite agree. He must have to exercise a great deal of Christian charity in his own home, and it's remarkable he has so much to spare for the rest of us," Jenny said with a roguish smile. But she was thinking furiously, the major had not really explained his presence in the churchyard to her satisfaction. "I see Robert here tonight, but his sister is not among the guests. Surely she was invited," Jenny persisted.

"I believe so, but Herron told me she was feeling unwell. I think perhaps she felt unable to face so many august beings. They do tend to intimidate one," the major confessed, rather like a small boy.

Jenny chuckled. Really, he was most disarming, and she decided to acquit him of any wrongdoing. His countenance was too open, his conversation too candid for a deep-dyed conspirator. But before she could continue her inquiry into the major's motives, they were interrupted by their host.

"Come now, Bosworth, you cannot be allowed to monopolize one of our most attractive guests. Go on, man, do your duty and chat with Mme. La Soutaine. And Jenny, come along. You have not met my other guest, Admiral Coniston, my former commander when I was serving in the Navy. He quite agrees with you about my regrettable character, and you can have a fine time exchanging tales of my iniquities," Piers laughed down into her set face.

Really, he was unmanageable. But Jenny refused

to give ground. "Of course, Lord Trevarris, I would enjoy meeting the admiral, but I am sure he is much too clever to tell me anything which would reflect on you unfavorably. You seem to have the ability to act outrageously and then pay no penalty."

"Ah, Jenny, your standards are so strict. I fear I can never live up to your ideas of chivalry and proper conduct. You are still angry about our session in the gallery. I remember it with the most enjoyment, and I thought at the time you were not resisting," he murmured in her ear, giving several of the guests the impression that he found little Miss Dryden most provocative. Jenny could have stamped her foot with rage. How dare he make her the cynosure of all eyes and then imply she had been a willing participant in his caresses!

"I do not enjoy being made the object of your casual flirtation, sir, nor do I appreciate you embarrassing me before your guests. Look, they are all staring," she said, trying to avoid the gaze of the censorious Mme. La Soutaine. "What can your aunt be thinking of me?"

"That you are adorable, as I do," Piers replied, taking unfair advantage of her inability to give him the rebuff he deserved. "Ah, here is the admiral," he said, propelling Jenny toward the white-haired gentleman who Jenny recognized at once as a naval man. The introductions made, Jenny avoided any mention of her host and confided in the admiral that her brother Richard was currently on station in the Caribbean, so she had a deep interest in all matters concerning His Majesty's Navy.

"Alas, sir, I have made a grave mistake. In order to gain Jenny's approval I should have retained my commission. Perhaps if I lost an eye and an arm in some stirring engagement she would look more kindly on me," Piers teased.

"Lord Nelson was an exceptional man, a real hero, not at all like you," Jenny protested hotly, then blushed remembering that she should behave in a more seemly manner before the admiral.

But he appeared to find the comparison amusing. "Quite right, Miss Dryden. Piers shares only an appreciation of beautiful women with the great Nelson. But I must admit, loath as I am to cause any conceit, that Piers was a perfectly competent officer when I had him aboard my ship," he twinkled at her. If this young woman had managed to engage Piers's interest to the point of matrimony, the admiral decided that she must be an unusual woman. Piers would not be trapped by an empty-headed beauty, and this girl was not a beauty in the acceptable sense of the word.

"Do put in a good word for me, sir. She believes me the most rubbishy fellow and try as I might I cannot seem to alter her opinion," Piers confided. Then bowing, he left Jenny with the admiral and wandered off to play host to his other guests.

"He is not, you know. Actually Piers was a fine officer and I was most disappointed when he resigned his commission, although I understood the reason. We need more like him now with Napoleon threatening our shores." The admiral spoke seriously, intent on impressing Jenny with Piers's hidden qualities.

"He appears to be a most conscientious landlord, but is a bit arrogant," Jenny returned, feeling that the admiral was a kindred soul, a man very much like her father, who held to his own values.

"He had responsibility and duty drilled into him at an early age by the old earl and naval life is quite demanding. I think we can forgive him wanting his own way. He is accustomed to command," the admiral explained, anxious for some reason that Jenny admire Piers. A sensible girl, bred to country life, and not impressed with Piers' rank and wealth was just what he needed, not one of those vapid belles who embellished the London scene.

"I believe you have seen a different side to our host than has been my privilege, sir. But I must say Piers has a doughty champion in you," Jenny conceded, liking this bluff Navy man, whose shrewd blue eyes, used to scanning the wide horizon, she suspected now looked with equal penetration on society's sins and virtues. She wondered if he had come to Cornwall at Piers's request to advise him on the problem facing him. If Admiral Coniston had retired from the Navy she did not think he had lost all interest in the nation's affairs. He appeared to be a man at the center of events. In this she was wiser than she knew.

"I believe I am to take you into dinner, mademoiselle." The marquess de Lisle had materialized by Jenny's side as she was pondering the admiral's motives.

"Well, Theron, you are a lucky devil." The admiral greeted him as an old friend. "But then, you always have been. And how is the family? I can see for myself that Melissa is in fine fig. And I will learn all about your sins at dinner for I believe I am her partner," the admiral said with a jovial twinkle in his eye.

"Now, Coniston, no flirting with Melissa. She much prefers older men, says they understand her. Now what is a poor besieged husband to make of that?" he asked Jenny whimsically.

"I am sure the marchionese appreciates her good fortune," Jenny replied diplomatically, liking the marquess. He had a sense of humor with a good dose of self-deprecation, which was always unusual. She noticed the exchange of respect between the admiral and the marquess. She imagined the dark nobleman had been quite a success with the ladies before being tamed by his Melissa. The admiral departed to claim the petite marchionese, leaving Jenny with the marquess who extended his arm to escort her to the dining room.

Chatting easily, he asked her a bit about her presence in Cornwall and laughed when she confided artlessly that she had been sent to the ends of the country to recover from a blighted romance.

"And I see the cure has been effective. There is nothing about the declining spinster in you, Miss Dryden. I fear it is the former suitor who is declining, cursing his bad judgment," the marquess responded gallantly as he seated her.

"How nice of you to say so, but I think he is very happy with his choice," Jenny protested demurely, shaking out her napkin and giving him a dulcet look beneath her lashes.

"And I suspect you are a bit ofa minx, which is all to the good. My Melissa is just such a one, quite a handful." He indicated his wife, who was chatting away gaily to Admiral Coniston and completely captivating the gentleman.

"She's very lovely, so chic," Jenny sighed, as if wishing she could emulate such style.

"Underneath all those fine feathers she's still very much of an adventurous urchin. When I met her she was disguised as a boy. Badly I might say," he admitted.

"And you penetrated the disguise with all your vast experience, sir, I am sure," Jenny riposted, enjoying sparring with this witty and sophisticated man. He shared some of Piers's manner and she surmised that he could behave quite as arrogantly when the occasion warranted it, but she was surprised at the ease in which she could parry his thrusts.

"I think you will do very well, my girl. And now I suppose we had better concentrate on this delicious turbot," the marquess said.

Jenny thoroughly enjoyed the dinner which featured saddle of mutton, Davenport fowl with petit pois, and broiled mushrooms. Her neighbor on the other side was Robert Herron, and she took the opportunity on the arrival of the Renish cream and Savoy cake to ask him about his sister.

"I understand that Miss Herron is feeling not quite the thing and had to beg off this evening. I saw her this morning and she seemed quite as usual," Jenny mentioned to Robert.

"Oh dear, I suppose you mean she was tart and testy, her usual manner, I fear. Evelyn is a trial to me, I must admit, but there are reasons for her jaundiced attitude, poor girl. She was engaged to a lieutenant in a foot regiment, who basely deserted her and married a girl he met at Tunbridge Wells. It quite soured her on men. She used to be fairly pleasant looking, but since his rejection she has done her best to repel all males. I have tried to comfort and help her, but she turns aside all my best efforts with caustic words," he sighed, looking even more like the puzzled woolly bear, Jenny often thought he resembled. Then recollecting that Jenny herself had been deserted, he stammered and attempted an apology.

Taking pity on him, Jenny soothed, "Don't worry, Robert. I have almost forgotten that I, too, was disappointed in love, as dear Babs puts it. Makes me sound like a dying violet, but I have recovered and am apt to think it was all for the best."

"Ah, yes, but you are so different from Evelyn. The man must have been mad. Surely he regrets his choice," Robert responded with somewhat heavy gallantry.

"That's kind of you, Robert, but I believe he is very happy. I only hope he is perfectly comfortable with Amelia," Jenny responded cheerfully, showing none of the symptoms of a suffering female as she finished up her second slice of cake.

Lady Lashford signaled that the ladies should withdraw and leave the men to their port, so Jenny rose, thankful to escape Robert's pitying look. No doubt he thought she was putting a brave face on her unhappy past when in reality she had discovered she owed Harry a great deal of gratitude. If she had not come to Cornwall she would not have met with all these adventures—gypsies, smugglers, spies, and, of course, the enigmatic Earl of Trevarris.

In the drawing room, Jenny was joined by Melissa de Lisle, who charmed her immediately. The marchionese was not at all haughty, having a merry smile and an interest in her fellows which she displayed with disarming questions.

"I see you had Theron as your dinner partner. Now he knows all about you, but I know nothing. I understand you are not from Cornwall. Piers mentioned that you are visiting the lovely Amy Morstan. She is a real beauty, having all the assets I crave," Melissa said.

"It seems to me you have enough to satisfy anyone," Jenny replied a bit wistfully. Indeed, Melissa certainly had the affection of her husband and that was no mean feat, for Jenny suspected that many women had tried to capture the marquess.

"Oh, no. I would like to be tall and willowy with a serene character. Not possible. Theron says I am irrespressible and undignified," she confided.

"And irresistible, I fancy," Jenny laughed. "Alas, I am quite boring, a vicar's daughter from Wiltshire, who suffered a broken engagement and came to Trevarris to recover," Jenny said candidly.

"Well, you seem to have done that nicely, and engaged the interest of the cautious Piers, not an easy thing to do. He has eluded some very clever matrimonial traps, let me tell you," Melissa informed her with a knowing air.

"I have recovered from the engagement, but I am

not intent on luring Lord Trevarris into the parson's mousetrap. Actually, I find him most provoking and he treats me as if I were still in the nursery," Jenny said with some disgust.

"Capital. That's very encouraging. These rakish types always respond to resistance," Melissa said cheerfully. "Look at Theron, poor dear. I had him firmly in my clutches while he thought he was doing all the chasing. He's never quite recovered."

Jenny did not believe that for a moment, but Melissa's romance fascinated her. "Your husband told me you were disguised as a boy when he met you," she said.

"Yes, it was too shocking. I was escaping from a wicked guardian. After Theron unmasked me, it was a duel of wits. I am an adventuress at heart, I guess," Melissa conceded with a roguish smile.

"But it has all turned out happily, I can see. Do you have any children, ma'am?"

"Oh, yes. A boy eight, just like his father, the imp, and a dear little four-year-old girl. I miss the children when we are away from them for long."

"Does that happen often?" Jenny asked, curious.

"Oh, yes. Theron accepts mysterious assignments from Whitehall and delves about in conspiracies. Sometimes I help him," she explained modestly.

Jenny repressed a gasp. Was that why the de Lisles were in Cornwall? And how imprudent of Melissa to tell her all this. But perhaps her confiding air had a purpose. Really, she must try not to be so suspicious of everyone's motives. She was about to probe further when the door opened and the gentlemen entered the room. To her surprise, Piers came directly over to where they were sitting on a small settee a bit removed from the general conversation.

"Ah, Melissa. I see you are cultivating the intransigent Miss Dryden. I hope you are putting in a good word for me. She is very angry at me right now," he said wryly.

"Not at all. I am telling her what a wicked fellow you are and that she would do well to be on her guard," Melissa mocked.

"Oh, dear. I knew you were not to be trusted. How Theron manages you, I will never understand. The poor chap is under the cat's paw, I believe." Looking at her host in his dark evening dress, Jenny conceded that he was a figure which could draw the gaze of any girl. His suntanned face and heavy-lidded eyes surveyed them with deceiving candor. Piers might appear to be a gentleman of the first stare, content with his vast wealth and his position as one of London's most eligible bachelors, but she saw him differently. She had once drawn him as a sleek tiger, and now she felt very much like a helpless stoat caught in his trap.

"I am a very obedient wife, Piers. You wrong me," Melissa quipped. As her husband approached, she enlisted his aid. "Isn't that true, Theron? Piers is insisting to this charming child that I am the veriest shrew, but you know how conformable I am."

"You are a minx, Melissa, so don't feed Miss Dryden this gammon," the marquess replied. As the four continued to bandy words, Jenny decided that while Piers might be a tiger, the suave marquess was probably his cousin, the leopard, an equal threat, even if slightly tamed by his delightful Melissa.

"Lucia is going to sing for us. She has a trained and charming voice," Piers informed them, and then left to escort the lady to the pianoforte. He drew the draperies to allow a breeze from beyond the open French windows to alleviate the closeness. Jenny thought the air was dreadfully still, almost ominous. Could a storm be on the horizon? It was uncommonly warm for Cornwall.

As Lucia entertained them with a skilled rendition of a country air, Jenny's thoughts roamed restlessly. She wished she could escape from this formal group and continue her investigation into the spy ring, which might be operating at this very moment while she sat here helplessly listening to the music. Why had Piers arranged this party? She had noticed Henri d'Aubisson chatting with practiced bonhomie to Mme. La Soutaine. Had Piers hoped his dignified and proper guest would expose Henri as an imposter? If so, his ploy had not succeeded, for d'Aubisson, turning the pages of the music for Lucia, seemed very composed and relaxed. After two songs, Lucia laughingly demurred, receiving her applause graciously, but refusing any more performance. Just as well, for as they argued amiably, a sudden crack of thunder beyond the windows startled them all and a searing flash of lightning split the sky.

The threatening weather brought an end to Piers's gathering. As he escorted Jenny and her cousins to the entrance, she wondered if his party had brought him the results he hoped to achieve.

So taken with thoughts of spies and concealed identities, Jenny was hardly aware of Piers's farewells and his intention of calling upon her the next day to discuss a matter of some import. Nodding distractedly, which brought a frown to Piers's face, she jointly thanked him with Amy and Francis and within moments they were on their way home. Amy jumped as a shaft of lightning rent the dark sky and Francis reassured her.

"I hope we reach home before the rain comes. It appears we are in for a violent summer storm. We sometimes have these tempests in the hotter months. They can be terrifying, but pass quickly," Francis informed Jenny, while taking both Amy's hands in his and holding them comfortingly.

"Poor Major Bosworth, riding unprotected in this nasty weather." Jenny, who was not at all afraid of storms, could not help thinking of others less fortunate who must brave the storm in the open.

"As an old campaigner I am sure he is used to such vagaries of nature," Francis soothed. "Ah, here we are, and just before the deluge, I warrant." He shepherded his womenfolk into the house just as the first few drops of rain were falling.

Bidding her cousins a warm good night, Jenny went to her bedroom to mull over the events of the evening, disappointed that she could not carry out her plan to investigate the cove. Of course, the weather might prevent the smugglers from carrying out the rendezvous. As the first gusts of sweeping rain burst over Pencairn she could only breathe a sigh of relief that her plan had been postponed. It was no night to be scurrying about the cliffs. Storms might not frighten her, but she lay awake a long time that night thinking about the recent developments, the dramatic events heightened by the crash of the thunder and the piercing bolts of lightning which accompanied the driving rain beyond her windows. She slept fitfully, her mind disturbed by images far more intimidating than the storm.

Chapter Fifteen

The morning dawned shimmering white under a benign sun, only a slight breeze from the southeast gently lifting the branches of the trees protecting Pencairn. Nature's capricious hand had left disorder in the wake of the storm. Flattened shrubs and fallen limbs were strewn about the grounds, but as Jenny surveyed the landscape from her window all looked peaceful and promising, a day for exploring, she decided. Unwilling to waste a moment, she gulped her morning chocolate and hurried into her riding dress, too impatient to wait for Polly, who arrived to find her mistress dressed. Behind her came Babs, wanting to hear all the details of the night's party.

"Breakfast first, Babs. I am starving this morning despite all the elegant food at Arthmore," Jenny insisted, shepherding the little girl down the stairs toward the dining room. "You may sit with me while I eat and I will endeavor to satisfy your curiosity. Have you had breakfast already?" she asked as they walked companionably across the hall.

"Oh, yes, hateful porridge. I wish I could have lots of toast and strawberry jam and no nasty gruel. I might as well be an orphan in a workhouse," Babs complained, eyeing the interesting dishes kept hot on the sideboard. "Ham, too. You are lucky to be grown-up, Jenny."

"By the time you have achieved my great age you will be thoroughly sick of strawberry jam, I am sure," Jenny laughed, her spirits rising as they usually did in Babs's company. Amused by the little girl, Jenny allowed her to sample some of the hot breakfast. Obviously Francis had eaten earlier and Amy always breakfasted in her room, so the two were able to have a cosy chat about the Trevarris party.

"A marquess and an admiral—how exciting! We never have such fine visitors, only dull mine owners or Parliament people. Cornwall is very prosy," Babs concluded after listening to the details of the menu, the ladies' gowns, and other tidbits Jenny thought suitable for her ears. *Prosy* would not be Jenny's choice of words, certainly.

"Well, come along. I will walk you down to the vicarage, for after yesterday's holiday, you will be wanting to get at your lessons," she teased, knowing how Babs would like to extend her freedom and spend the day outdoors. And who could blame her? But Jenny felt she must supply some discipline.

After some grumbling they set off, walking slowly through the glistening morning to the village. For once the villagers appeared in a cheerful mood. Several of them nodded a good morning and commented on the storm. Robert Herron, leaning on his gate and watching their approach, hailed them with a great smile.

"A beautiful morning. We must savor it, for by nighttime we could be enveloped in mist or yet another cloudburst. Come, Babs, I think we will set your sums in the garden. Could I tempt you to stop for some chocolate, Jenny?" he pleaded, looking wistfully at the glowing girl.

Jenny, much as she would have liked to oblige Robert, could not face Evelyn's vinegary face on that perfect morning and refused gently, pleading errands for Amy. Behind his back Babs grimaced as if to say she knew Jenny was fibbing.

After a few moments' conversation about the party, Jenny took her leave, spying Evelyn hurrying from the back garden intent on breaking up the tête à tête. Really, she did make life difficult for Robert. He should take her in hand instead of dealing out sympathy and charity to his thorny sister. Still, it was no business of hers, and Jenny stepped briskly along the street, intent on returning to Pencairn. She had a mission this morning and no time for idle chat with the Herrons.

Avoiding the house, she went directly to the stables, requested her mare, and was soon galloping across the littered fields toward the cove. She had been avoiding the isolated spot since she and Babs had been trapped by the tide, but today she conquered her uneasiness and ventured down onto the beach. It was fruitless to look for any signs of the smugglers. Even if they had braved the storm, the winds and rain would have washed away any evidence of their activity.

Jenny poked about, pushing with her foot at stray shells and seaweed thrown up by the tide. She wondered what alternative plans Black Jack and his chief had made due to the weather. And what of the boats from France which may have set off in calm seas only to encounter last night's tempest? They could not land and must have turned back. Oh, dear, if it were to be rescheduled, Jenny would have little luck discovering the time and date of the next consignment.

She sat down on a lichened rock and contemplated the sea which hid so many secrets. The water lapped gently across the shale, looking tempting and peaceful, but the current was moving swiftly for all that.

Jenny rose disconsolately, thinking she might try to get around the rocks and explore the cave in which she and Babs had sheltered. The tide was low and although the sand wet and rocky, she should have little difficulty. Picking her way carefully around the edges of the cove she remembered Piers's warning about exploring beyond the edges of the protected inlet, but somehow the pleasant skies and blue sea did not hint of any sudden calamity. Yes, there was the entrance to the cave.

Peering into the dark recess, for no sunshine penetrated the cave, she thought she saw a bundle of clothes in the corner pushed up against the slimy walls. Could this be evidence of the smugglers business, left behind in a hurried exodus? She approached it cautiously and then recoiled in horror. It was not a bundle of rags, but a body of a woman, her long black hair streaming water soaked and caked down to her waist, a white flaccid hand thrown out as if to save herself from the watery depths which had claimed her. How could she have come here?

Jenny hesitated. She did not want to investigate any farther. The idea of examining the cold salty corpse repulsed her, but what should she do? Gingerly she laid a hand on the woman's body, although Jenny had no doubt that life had long left the poor soul. The cadaver felt cold, clammy, her eyes glassy and fixed, her mouth thinned in a grimace. In life she must have been attractive. A young woman, not more than twenty at the most, she was dressed plainly in a kersey gray skirt and white muslin blouse, her only ornament a locket around her neck. It was finely chased, obviously valuable, and the woman's other hand clutched it as if for reassurance.

Shuddering, but almost without knowing what she did, Jenny removed the locket and wrapped it in a clean handkerchief which she took from her pocket. She had a feeling that the locket might be important and she had every intention of turning it over to the authorities. But her first task must be to find help. She could not leave the woman there unattended.

Taking one last sorrowful look at the pathetic figure, she scurried from the cave and made her way around to the rocks, eager to reach her horse and ride to the village.

Her first instinct was to locate Major Bosworth, who would know how to deal with the aftermath of the tragedy, but when she arrived breathless at his headquarters, a small cottage near the quay, it was to learn he had gone out on some military business. Reluctant to explain her discovery to the rather sullen soldier lounging on the doorstep of the cottage, she hesitated. The man appeared to think she was seeking the major for some suggestive purpose. She did not like his shifty eye nor his leering smile. Turning away, she wondered what she should do. Her desperation was solved by the timely appearance of Piers, who rode up to the cottage as she was leaving.

"There you are, Jenny. Had you forgotten we were to ride this morning?" he asked her with a hint of chagrin.

"Yes. No, it doesn't matter," Jenny replied distractedly. Abandoning her decision to solve any mysteries on her own, as she was considerably shaken by her discovery, she wanted only to throw the whole miserable affair onto Piers's broad shoulders. Only later was she to wonder why she felt so reassured by his presence. Seeing her agitation and not understanding it, he nevertheless attempted to soothe her.

"Come, Jenny, whatever is troubling you cannot be that serious," he said, securing his horse and taking her hand. "Tell me what bothers you." Taking a last disgusted look at the soldier who was watching them avidly, she pushed Piers down the street away from prying eyes and ears.

"Piers, the most dreadful thing. I went down to the cove this morning, thinking to do a little detective work on my own because of something I overheard yesterday in the church, and I found a woman's dead body in that cave where you rescued Babs and me the other day. It was ghastly, the poor young thing. Could she be a victim of the storm or some other tragedy? We must get help, remove her for a proper burial," she blurted out.

With commendable calm, Piers took charge. "Well, come show me this woman and then we will arrange to have her carried to the church. I take it Bosworth is away, and that lout will not be of much help, but first I must see the body." He said this all in a matter-of-fact tone, as if the discovery of strange young women drowned in a cove was not an exceptional occurrence.

"Yes, yes, I will take you there," Jenny replied in relief, Piers's controlled acceptance of her news steadying her. Of what use were hysterics? and she despised females who acted in that gooselike way. Obviously the business must be investigated, but the most pressing concern was to give the poor woman a Christian burial.

"Come, Jenny, let us ride out there now. No doubt the woman is the victim of a wreck at sea. Last night's storm must have caused havoc up and down the coast, and any ship unfortunate enough to be at sea during the worst of it might have floundered and lost her passengers and crew," Piers explained as they cantered away from the village and across the fields.

Under Piers's bracing tones much of Jenny's fear quieted. She did not think she would soon forget her first glimpse of the woman, but Piers's strong male presence by her side dissipated much of her horror as they rode through the bright sun-dappled fields toward the cove.

Arriving at the scene, he dismounted and helped Jenny from her mare, securing the two horses to a nearby tree. They scrambled down onto the beach and made their way around the inlet across the rocks and onto the next point that led to the cave. Jenny paused for a moment, dreading the sight she knew she must see. Piers went first, entering the cave with brisk steps, his boots soundless on the sandy floor.

"Dark in here. Nasty place," he muttered, casting around to see what Jenny had found, but the cave was empty.

Jenny, at first averting her eyes, scurried to his side, indicating the spot where she had found the body. Not a sign of the woman was evident. Piers bent down to look at the floor of the cave, but could see nothing.

"Are you sure she was dead, Jenny? She might have recovered and wandered off," he asked, concerned.

But Jenny would entertain no such doubts. "I did not dream it you know. I felt the woman's body. There was no sign of life. She was cold, clammy, white. I can tell you exactly how she looked, what she was wearing. It was a dreadful sight," she said with some heat, believing he thought she was imagining it all. And then remembering the locket, she took the wrapped trinket from her pocket.

"She was wearing this, one hand clutching it. I don't know why I removed it, but it's as well I did, for now there is proof of her presence here. You surely don't think I made it up?" Jenny asked indignantly, her irritation at his skepticism banishing the last lingering frissons of fear she had felt.

Taking the locket, Piers looked at it carefully. "Of course not, Jenny. I believe you saw the woman. What I am not sure of is whether she was actually dead. And if she was it is obvious someone has removed her body." While he was reassuring Jenny, he was turning the locket over and examining it with a practiced eye. "Quite a valuable piece. Old, I think, and no doubt some family heirloom. I think we would not be amiss to open it." He had some difficulty, the salt water having jammed the snap which fastened the locket, but at last he pried the pieces apart.

Jenny peered over his shoulder, fascinated. On one section of the locket under glass was a miniature of a young dark-haired man in the uniform of a French officer. But in the other section, also protected by glass, was a folded bit of paper. Piers removed it painstakingly, determined not to damage it. Unwrapping the paper, they saw in minute writing a row of numbers, meaningless to them, but Piers gasped.

"Your young woman was French, I think, and on her way here for no good purpose. Whoever was to meet her may have discovered her dead and removed her to prevent any questions. You were fortunate that you were not found near the body or you, too, might have suffered a nasty fate," Piers said gravely. "Damn it, Jenny, when will you use a little prudence? You have no business being involved in these goings-on, and I want a report on that conversation you heard in the church. These are desperate times and if we are to foil Napoleon's invasion we must make every effort. We can't have amateurs roving about the countryside muddling up our attempts to catch the culprits," he finished with some irritation.

He must take this paper to the admiral and see what he made of it and then there was the matter of the woman. And Jenny. She was in real peril if the smugglers or spy chief knew she discovered the locket. How could he protect her? With commendable restraint he mastered his vexation and said more kindly, "I know you want to help and I think you probably want to show me that you are as capable as any man of serving your country, exposing her enemies, but believe me, Jenny, this is not some storybook affair, with the hero rescuing the damsel in the nick of time. There is much that is puzzling, but you must rely on more experienced hands to solve the enigma."

Although she was loath to admit the sense of Piers's argument she had to accept the justice of it. She was out of her depth in this tangled web of duplicity and treason. The danger to her personally she discounted, but she found the mystery puzzling, the motive of the conspirators inconceivable, and the invulnerability of Black Jack to prosecution unclear. She voiced some of these questions to Piers.

"If you know that Black Jack is in league with the French, conniving at betraying his country, why can you not prevail upon Major Bosworth to arrest him and have him up for trial?" she asked with a certain telling simplicity.

"Well, for one thing we have no proof and, for another, to arrest Black Jack now would bring us no closer to the real culprit," Piers explained, meanwhile turning over the locket carefully as if searching for some abstruse clue to its owner.

"Wouldn't he reveal the name hoping to receive some mitigation of his sentence?" Jenny asked.

"Perhaps he doesn't know it," Piers answered vaguely, his mind evidently elsewhere.

Jenny, concluding that men unnecessarily complicated the simplest matters, abandoned her questions and returned to the most pressing problem, the disappearance of the woman's body. Could she have been wrong, that the stranger she had discovered had merely fainted from her immersion in the sea, recovered, and wandered away? That seemed very unlikely to her, although she thought Piers doubted her evidence of the woman's death. Perhaps he even doubted there had been a woman, thinking Jenny had imagined it in some hysterical fit.

"I think we ought to make an effort to find the woman," she informed him with some hauteur. "Then you will accept my story." She did not like the idea that Piers thought her so foolish that she would have mistaken a fainting woman for a dead one.

Piers, who had been trying to decipher the paper, had paid little attention to Jenny's of the situation and suddenly was recalled by her sharp tone. He smiled at her with affection.

"Dear Jenny, you are annoyed with me, aren't you? I do believe you found the woman. It could be quite important, this locket, if we could solve the enigma of this code. And you are right. We must find her, dead or alive. Obviously someone has removed her or she has gone off on her own. What concerns me even more is that someone may have seen you poking about in here and will take steps to silence you. I don't want to frighten you, but you must be aware that you represent a threat to these people. They are a ruthless, brutal lot who will stop at nothing." He did not want to catapult her into a state of mindless fear, but was concerned for her safety. She was such a reckless girl, throwing herself into escapades without really understanding what was at stake, and he felt powerless to protect her.

Suddenly, standing there with the mysterious locket in his hand, watching the varying expressions of perplexity, determination, and curiosity cross Jenny's open face, he knew he desperately wanted to protect her from the present menace which threatened to disrupt her young life, to stand between her and any future peril or problem which could cause her unhappiness. He was startled by this discovery, by the fact that standing there in the dank cove, apparently concerned only with the apprehension of a traitor, he should realize with blinding clarity that Jenny was more important than anything else.

Evidently some fleeting sense of his sudden uprush of feeling must have penetrated Jenny's awareness, for she asked him, "Have you had an idea, Piers?" referring, of course, to the locket which he still grasped. But he, surprised by the sudden knowledge which had come to him, for once did not know how to react. Certainly he could not blurt out his feelings there in the depressing dark den of smugglers. Jenny deserved better of him. Self-control was a long ingrained habit with Piers, as was the ability to show an impassive face to the world, so he answered her casually. "I have several, Jenny, but most important now is to find Bosworth and put him and his troop on the track of this woman. And to escort you home before you can come up with any more surprises." Underneath the teasing tone Jenny sensed his purpose and she did not, for once, argue with him.

As they walked quickly away from the cave, Piers pocketed the locket, having replaced the paper with the meaningless numbers. His eyes scanned the horizon, searching for a ship or fishing skiff, peering behind outcroppings in case any hostile eyes were watching them. There were too many hiding places on the rocky shores. Piers would be relieved to get atop the cliff and safely onto their horses. And he lost no time in doing just that. As they rode away from the cove, Jenny pleaded, "You will inform me about the woman if you find her, won't you, Piers?"

"Yes, I will, if in turn you promise to stay close to Pencairn and not indulge in any wild freaks of investigation on your own. I am just wondering if it might not be better to insist that Francis send you home to Wiltshire," he pondered, thinking that Jenny's presence now could only distract him from the business at hand. Then, when he had helped to catch the traitor and put a stop to Black Jack's more outrageous stunts, he could safely turn his attention to Jenny. He would travel to Wiltshire, court her in an approved fashion, win her parents' approval. After all, he thought, they must welcome me. Piers had no illusions about his considerable assets as a husband. Too many marriageable girls and their mamas had assured him of his eligibility. But, of course, an unworldly country vicar and his wife might judge him differently. Brooding over the possibility of the Drydens rejecting his suit he did not at first appreciate the strength of Jenny's anger at the thought of being exiled to Wiltshire.

"If you persuade Francis to send me home and miss all the excitement, I will never forgive you, Piers. Besides it's most unfair, since I have made the most telling discovery of this whole business." Jenny's outrage was evident and she turned a most disapproving eye upon her companion. "It's just like you, Piers, to want to take over and manage everything in your usual arrogant fashion. Well, I won't have it. If you suggest anything to Francis about sending me home I'll make you regret it."

"And I wonder how you would do that," he mused with infuriating aplomb. Then seeing that Jenny really was in a state that did not entertain any light-hearted teasing, he hurried to calm her fears but with a cautionary note. "All right, Jenny, I will not insist on you going back to Wiltshire, if you promise to behave with some circumspection." Seeing she was not entirely appeased, he added with a wicked grin, "I would miss your infuriating ways and become bored beyond measure."

But Jenny, realizing that she had made a cake of herself, refused to be drawn. Averting her head, she remarked in tones which would have done justice to a duchess, "I have some demands of my own, Piers. I want to know what is happening. You should share your information with me, as I have with you. That's only fair."

"Oh, Jenny, can't you see that I am afraid you will rush into some dreadful situation before I can solve this problem? It distracts me from the task in hand to worry over you," he pleaded, wondering how far he could go, realizing that Jenny had no idea that he entertained warm feelings for her, believing him to be merely amusing himself.

"You have no reason to concern yourself over me. I can take care of myself," Jenny said resolutely, loath to admit that Piers had been conveniently available to rescue her before and kind enough not to remind her of it. Shaking off the passing thought that it would be pleasant to have him always around to save her from the consequences of her rash actions, she returned to the problem which concerned them.

"You have told me nothing about your investigation into Henri d'Aubisson. Have you discovered whether he is an imposter or not?" Jenny asked in a businesslike tone, implying she would listen to no more objections or suggestions as to her behavior.

"Yes, well, Henri is not all he professes to be, but now is not the time for that. Here we are at Bosworth's headquarters, and by the activity about, I assume he has returned from wherever duty called him. Very conscientious the major," Piers said, with what Jenny thought a good deal of condescension. But she was willing to overlook that for the moment if they could gain some cooperation in the hunt for the drowned woman.

Seeing no evidence of the sullen soldier who had treated her so shabbily before, Jenny accompanied Piers into the building, although she suspected he would have preferred to have left her outside the discussion. Still, she was the one who had found the body and she did not trust him to give an accurate report to Major Bosworth.

The major received them with pleasure, which masked a certain surprise. Piers soon satisfied his curiosity and told of Jenny's discovery. His account was precise and made no reference to his own doubts about the woman's death. The major appeared to accept the situation and only asked Jenny for her own observations, without implying he found this account of the disappearing corpse at all dubious.

"Bosworth, I think you should send your men

around the village to try to find this woman. Of course, I would not presume to tell you how to carry out your duties, but it is obvious she intended to come here secretly and we should try to discover what she intended to do," Piers said a bit curtly, Jenny thought. After all, Major Bosworth must know how to mount a search. He might take umbrage at Piers telling him how to proceed no matter how silkily the earl made the suggestion.

"Quite right, Lord Trevarris. I will attend to it immediately. And perhaps later you can tell me a bit more about what you noticed when you first saw the woman," Bosworth said to Jenny, implying that he was not completely satisfied with her story.

"Yes, of course," she agreed. Jenny would have gone on to discuss the finding of the locket and its meaning, but since Piers had not mentioned it, she decided he had a reason not to give this information to the major. What did that mean?

Jenny waited until they were well beyond the village, riding toward Pencairn, before she asked, "Piers, why didn't you show the major the locket as proof that the woman was really there? I think he might believe she was the product of my overheated imagination, although too polite to say so, while the locket would be telling evidence that she really was in the cave."

"Yes, you are right, but I am glad you did not blurt it out right then. I want to discuss this latest development with the admiral before confiding in the major. Bosworth appears to be well up to his job, a dependable fellow, but a good campaigner never reveals all his strategy until he has to," Piers informed her sternly, causing Jenny to gaze at him in stupification. Could Piers distrust the major? She remembered stories that smugglers often enlisted the aid of the soldiers and Customs men with large bribes. Did Piers believe the major was vulnerable to such corruption? And certainly abetting treason was far more serious than allowing a few illegal cases of brandy and silks into the country. Not for one moment did Jenny think the major venal, but Piers evidently preferred to keep his own counsel, and he must have had valid reasons. Jenny, troubled and confused, felt that even Piers fell under the cloud of duplicity and mystery.

Arriving at Pencairn, she bid him a rather abrupt farewell after thanking him for his escort, wanting to escape as he suddenly seemed strange and rather frightening. Sensing her withdrawal, and suspecting the emotions behind it, he made no demur, having business of his own to accomplish, but determined to settle their relationship before much more time had passed.

He left her with the promise to return with any new information after his conference with the admiral. And he warned her again to behave prudently.

Raising her hand to his lips, he kissed it lingeringly. "Please, Jenny, take care. You matter to me and I don't want you to suffer any harm from this adventure into which you have so heedlessly fallen. Trust me to solve it. And, remember, next time you tumble into trouble I might not be available to rescue you, although I pray I will always be on hand when you need me," he said, causing her heart to quicken.

Before she could manage any reply, he had leapt on his horse and galloped down the driveway eager to reach Arthmore and the admiral. Jenny, staring bemusedly at the retreating horseman, for the moment forgot all about traitors, mysterious drowned women, cryptic messages, and brutal smugglers. Piers's parting words had caused an excitement which blinded her to any concern but the desires of her own heart.

Chapter Sixteen

Left alone to ruminate on Piers's words, Jenny retired to her room, settling down by the window to ponder his meaning. Was she imagining that Piers cared for her in a significant way? She could hardly allow herself to hope that the arrogant earl found her attractive, that he intended to offer for her. For weeks she had been confused about her own feelings for him, denying his appeal and fighting what she believed were his flirtatious ploys, unwilling to think he meant anything serious by them.

From their very first meeting he had challenged her resolution to dismiss him as a womanizer. She wondered if he made these provocative approaches because he could not entertain the idea that any woman found him less than acceptable. If he had been the rake she at first thought, would he have involved himself in this dangerous investigation, denying himself the pleasures of London to bury himself in Cornwall and chase enemy agents? Remembering his kisses, his last words, and the passion he could so easily arouse in her, she struggled to find her equilibrium.

She shook her head angrily. Had she learned nothing from Harry's false avowals, that she would rush into a hopeless yearning for a man who would abandon her when she had served his purpose? Wary of yet another blow to both her pride and her affection, Jenny abandoned these fruitless musings and turned instead to the prospect of unmasking the traitor in their midst.

She was convinced that the smugglers, under the orders of this mysterious agent, had removed the body of the Frenchwoman. Perhaps she represented some threat to their safety. But how had she come to be washed ashore at the cave? Where was she coming from, and what was her mission? Did the numbers in the locket represent a message from her masters revealing the date, time, and target of the invasion as Piers suspected? If so, and if the smugglers knew she had seen the body and discovered the locket, Jenny was indeed in danger, but somehow she could not take the threat seriously. Surely no one would attempt to remove her, a visitor and relative of one of the county's most prominent magistrates and land owners. Her very presence in Francis's household must offer protection.

She had every reason to believe that these people were ruthless with so much at stake. And Black Jack, for one, would stop at little if he thought his income and way of life was in jeopardy. Piers discounted Henri d'Aubisson as the traitor and, based on her own observation of his character, she could only agree. But she was not quite so certain of the

Pencrists. Both Lucia and Austen seemed well placed, amoral, and shrewd enough to be conspirators. Austen needed money and Lucia wanted to return to society where her many talents could be appreciated. It was ridiculous to even consider Robert Herron, a kindly, generous, if slightly muddled, dedicated pastor to his flock.

While she was sorting out this cast of characters, Jenny idly sketched animal caricatures. If Lucia had the characteristics of a sleek feline, Robert those of a woolly bear, what of Major Bosworth, competent but unimaginative? Rather like a St. Bernard dog, she imagined. No, none of them fit the picture of a master spy.

Suddenly, almost without volition, her nimble fingers drew a nasty sneering ferret with the lineaments of Evelyn Herron. Jenny drew back from the picture with a sudden gasp. Was it possible? Could Evelyn, with her warped sense of injustice, her bitter outlook, her crabbed nature, be the traitor?

Once the idea took hold, Jenny could not abandon it. There was no reason a woman could not have organized this intricate plot. Of course, she would have to gain ascendancy over Black Jack. Jenny faltered a bit there. Would he be willing to take orders from a woman? Of course, he might not know the identity of his chief. Jenny, however, recalled the overheard conversation in the church, Black Jack protesting some arrangement he felt too dangerous or too impractical, and his eventual agreement. If Evelyn were the traitor she must have powers that Jenny could only guess. Would greed alone motivate Black Jack to obey her commands?

Now that the idea of Evelyn as the chief of the smugglers, the conspirator who would welcome French soldiers to the shores of her country, had surfaced, Jenny could barely contain her impatience to test her theory. She had told Piers she would wait to hear the results of Major Bosworth's search for the drowned woman, but the thought of idly sitting there when she could be finding the evidence which would prove Evelyn's guilt was anathema. Still, it would be best to give some thought to her next move. Jenny doubted that the cove, now revealed as a former cache for the smugglers, would be used by Black Jack and his men again. Too many people, including the military and Piers, knew of its past. No, the smugglers must have discovered a new hiding place, not obvious to searchers who understood the practices of the smugglers. Jenny frowned. She was at a disadvantage, not knowing the area with the intimacy of a longtime resident.

She might be on entirely the wrong tack when it came to Evelyn Herron, but she felt the vicar's sister was worth investigating. Surely Jenny was clever enough to wring some damaging evidence from Evelyn, if in fact it existed, and Jenny knew that proof of Evelyn's guilt would be needed before either Piers or Major Bosworth would act. And that proof must lie in the church somewhere. If she told Piers of her suspicions he would, in his usual arrogant fashion, take charge of the whole business, and although Jenny did not doubt his astuteness or courage, she believed a woman, herself, would be more apt to force Evelyn to reveal her iniquity.

Jenny hesitated. Was she viewing Evelyn as the traitor because Jenny disliked her, found her character, manner, and appearance repellent, or was there every reason to suspect her? At any rate she felt she must choose both her time and her actions carefully. The secretive Miss Herron would not easily be tricked into a confession or even an admission which hinted at her guilt. Jenny felt in her innermost being that Evelyn Herron could behave as viciously as Black Jack. She might even be responsible for the death of the woman in the cave. Well, she must plan her approach to Evelyn carefully and not rush boldly to confront her.

If Jenny was impatient to challenge her adversary, she managed to behave circumspectly at luncheon. Both Francis and Amy were present, and Jenny was happy to see that their improved relationship continued. Francis had heard of Jenny's discovery and questioned her sternly.

"After the frightening experience you and Babs had in the cave, Jenny, I am surprised that you visited the wretched place again," Amy said after learning of the mystery of the disappearing woman.

"Yes, well, it's obvious that something unusual is going on in this village and my curiosity was aroused. All those tales of smuggling and the reputation of Black Jack are very intriguing," Jenny replied with a deceptive meekness.

"Not just intriguing, Jenny, but dangerous. Why do you suppose Piers requested Bosworth and his troop? He intends to find out what is going on and we are both certain it is more than just the usual illegal trading. Which is why you must be careful. The body of the woman has not been found," Francis said with a worried frown.

Jenny, irritated that Francis might not believe her story, protested. "You do believe that I saw the body, Francis? She was dead—cold and rigid."

"Oh, Jenny, how could you touch her?" Amy shuddered with delicate revulsion.

"Well, I had to find out if she was alive and needed help. I couldn't just turn away," Jenny explained patiently.

"I applaud your charity, Jenny, but again let me warn you that meddling in this business is not just some holiday exercise. If anything happened to you, how would I explain to your parents that I did not protect you, letting you roam about the countryside and getting yourself into trouble?" Francis reasoned. "I would not want to deny you freedom, to insist you take a groom wherever you ride, placing certain areas of the estate and countryside out of bounds, but you must see my position."

"Oh, Francis, I will be most careful, and I am grateful for your care and concern," Jenny soothed. She added whimsically, "My mother and father would sympathize with you. They have tried to restrain my exploits for years with little success. I am just a nosy interfering female with an insatiable taste for adventure, I guess."

"Jenny, you will not take Babs into any dangerous places, will you?" Amy pleaded, remembering how much time the two cousins spent together, and how enterprising her small daughter could be.

"Of course not, Amy. I wouldn't dream of risking

her safety. You know how fond I am of her," Jenny protested, appalled that Amy could entertain such a notion. "But don't you see that as long as all this suspicion and intimidation exists in the village and at your mine, Francis, we are all living under a threat. It must be stopped." Jenny set her chin and looked quite fierce, as if she would brook no further attempts to restrain her from doing her duty.

"She has a good point there, Amy, but I must ask you both to be on your guard when going about your daily affairs. I do not like the atmosphere in Trevarris. These are difficult times. I wish I could believe that Piers will solve the dilemma, unmask the villains, and return our village to a measure of peace." Francis sighed for he was encountering his own problems with unruly and sullen workers, stirred up, he thought, by Black Jack, although there was no proof of that.

"There will never be peace until Napoleon and all his minions are defeated," Jenny said stoutly and, as both Amy and Francis were forced to agree, the discussion ended.

Piers did not come by during the afternoon with a report on the search for the woman, so Jenny concluded they had not found the body. She began to have doubts. *Could* the woman have been alive? And if she were, where could she have gone to elude discovery? Jenny had promised to remain at home and wait for Piers, but the inactivity irked her. She was tempted to ride out to see Maritza. Would the troops have investigated the gypsy camp? She did not really think the woman would be there, but where could she be?

The afternoon and evening passed slowly. Even Babs's arrival after tea and the girl's eagerness to tell of her ascendancy over Johnny Grathum did not dispell Jenny's impatience nor distract her from a lowering feeling that time was passing. She felt every moment was vital to solving the dilemma of the missing Frenchwoman. Evidently the admiral had not solved the enigma of the locket or certainly Piers would have let her know.

In this supposition she was correct. Admiral Coniston, at first excited by the odd paper, as the hours went by in a fruitless attempt to decipher the numbers, shared Jenny's frustration. 12-2-10. They must have some meaning, a cryptic reference to a possible invasion date? Piers, the admiral, and the Marquess de Lisle, locked up in the library at Arthmore, figured every possible permutation, but came up with no answer. At last, disgusted, Piers stood up from behind his desk and began to pace the room.

"At first I believed we had discovered the date of the invasion. But these numbers make no sense in that context, since that date would be two years away."

"The numbers refer to a code, possibly solved by a book," the marquess suggested. "Without the code book we are at a standstill."

"Yes, no doubt the spy has the book. But whoever the villain is he is equally checkmated. Without the message in the locket he cannot know when to expect the ships," the marquess explained shrewdly.

The admiral looked at de Lisle with admiration. "You are absolutely right, Theron. We must find that book. It is even more vital than the name of the spy."

"I want them all: the book, the spy, the organization, whatever will put a stop to this threat. Lives are at stake here and I don't mean just the people of England, but nearer to home," Piers protested in some desperation.

"You are afraid for the intrepid Miss Dryden?" the marquess inquired, immediately grasping Piers's fear.

"Yes, she is constant peril until we capture the perpetrator of this treachery. If indeed the woman Jenny found is alive, she knows Jenny has the precious locket. If the woman is dead, her allies realize that whatever message she brought has been removed. Unless, of course, they expected a verbal report, and that is a possibility. This locket and message may have an entirely different meaning than the one we are trying to interpret," he said in some confusion, the perplexities mounting.

"No, I don't think that is so, Piers. I believe the woman would not have been entrusted with only an oral message. This paper must have a deeper significance," the admiral protested.

"Well, I cannot sit here doing nothing. I will have to tackle Black Jack again," Piers decided. And, then, following Jenny's reasoning, he remembered the gypsies. They kept their secrets well and had no reason to love the English. Could the tribe be part of the conspiracy?

"I cannot remain here any longer worrying over these damned numbers. I will leave you to it. Perhaps, Theron, you could enlist Melissa's aid.

Once before she solved the mystery of French messages delivered under our very noses," he reminded the marquess. "At any rate, I am going to ride out and see what is happening to the search. Obviously Bosworth has found nothing and he may believe Jenny's story was all a hum," he finished bleakly.

The admiral and the marquess agreed to continue their efforts with the numbers. But they were becoming desperate, so close yet still so far from deciphering the paper which they were convinced held the secret to the upcoming invasion.

Piers, riding impatiently toward the gypsy camp, met Bosworth and his men galloping down the road. He stopped the major for a progress report.

"What have you found, Bosworth?" he asked, stilling his restless horse with iron knees.

"Not a sign of the woman, either alive or dead. We have searched every likely looking spot, even delved into the surrounding caves, but that is hopeless, there are so many. We turned out that disreputable inn, the Bull's Head, but all we discovered was dirt and a sullen landlord. We have just returned from the gypsy camp. They were most uncooperative, but I honestly believe they had no idea of what we were after. I want to apprehend that smuggler chief, Black Jack, and make him sweat a bit. We are on our way to his cottage now." Bosworth looked hot and harried.

"Leave Black Jack to me. I have the means to force some admissions from him and I think I can persuade the gypsies to tell me whatever they know. Unfortunately, soldiers have a quelling effect on them and they will not help you," Piers replied brusquely.

"Of course, sir, if you think you can succeed where I have failed," Bosworth said stiffly, not liking the idea that Piers might usurp his duty and apprehend the culprits.

"Don't be so touchy, Bosworth. I meant no slight on your prowess, but you must remember, I know this part of the country well. And I know the people—a stubborn, unfriendly lot they can be, too. I suspect they see you as interlopers harassing them unduly. But I am in no doubt that your presence here will help to flush out our traitors. I am grateful that you came," Piers responded with the charm he could summon so easily to beguile those who opposed him. He would have his own way, but he did not want to antagonize Bosworth, whose cooperation was vital, in case of any action or the possible arrest. Bosworth must be available to whisk the spy away to the safety of a Penzance jail. Piers had neither the authority nor the resources to hold the enemy in custody.

Major Bosworth, by nature amiable and optimistic, gave a grudging smile, acknowledging that he had been too quick to take umbrage.

"Sorry, sir, but this duty is frustrating. We don't seem to be making much progress," he complained. "But I will be grateful for whatever you discover." Then saluting, he spurred his horse and calling to his troop, disappeared rapidly in the direction of the village. Piers trotted on thoughtfully to the gypsy encampment.

After greeting the headman and assuring him that

the tribe was welcome to extend their stay as long as they wished, Piers sought out Maritza. Surely she would have some knowledge of Black Jack's accomplices. He just might get her to reveal it, now that her previous loyalty to the smuggler had been destroyed by his brutal treatment of her and his rejection of their child.

As usual, she was sitting on the steps of her caravan, dandling the baby and surveying the camp with a somewhat bitter eye. Her caravan had been placed at a suitable distance from the others and she was generally ostracized by the women of the camp. She must be lonely and Piers wondered why she did not leave and try to find employment in some town, and settle into a more rewarding life for herself and her child. But he remembered that the gypsy exiled either by choice or by edict of the tribe had a grim time of it. *Gorgios* distrusted them and once they had left the tribe to live among the alien population they were not welcomed back. She had certainly paid dearly for her alliance with Black Jack.

"Good day, noble lord. Have you come to take pity on poor Maritza? How can I be of service to you?" she asked extravagantly, her dark eyes flashing suggestively.

Piers ignored her provocative look, but could not help thinking what a temptation she was to any vulnerable male, with her bold, flaunted figure, her mane of careless black hair, and that air of sexuality which was in no way diminished by her maternal cares. "How is the baby today, Maritza?" he asked prosaically.

"Ah, the little one fares well, now that your lady has cured him. A saint she is to bother with a gypsy brat, but Maritza does not forget and I will repay her kindness," she promised, tossing her head and jingling her bracelets dramatically.

Indeed, the baby, to Piers untutored eyes, looked healthy and for once clean and content. "She does not want payment. She helped you because she is good-hearted," he answered shortly, not wanting to discuss Jenny with Maritza.

The gypsy seemed to sense his reservation, for she smiled lazily and said, "Ah, Maritza understands. I will read your hand and reveal the future. You will learn your lady's dreams and hopes. Perhaps Fate will promise many sons and great fame for you. Maritza will tell you and you need not fill my palm with silver for this vision," she chanted, standing up and coming closer to Piers, her baby held negligently on one hip.

"Some other time, Maritza. What I would like to hear now is some information about Black Jack," he said. Really, she was a brazen creature, ready to bed any man who took her fancy. No wonder the tribe scorned her. Gypsies had rigid ideas about women like Maritza and she was fortunate a more stringent punishment had not been meted out to her for her transgressions.

She spat contempuously on the ground. "Bah, that black-hearted bastard. He is evil that one and will come to no good end. Then Maritza will have her own back. She will laugh at his hanging," she chortled venomously.

"Well, he can hardly be hanged if he is not caught in some lawbreaking. Now what do you know about his smuggling?" Piers asked bluntly, weary of all the posturing.

Maritza was more than ready to betray her former lover, but she knew little about Black Jack's secretive chief. She remembered one episode when he had left in the middle of the night on some mysterious errand which had angered him a great deal.

"Brandy and silks is what we bring in, not these blasted Frenchies," he had muttered before throwing on his boots and rushing from the cottage on receipt of a whispered message from some unknown source. All the information did was confirm Piers's belief that Black Jack was in league with the spies, but he was certain of that already. Had he not seen the muffled figure whisked away on his midnight vigil at the cove?

"There must be something else, something Black Jack said which would give us a clue to this business," he muttered more to himself than to Maritza.

She looked at him slyly and then, tossing back her head revealed, "There is something else, but you *gorgios* have no faith in the second sight. I do not know whether you believe in my powers," she hissed, her eyes glittering.

Piers, not particularly impressed by this act intended to fascinate the gullible, was still interested in whatever she suggested.

"When he left, I was angry and wanted to know more, but when I questioned him, he hit me, saying to shut my mouth or it would be the worse for me.

But later I heard him muttering in his sleep about 'the sacred stones.' That was all, just sacred stones, whatever they may be. The sacred stones I know of are far away, many leagues from here. He is mad that one, mad and bad."

Piers thought she might be referring to Stonehenge, a magnet for gypsies, but he could see no relevance to this latest information. Abandoning that line of questioning, he asked Maritza about any strangers visiting the camp.

"We do not welcome strangers, my lord. If they persist, we have ways of warning them off. No one has entered our circle in the past few days. I would know. My uncle is the headman and hides little from me," she said proudly.

"Perhaps this stranger stole quietly into camp and few know of it," Piers persisted, trying to force some admission from her.

"Impossible. Gypsies have no secrets with *gorgios*. The tribe shares all knowledge. If anyone came here from the outside we all would learn of it." Maritza was adamant in her scorn of such a suggestion, and Piers was forced to agree that it would be unusual for a stranger to penetrate the camp without her discovering it. Finally, he decided he would learn no more from Maritza and, tossing her a few coins which she pocketed greedily, he took his leave.

But before he could mount his horse, she ran to his side, placing an urgent hand on his arm, her breast heaving and her eyes staring wildly into the distance.

"Take care of your lady, my lord. She is in great danger. Maritza sees evil in a halo about her head. Beware. Maritza has spoken the true word," she intoned. Before he could question her further she ran into her caravan and slammed the door, as if running from an unnamed menace.

As Piers rode away from the camp to seek out Black Jack, he frowned, his apprehension mounting despite his best effort to shake off the feeling. Of course, he did not believe that gypsy nonsense of divining the future, the act assumed for credulous fools, but he was enough of a Celt to have a certain respect for the second sight, the ability to see some portentous future event. Maritza's dire warning was not more than he had felt himself and tried to convey to Jenny. If only she would heed him. He was not surprised that Maritza had realized his feeling for Jenny. Probably everyone sensed that, except for the object of his affection. Piers smiled sardonically. Before he could ask her to be his wife he must solve this damnable intrigue. She would never take orders meekly, but at least as his wife she must *promise* to obey.

He sighed. He doubted he could ever compel her obedience. He must rely on her love and respect, both of which he had yet to earn. But he would have her no differently. He must just redouble his efforts to prevent disaster from falling on her innocent head and protect her from her own folly, a prospect which appeared quite daunting.

Chapter Seventeen

Since Piers had not seen fit to return with any information about Major Bosworth's search for the Frenchwoman or the results of deciphering the message in the locket, Jenny had no compunction about going ahead with her own investigation. Thus, she set off to escort Babs to the vicarage with determination writ on every lineament.

Babs, sensing her cousin's distraction, made her displeasure known. "Jenny, you are not listening to me. I think it's a wonderful joke to put a dead frog in Miss Herron's bed. I will sneak up there pretending to tidy myself after lessons. I have the frog right here in my book satchel. Johnny and I captured it yesterday, although he was such a sissy about killing it. For a boy, he is very fainthearted, spoiled no doubt by his silly mother." Babs rattled on, but all Jenny really grasped was that Babs intended to perpetrate some horrid trick on Evelyn Herron. That would never do. Jenny wrenched her thoughts from her own pressing concerns and concentrated on Babs.

"Really, Babs, you must not call Mrs. Granthum a silly woman, even if she is. And you must not play such a nasty joke on Miss Herron. Your father would be very angry. There would be no strawberry jam for days," she added as clinching argument.

"Oh, Jenny, I am disappointed in you. I bet you played much worse jokes when you were my age, and now you want to spoil my fun. Grownups are so tedious," she said, swinging her satchel carelessly as she skipped along, her golden brown hair bouncing.

Jenny could not help but laugh, seeing the justice of Babs's complaints. "You are quite right. We are tedious, but on the whole not too unobliging. If you will give me the frog, I will say no more about it and instead take you down to the badger set I discovered at the very bottom of your garden. Kipp hasn't found it yet," she said, mentioning the Morstans' gardener with whom Babs enjoyed a continuing vendetta.

Babs put her square little head on one side, considering the offer. A badger set was quite a find, but then to sacrifice the opportunity of plaguing Miss Herron was quite attractive, too. Babs, like Jenny, found the vicar's sister irksome, much too apt to criticize and behave in a tyrannical way. Babs thought, too, that Miss Herron really disliked children, not at all like the jolly vicar who was kind and sometimes told her stories instead of drumming the hateful multiplication tables into her resistant head.

On the other hand, Babs pondered, if she refused Jenny's offer, her cousin might be really provoked and their relationship would be flawed. Not that Babs thought Jenny would snitch on her, but her older cousin would disapprove and then the badger outing would have to be abandoned. Oh, dear, it was a dilemma, but Babs decided she must accept Jenny's offer.

She stopped midway down the lane, still swinging her satchel and said soberly, "You drive a hard bargain, Jenny, but I cannot miss the badgers, and you are probably right about Papa and the strawberry jam."

Jenny, relieved, thanked Babs soberly and without blanching took charge of the dead frog, wrapping it in her handkerchief and promising that Babs could have an impressive funeral for the poor thing later. All these promises would have to be fulfilled, Jenny sighed to herself. Normally she enjoyed excursions with Babs and the little girl's amusing tales, but today she felt impatient, eager to discharge her self-imposed task of delivering her to the vicarage. Not fair really. It was not Babs's fault that her elders had become involved in all these mysteries. But Jenny could not have Babs raising Evelyn Herron's wrath when she hoped to disarm that lady's intrigues.

"You are a great gun, Jenny, even if you won't let me frighten Miss Herron with the frog, which she deserves. Mama would shriek and go into hysterics if I handed her a dead frog." Babs nodded her head vigorously in approval.

"Your mama did not have a brother who quickly taught me not to be missish over dead frogs, rats, and other denizens of barn and field," Jenny replied, laughing, remembering Robert's scorn of any faint-heartedness from Jenny. To accompany Robert and Harry on their various adventures she would have endured much more than a dead frog. She thought longingly of those former days when she was Babs's age, halcyon times without the complications and dangers of the adult world.

"Well, I think it's a shame not to use my frog to good advantage, but as a favor to you, Jenny, I will refrain from tampering with Miss Herron's bed," Babs sighed sadly.

"I am most appreciative, Babs. And, do think, you would be immediately suspect. For who else would have the courage to dare such a feat?"

"True," Babs conceded. "And I would not be present to watch her discovery which would spoil a great deal of the pleasure."

Jenny and Babs looked at each other and burst into gales of laughter. The picture of the austere Miss Herron encountering a dead frog as she retired for the night appealed to them both. So they reached the vicarage all smiles and giggles, causing Robert Herron to ask why they were so merry. This only set off another spasm of laughter and the explanation that it was a secret joke, not to be shared, which he accepted in good part.

"But I will have my revenge, Babs, as it is Geography today, and I will put you onto the map of Africa," he promised.

"Better than multiplication tables," Babs decided and went off to her lessons. Robert, inclined to keep Jenny chatting, realized she was eager to be on her way and so followed his charge slowly, looking back wistfully on Jenny as she walked purposefully down the lane toward the main street of Trevarris.

Jenny meant to look busily intent on some errand

to avoid any interview with Robert which could be misconstrued by his sister, who probably lurked inside the vicarage ready to pounce on any suggested intimacy. Poor Robert. If Jenny's ideas about his sister should prove correct he would suffer a great deal, although himself innocent, as much duped as anyone by her wicked behavior.

Jenny idled by the quay for a while, waiting until both Herrons were convinced she had left the vicinity. She saw no sign of Black Jack which was reassuring. Probably Major Bosworth and his soldiers had forced him to go into hiding or at least refrain from swaggering about the village striking fear into the hearts of the townspeople. Like most bullies, when he felt threatened himself he retreated, but Jenny wondered if he would make some effort to revenge himself. She did not want to tangle with him.

Finally, believing herself safe from scrutiny, Jenny wandered back to the church, sketchbook in hand. If she were noticed by anyone she could claim she was pursuing her hobby of drawing the local sights. But she did not want to be observed by the Herrons entering the church. She decided after a preliminary survey to enter the church by a side door well screened from the vicarage by yews.

Carefully opening the door, pleased to notice it had no revealing squeak, she entered and slowly pulled the door shut behind her, temporarily blinded by the darkness of the interior of St. Dunstan's. The building was an old one dating back to the fourteenth century and had happily escaped the depredations of the Roundhead troops, Cornwall until the last remaining safely in Royalist hands.

Stepping quietly in her soft kid slippers, she slipped noiselessly about the pews. Aside from the Trevarris and Morstan enclosed seats there was little room here for a hiding place of any substance. In the gentry's pews of solid oak, she could find no secrets. What she was looking for was a sizable space which could conceal a cache of crates or even a body. The church was singularly bare of any such possibilities.

She wandered over to the altar and pulpit, tapping the wooden rails and mounting the steps to poke about the pulpit, with its stark carvings and heavy Bible, open to the previous Sunday's lesson, Matthew 10:16. "Behold, I send you out as sheep in the midst of wolves; so be wise as serpents, and as innocent as doves." How apt, Jenny thought, wishing she could be as wise as a serpent, but knowing she could only claim the innocence.

Tiptoeing down the steps of the pulpit she felt drawn to the tomb of the Crusader, Piers's doughty ancestor, which had attracted her on the previous visit when she had heard Black Jack reproved by the mysterious voice. The small side chapel, which was halfway down the nave on the left, had a vaulted arch doorway. Inside, the chastely decorated tomb of the lord of Trevarris and his wife, Elfrida, stretched side by side in eternity. An intricately carved rail enclosed the stone crypt and showed little deterioriation in the centuries since its construction.

The chapel itself was spartan, and looked as if it had just been swept, which aroused Jenny's curiosity. Somehow she could not believe that the aged man who served as sexton and gravedigger and who she had seen pottering about the churchyard had cleaned the

Crusader's chapel so well. And how often would worshippers visit this crypt? From her own experience Jenny knew that parish members could only be lured to church on Sunday unless some special event occurred. Of course, the Altar Guild or other dedicated women's groups might consider the housekeeping of the church under their purview, but Jenny doubted that. No flowers graced the altar, which would surely be the case if the Altar Guild had charge. Her suspicions aroused not only by the tidiness of the chapel, but by an indefinable aura pervading that chapel and crypt, she renewed her investigation.

Jenny ran a tentative hand around the crypt carving above the iron railing which protected it. Neat scallops edged the lid of the tomb, and Jenny pressed each one firmly, but they did not give. In the center, the line of scalloping was broken by a bas-relief of an archangel. Jenny passed her hand over the wings with a frisson of expectation.

The left wing gave into her touch, causing the lid of the tomb to rise silently, exposing steps leading down into the depths of the church, obviously a cellar. The steps were clean and steep, beckoning to the bottom, but Jenny hesitated. To descend into that cellar and perhaps be trapped there was not a prospect she viewed with any enthusiasm. Surely her wisest course was to seek help, to reveal her discovery to Piers or Major Bosworth. Who knew what lay below? The tombs of the Crusader and his gentle wife, of course. Probably remains of the smugglers' cargo or even the body of the missing woman. Jenny had her share of courage, but even her valiant spirit was daunted by the thought of descending those steps.

As she pondered her next move, her heart caught in her throat. She heard a stealthy movement in the recesses of the church. Quickly depressing the wing again she saw the lid of the tomb lower, making no noise, surely proof it was often used. No sooner had she begun hurriedly sketching than Evelyn Herron appeared in the entrance to the chapel.

"Good morning, Miss Dryden. You seem inordinately interested in our chapel. Really, it is quite a common crypt with no unusual features." The stern woman's eyes pierced the gloom. Was it Jenny's imagination that Evelyn suspected her discovery? If the other woman knew of the tomb's secret, her hard cold eyes did not betray her.

Barely able to conceal her trepidation at the appearance of the woman she believed a conspirator, Jenny assumed an air of naive confusion.

"Is there some reason why I should not sketch the crypt, Miss Herron, or for that matter be in the church? Surely St. Dunstan's is open to all who wish to visit." She could not allow Evelyn to get the upper hand and intimidate her.

"Not at all, if that is what you are here for. But I rather think you are a busybody, Miss Dryden, poking about where you have no business." There was menace in her dry flat tone.

"I don't understand what you mean," Jenny answered bravely. Then thinking that she might distract the woman from probing further, she attacked. "Why is it, Miss Herron, that you think I am a threat to you? Do you have something to hide?

Surely my sketching forays in the church do not concern you?"

"You are a meddler, stirring up trouble in your wake, and if you have any idea of luring my brother into your toils, put it from your mind. I would never allow it," Evelyn replied.

"I assure you I have no designs on your brother. The prospect of having you as a sister-in-law would deter me even if I had fallen madly in love with Robert, which I can tell you is not the case," Jenny said loftily, hoping her snide remark would distract Evelyn. Jenny had to disarm her in order to make an escape, somehow without revealing what she had found.

"Perhaps you have your eye on a more impressive party, Lord Trevarris. I have noticed you making sheep's eyes at him," Evelyn returned, her spite rising as she realized she was not cowing her adversary.

Jenny bit back a disclaimer. Really, the woman was mad, so filled with hate and revenge she would say or attempt any black deed. But Jenny must get away. To her horror, Evelyn edged nearer.

"Since you are so interested in the Trevarris crypt, let me show you one of its secrets," she offered, her voice laden with meaning which did not escape Jenny.

"Some other time, perhaps. I must return to Pencairn. Amy is waiting for me," Jenny insisted, backing away. But to no avail, for Evelyn grasped her arm. Surely she would not attempt to force Jenny down those dreadful steps. Jenny barely repressed her fear and knowlege. She must pretend an innocence which she was far from feeling. Trying to shake off

Evelyn's hand she heard, to her relief, the sound of the church door slamming shut and Robert's voice calling, "Evelyn, are you here?"

If Evelyn was angered by the interruption, she concealed it well. For a moment she hesitated, as if unwilling to answer Robert, but then seeing the futility of hiding their presence, called to him, "I am in the crypt with Miss Dryden, Robert."

Robert bustled in, delighted to see Jenny, but preoccupied by whatever business had brought him in search of his sister. He seemed unaware of the aura of malevolence that permeated the chapel. Evelyn had released Jenny's arm and stepped back, and it appeared that the two were having a friendly conversation. Jenny would have liked to have warned Robert, but her first instinct was to remove herself as quickly as possible.

"Has Babs finished with her lesson, Robert? If so, I will take her home," Jenny said a bit breathlessly. She was not as good an actress as Evelyn who had resumed her usual aloof manner.

"Yes, Jenny. We had to stop early today as I must make an urgent parish visit, and Mrs. Polson is inquiring for my sister. I am so happy you take such an interest in St. Dunstan's. Please feel free to roam about all you wish. If you have any questions, don't hesitate to ask me," Robert insisted in his friendly way. Unobservant to the last, he wondered if perhaps Evelyn was warming to Jenny.

"I will just collect Babs and be on my way," she said quickly, then sidled past Robert to the door.

Evelyn watched her go with basilisk eyes but made no move to stop her. Instead she turned to Robert and complained, "Why does Mrs. Polson always need my advice? She is perfectly capable of running the choir without my assistance."

"Of course, my dear, but you must just soothe her down a bit. She wants to eject Robbie Balscomb from the choir because he is so disruptive," Robert explained as he followed Jenny from the church and through the side door to the vicarage.

Evelyn snorted. "The best tenor in the group. She will certainly have to be persuaded to keep him." She chatted on to her brother about the choir's problems, just as if ten minutes before she had not been threatening Jenny. Of course, Jenny might have mistaken Evelyn's general dislike and bad temper for menace, but Jenny could only be grateful for Robert's sudden appearance, for she had a sense that Evelyn would have actually attacked her. That would certainly have added weight to Jenny's case, that the vicar's sister was the master conspirator, but somehow that did not comfort her.

Hurrying to put as much distance as possible between herself and Evelyn, she chevied Babs into making her farewells and the cousins were soon on their way home. But as they left Evelyn and Robert standing in the doorway, Jenny was reminded of that eerie scene in the crypt again.

"Take care, Miss Dryden. You seem to have a penchant for adventure. It might lead you onto dangerous paths," Evelyn said calmly, a friendly warning. At least Robert took it as such.

"Really, Evelyn, of what can you be thinking? Jenny is just interested in her fellow creatures, a very endearing trait." Then to Babs, "And see to it, young lady, that you draw me an accurate map of Africa since we had to cut short our lesson today."

As the yards lengthened between the vicarage and Pencairn, Jenny wondered if her imagination had read more into their confrontation at the Trevarris tomb than was warranted. Was she allowing her dislike of Evelyn Herron to cloud her judgment? There was certainly animosity in Evelyn's attitude toward Jenny. Robert had explained the cause of his sister's bitterness and tried to enlist Jenny's sympathy, but somehow her natural charity failed in this case. And certainly Evelyn's actions at the crypt had been meant to frighten her. No, she was certain Evelyn was the conspirator they were all seeking and that something was concealed in that crypt. The sooner she shared her knowledge with Piers the better.

She was so abstracted she barely heard Babs's artless chatter as they hurriedly walked along, until the little girl plucked at her arm, gasping, "What is your hurry, Jenny? I can't keep up. You are racing along at such a speed."

Jenny, pulled from her troubled thoughts, smiled at the little girl, welcoming the distraction. "I am sorry, pet. There, we will amble along and you can tell me about the geography lesson."

"Not much to tell. Africa sounds very exciting, but as I have not much chance of going there, I can't see the use of learning its shape and location. I suppose I will never leave Cornwall," Babs moaned, for her taste for adventure was continuing.

"Nonsense. You will be off to London before long, and when you have made your come-out you will travel all over England. Of course, until Napoleon is defeated you cannot go to the Continent," Jenny advised practically, then remembered that enemies of her country were preparing the ground for Napoleon to attack nearby. Not even here were they safe from the dreaded Corsican who controlled all of Europe and wanted to extend his sway to England.

"Well, I wish he would be disposed of soon. I like the idea of traveling, but I am afraid Papa would think Africa too far. I would much rather see lions and tigers than churches and historic sights," Babs informed her sagely.

"Perhaps you will marry a missionary and he will take you off to convert the heathens," Jenny suggested outrageously.

Babs responded indignantly, "More apt to end up in a cannibal's pot, and serve me right if I were to do such a daft thing."

They had now reached Pencairn and Jenny sighed with relief, much cheered by Babs's chatter and disgusted with herself for the fear which had almost overcome her at St. Dunstan's. Really, she was behaving like one of Mrs. Radcliffe's vapid heroines, giving way to silly imaginings and not using the sense God gave her. After lunch she would send off a message to Piers to come immediately. Now that she was away from the brooding atmosphere of the chapel she was able to view her discovery with some objectivity. There was every reason to suppose that the missing woman could be in the tomb with Piers's ancestors. Jenny felt she had made a major step forward in solving the mystery of the traitor.

Eating her luncheon with a hearty appetite, Jenny

was quite pleased with herself, and listened to Amy's gossip about the house party at Arthmore with gentle indulgence. She had no intention of telling her cousin about the secret of the church until Piers had been informed and taken some decisive action. Despite her dislike of his arrogance and his managing ways, Jenny was content to have him manage this aspect of the search.

Her first instinct had been to ride directly to Arthmore and blurt out her theories, but wisdom had prevailed. She decided instead that she would send off a note requesting he call as soon as was convenient. She doubted that the body would be moved again, if indeed it were there, but even if he found the crypt empty, there would be some evidence of illicit cargo or worse, she was convinced. And she had a certain amount of hesitation in interrupting Piers's house party. Lady Lashford and the guests would think her a veritable harum-scarum, riding up to Arthmore without an invitation.

She repaired to her room to write a note, which she then gave to a groom to carry to Arthmore. After the servant left, she sat herself down and prepared to wait for an answer.

Chapter Eighteen

Piers had every intention of calling on Jenny after interviewing Black Jack, but his attempt to find the smuggler was unavailing. Obviously the rogue had learned from his many sources that Major Bosworth and his men were searching the village for some reason, and he thought it prudent to make himself scarce. Whether the smuggler was involved with the removal of the mysterious Frenchwoman or had some other reason to evade the military, as was entirely possible, Black Jack had decided to go into hiding. As he knew the neighborhood in a way that Bosworth could never fathom, the major's search would be fruitless. Black Jack would appear when it suited him.

But before Piers saw Jenny he had to find out if de Lisle and the admiral had solved the puzzle of the locket. He wanted time, too, to plan his approach to Jenny. He had every intention of telling her he loved her, of asking her to be his wife, but he wanted the conspiracy solved before he ventured a proposal.

Experienced enough to know that Jenny's warm response to his kisses meant she did not really dislike him, he still had some doubt that she cared enough for him to make a commitment. She might still be hankering for her former betrothed or be so wary of men that she did not trust Piers. Sophisticated and assured in the conduct of casual affairs, in this the most important decision of his life, Piers felt insecure, as callow as the veriest stripling.

Abandoning fruitless conjecture, Piers hurried to Arthmore for a conference with his allies.

And his confidence in the sagacity of his confederates was well placed. Upon entering the library he was hailed with excitement by the admiral and complaisance by de Lisle, who had been joined by his wife.

"Well, Piers, you were quite right. Melissa has solved the mystery of the numbers and we were sapskulls not to have seen it," Theron exclaimed, throwing a glance of admiration to his wife. "I will let her tell you."

Melissa looked grave, unlike her usual insouciant manner. "I believe the numbers twelve-two-ten refer to the French Revolutionary Calendar, which Robespierre instituted to replace the regular Gregorian calendar in use by most countries. The Assembly abandoned the old calendar and dated the years and months from September 22, 1792, the date of the establishment of the new French Republic. There are twelve thirty-day months of three weeks with ten days each, ending in a rest day, for they have done away with Sunday, disgusted with the clerical influence which is supposed to support the ancient regime. So twelve-two-ten turns out to be the second week of Fructidor, corresponding to our August and the tenth day which works out, I think, to the twelfth of September," she explained breathlessly and with an air of triumph.

"Melissa, you are a genius," Piers said, hugging her with delight. "Why couldn't we have figured that out?"

Melissa smiled demurely, but could not resist a little dig at the men. "You are all so arrogant that you would never believe that there might be another way to calculate the months and days."

Theron looked at her with amused affection. "She couldn't resist that, Piers, and we can't complain, for I am sure she is right. And you need not continue your display of affection. Find your own wife to cuddle," Theron admonished, but not at all annoyed by Piers's approval of his elfin wife.

The admiral interrupted the mutual congratulations to advise, "We must let them know in Whitehall immediately. Valentine and Sterling-Hicks will be pleased."

"I think you should go yourself, Coniston," Theron de Lisle suggested. "Not that I wish to break up your house party, Piers, but this message is vital to the War Office arrangements. We may know the date of the expected invasion, but we are not sure of the landing site, although I suspect it must be nearby, certainly in Cornwall."

"You're right, Theron. Admiral, you must leave immediately for London. I will order a carriage.

After your business is completed we will be happy to see you back to continue your interrupted visit," Piers insisted hospitably.

In the hurry of getting the admiral off with suitable written evidence, a copy of the paper in the locket, and making arrangements for a relay of horses along the route to London, an arduous three hundred-odd mile journey, Piers's household was in such a flurry of activity that Jenny's note requesting Piers to call upon her was forgotten.

The young footman Charles, who received the note from the Pencairn groom, had every intention of delivering it forthwith, but just as he went to find a tray for the presentation, the butler ordered him to the first floor to help with the admiral's luggage. He pocketed the note and during the rush of the next hours Jenny's request went unread and unanswered due to the footman's negligence. Not until he sat down to his tea about four o'clock did he remember the note. Afraid to mention his carelessness to the butler, he finished his meal, and only then repaired to the library where Theron de Lisle and Piers were studying some coastal maps, and tendered Jenny's note formally.

Piers, reading her request, had no notion that it had been sent some four hours earlier. But he felt guilty that he had not given her a report on the latest developments and excused himself from Theron, eager to repair his ommission.

Jenny's impatience to confer with Piers was soon satisfied. Not an hour after she dispatched her note a reply came from Piers. He made no mention of her own demand for a meeting, which she never thought to query, but suggested that as he was so occupied with the admiral and the marquess, that she come to him at Arthmore. Seeing nothing unusual about this invitation and in any case in no state to wonder at the wording of the message which was written on the engraved Arthmore notepaper, she hastened to obey.

Neither Amy nor Francis were at home. Only Babs, who had hoped for an afternoon expedition with Jenny, was disappointed that her cousin had to beg off. Promising the little girl that she would certainly show her the badger set before the day was out, Jenny said she must answer an urgent summons from Arthmore and rushed away before Babs could ask any more questions.

Requesting a groom to saddle her usual mare, she rode toward the Trevarris mansion, veering off the main road within a mile of Pencairn. The bright sunshine of the morning had vanished in a sudden surge of lowering clouds which scudded across the sky, a dramatic change so typical of Cornwall. Heavy hawthorne trees lined the track on which she cantered. She was eager to arrive at her destination, only now remembering that she had been warned to take care and not venture out alone. But surely Piers would not have asked her to ride over to his house if he thought there was any danger. Still, she was conscious of a small shiver of apprehension as the atmosphere darkened and the roadway seemed heavy with menace.

Just as she emerged from the path, still hidden by a heavy growth of shrubs and wind-tossed trees, a horse and wagon burst across her path from the underbrush, causing her mare to rear frantically. Jenny, caught by surprise, lost her seat and tumbled to the ground. Momentarily stunned by the fall, she was grasped by rough hands and, to her horror, a coarse bag was thrown over her head and her hands bound behind her back. She did not submit to this rough treatment without a struggle, thrashing and squirming, kicking out at the man who threw her brutally into the back of the cart, although she felt suffocated by the constricting odorous bag, the paralyzing feeling of helplessness, and the suddenness of the attack. She was shocked and vulnerable.

One of her abductors, tiring of her fruitless efforts, cursed and growled, "I'll settle you, you little fool," giving her a hard clip on the head which silenced her protests. Ordering his companion to hurry and tie the mare to a nearby tree, he looked impatiently about, eager to be gone. The mare would be found or break free eventually, but that would give him the necessary time to carry the unconscious girl to the prepared hiding place. Within moments the wagon was off down the road away from Arthmore and toward the village.

Despite their caution, Jenny's abductors had been seen. Maritza, with the quiet stealth for which her people were well-known, had tracked Black Jack from the beginning of his sinister mission. She had been determined on vengeance against this man who had denied their child, brought the scorn of her tribe upon her, then abandoned her. Black Jack had made a bad mistake in not taking Maritza into account, for she was now a committed enemy who had vowed to make him pay for his callous treatment.

She knew he was involved in some highly suspect activities, but not overly scrupulous about the law herself she had been indifferent until now. The presence of Major Bosworth and his troop in the village, Piers's questions, and a general feeling of uneasiness among the villagers had only confirmed her belief that Black Jack was up to his usual tricks, but this time she intended to catch him out and betray him to the authorities. She would have no compunction about using her knife on his wicked hide, but she felt his downfall would be greater if the law took him up. To this end she was willing to abet the soldiers and she could use methods of which they were ignorant.

Bringing Black Jack to her idea of justice also included discovering a share of his loot, and to this end she watched him hitch up the horse and wagon that afternoon. From her hiding place behind a convenient outbuilding near his cottage, she had decided he was off to collect some illegal cargo from a secret cache. Certainly this strange journey was worth an investigation, perhaps yielding some treasure which might help her regain acceptance from the tribe.

Although the men were watchful, keeping a wary eye out for passersby, they were no match for Maritza. She had been disappointed to see them hide in the trees and shrubs opposite the path to the great lord's mansion, but then she had witnessed their attack on Jenny. Recognizing the kind lady who had cured her Janos of the fever, her first instinct had been to try to rescue her, but a cautious regard for her own safety prevented her. She was no match for two armed men. No, her best plan was to follow them and then alert the lord or the soldiers.

She waited for a suitable time and then, cooing Romany words, mounted Jenny's restive mare and, moving to the grass edge of the path, which muffled the horse's hooves, followed after the wagon which she could hear in the distance.

Piers, arriving at Pencairn to tell Jenny about the code which Melissa de Lisle had deciphered, was disappointed to learn that she was not available. Having steeled himself for the interview which he hoped would decide his future, he felt baffled and annoyed. He had told her not to leave the house, not to wander about inviting danger, but she had seen fit to ignore his warning. Frustrated that he must postpone his proposal, he told Peabody to inform Jenny of his visit, and since neither the master nor the mistress of the house were on hand, he strode down the steps, irritated and balked. Really, Jenny was so unaccountable. But then he smiled. Would he have her any different?

Just as he was about to mount his horse, he heard Babs crying to him from an upper window, "Sir, did you bring Jenny home?" Jenny had promised to take her to see the badger set and instead had gone off to Arthmore and now had come back and ignored her.

"No, Babs, I haven't seen her," Piers answered, gazing up at the sturdy little girl. "Perhaps you had better come down. I fear you are in danger of falling from that window," he advised, unable to repress a grin at her indifference to her precarious perch.

"Yes, I will. I want to talk to you," Babs said seriously.

Within moments she had scampered down the stairway, ignoring her nurse's clucking and attempts to dissuade her. Piers, waiting for her impatiently, kept slapping his crop against his knees. A feeling of uneasiness began to dog him. There was some mystery here.

Babs, marching up to him, said, without any preamble, "Jenny said she had an urgent message to meet you at Arthmore and begged off our expedition, and now you say she never came. I do call that shabby of her."

Piers, now thoroughly alarmed, did his best to hide his fears from the little girl. "Well, we may have missed each other on the road or she may have had an errand in the village first," he explained, trying to soothe both Babs's disquiet and his own.

"She said it was urgent," Babs insisted. "And you couldn't have missed her on the road. I do hope she hasn't had an accident, although she is a very good rider."

"She took the mare, then?" Piers asked, trying to gain some information without arousing Babs's suspicions. He must not frighten her, but all he wanted was to ride pell-mell after Jenny. Obviously, there had been some mistake.

"Did she say she had received a note from me, Babs?" he inquired, keeping his tone level.

"Not exactly, she just said she had an urgent message from Arthmore," Babs insisted.

"Thank you, Babs. I will track her down and

return her to you," Piers promised gently, hoping he could do just that but now thoroughly apprehensive that Jenny might have come to some harm. Patting Babs on the head, he turned and leapt onto his horse, and before she could protest had galloped down the drive, surprising Babs with his haste.

Puckering up her face in a worried frown, Babs wondered if Jenny had suffered some mishap. Lord Trevarris appeared most concerned. Could Jenny have been captured by smugglers? Babs's vivid imagination conjured a picture of her admired cousin the victim of some horrid plot or perhaps lying injured down by the sea. She knew nothing of the disturbing events of the past few days, but she had sensed Jenny's abstraction and realized that the adults knew some secret which they were hiding from her. How she wished she was grown up and could aid Jenny in whatever adventures upon which she had embarked. Babs knew that Jenny was up to some rig and she thought it most unfair that she was excluded. After all, she had proved she was a game one when they had been marooned in the cave. Jenny should have trusted her and asked for her help. Babs was gravely disappointed in her cousin, repressing a niggling sense of disaster.

Shaking off her fear, she kicked at the gravel sadly, wishing she knew what was happening and yearning to discuss these troubling thoughts with some sympathetic confidant. But then nurse appeared, chevying her into the house and scolding her for bothering his lordship, threatening to disclose her bold behavior to her parents, and generally behaving in a silly manner which tried Babs's patience, but did not dispel her feeling that Jenny might be in grave trouble.

If Babs worried about her cousin's whereabouts, Piers was nearly frantic as he galloped up on the driveway to Arthmore. He doubted very much that Jenny had reached Arthmore, but had been lured to the suggested rendezvous by some ruse which had ended in disaster. Still, before he could institute a search he had to check at home. Perhaps she had eluded her enemies and managed to reach Arthmore although he doubted it.

His dark mood was not improved when he galloped up to the entrance and saw Maritza raging at his butler, who was intent on denying her entrance.

"You stupid, foolish old man, I must see the lord. Every minute you keep me out will add to the trouble, believe me, you damn *stupido, gili . . .*" Maritza cursed a long string of Romany words which only increased the man's determination to eject her from the property.

"Begone, woman, we want no gypsy trash about here," he insisted, manhandling Maritza down the steps despite her screaming and kicking. She heard the sound of Piers's horse before the butler and threw herself in front of the stallion as Piers dragged the horse to a halt.

"What is all this commotion, Evans?" And what's the trouble now, Maritza?" Piers asked impatiently. He had no time for Maritza's dramatic complaints when Jenny was in danger.

"Oh, my lord, you have come just in time. Black Jack has taken your lady to that old hut beside the

Morstan mine and he intends no good, I know. We must rescue her from him," Maritza babbled, almost beside herself with excitement. Although she genuinely wanted to extricate Jenny from her erstwhile lover's clutches, she also enjoyed the histrionics which accompanied her information. She wheeled up and stuck her tongue out at the shocked butler, her arms akimbo. "See, you bacon-brained dolt, the lord wishes to hear me. Go attend to your duties," she ordered arrogantly, stamping her foot.

"That will do, Maritza. And, Evans, you can safely leave this baggage to me." Then thinking over the possibilities, he added as the butler walked away, his back rigid with disapproval. "Please ask the Marquess de Lisle to come here, and send a groom to the stable for a mount for him." Then, turning to Maritza, he grasped her by the arm. "Now tell me exactly what you saw and no romancing, Maritza. Jenny's very life can depend on what you have learned. We have no time to waste if we are to rescue her."

Realizing that Piers would stand for no more delay, Maritza told of Black Jack's abduction of Jenny and her imprisonment at the deserted hut near the mine. The gypsy boasted about her cleverness and stealth in finding the hiding place and obviously expected not only praise but a goodly award of gold for her information. By the time she had concluded her narrative, Theron de Lisle had joined Piers on the entrance steps, fascinated by the creature who was engaging his host's rapt attention. Hurriedly Piers explained the situation to him.

"I think, Theron, I must not wait to contact Major Bosworth, but ride out to the mine immediately. Will you try to find the major and send his troop after me?" Piers asked distractedly, eager to be gone.

"That will never do, as they will not know where to find it, and, as I certainly don't, I will go with you now. We must send a message to Bosworth by one of your grooms who will know how to lead them to the hut or this Romany chit here can direct them," de Lisle advised. Piers's normal cool-headedness in the face of danger had vanished completely in his anxiety for Jenny's safety. But, taking a firm grip on his emotions, he agreed and dispatched the necessary orders. Delaying only another moment to snatch his pistols from the house, he rode off with de Lisle hot behind him, crying out a last command to Maritza to reach Bosworth in case his own messenger went astray.

As he pounded down the drive, turning sharply right to ride across his fields, he prayed he would be in time and that his intrepid Jenny would bite her tongue and not try to play the heroine in this latest, most deadly, of her escapades.

Chapter Nineteen

Piers need not have worried that Jenny would attempt to challenge her abductors. The blow on the head which Black Jack had delivered so callously had left her unconscious for some time, long enough for her assailant to carry her out to the abandoned shack and deposit her roughly on a pile of odorous blankets in one corner of the rude shelter. Maritza, who had watched the procedure from some distance to elude detection, had not told Piers of Jenny's condition. She had been too far away to see exactly what had happened. She only knew that the kind lady who had helped her Janos had suffered some assault and then been kidnapped.

Maritza, like most of her tribe, shunned the high moors where the tin mines lay, for the Romanies believed in the evil spirits or "Knackers" as the Cornish called the distorted devils they thought inhabited the dark world beneath the wasteland. Local folk swore that at night they heard the sound of the tinners' strange knocking and tapping underground and even testified to seeing the odd misshapen specters of bent old men darting from the sunken holes. Tinners had once been an independent group, considering themselves craftsmen offering their skill for hire, but with the boom in their product at the beginning of the war, uplanders had managed to form companies, employing their own men, and several families won fortunes from tin as Sir Francis Morstan had.

However, relics of the old freewheeling life of the itinerant tinner still remained and the scattered isolated moor houses stood as a reminder of the days when the tinners camped near their "set." They were sturdy structures but primitive, one large windowless room with a hearth for burning furze and turf, and straw piled carelessly for sleeping. Most of Sir Francis's workers lived in Trevarris and the few moor houses had long been abandoned, shunned by all but the most desperate vagrants, for they were thought to be haunted by the knackers. If Maritza had not followed Black Jack, it is doubtful if Piers or Bosworth and his troop would ever have thought to look at that derelict building some ten miles from the edge of the village as the current seam on which the men were working underground was some distance away from the moor house.

Jenny, coming slowly around from the blow which had rendered her senseless, did not at first realize her situation. In the dark and brooding atmosphere of the hut, the mutter of voices slowly penetrated her throbbing head and she remembered what had happened. Black Jack had frightened her horse. She had fallen and he had abducted her, throwing her into that cart and bringing her to what she was convinced was an isolated hiding place. But for what reason?

Hearing a door shut stealthily, she decided it was prudent to keep her eyes closed and feign unconsciousness. Frightened, but angry, her resilient spirits had temporarily deserted her, but if her captors thought she was without resources they were mistaken. Her hands remained tied but at least the noxious bag had been removed from her head, although she could see little in the shadowed room. She wiggled her hands in an attempt to loosen the bounds, but was not making much progress when she was stunned to hear a familiar voice say to Black Jack, "I see you were successful. I knew that ruse with the Arthmore writing paper would bring her out. What have you done to her?"

When Jenny had overheard the voice in the church it had been muffled, but now it was clearly identifiable as Evelyn Herron's. So it was as Jenny suspected. Evelyn was the organizer of this nefarious plot to betray her country to Napoleon.

Despite her own vulnerable situation, Jenny felt a satisfaction in having her suspicions proved. She realized that Evelyn had intended to push her into the Trevarris tomb and leave her to suffocate and die. However, Jenny realized she had gone from the proverbial frying pan to the fire, for she knew that Evelyn would never release her. Jenny could only hope to delay the inevitable end by plying the woman with questions. There was the possibility that Babs might tell her parents of Jenny's errand and when she did not return the alarm would be raised. But Jenny had small hope that any searchers could rescue her in time to thwart Evelyn's murderous intention.

"Just gave her a slight tap on the head. She was making a damned nuisance of herself, fighting, scratching, and squirming. Had to keep her quiet. Lots of spirit for a gentry mort, she has," Black Jack informed her with a trace of admiration.

"She is a danger to us both and must be silenced. But first I have to question her. We must know if she found the message on the body. We know she was creeping around that cave and certainly informed the military of what she saw. Fortunately, I don't think they believed her, thought she was imagining the whole thing. But we don't want that major poking his long nose into our activities. He might find some traces of what we are doing," Evelyn said in a matter-of-fact voice that Jenny found more alarming than any threat. Evidently Evelyn could contemplate murder without any hesitation.

Jenny kept her eyes shut as she heard Evelyn approach her corner, her heart beating so hard that she was convinced her enemy could hear it. Jenny had succeeded in loosening her hands somewhat, but was not yet ready to reveal that small victory. She awaited Evelyn's inspection with a determination not to show her fear. She would never give Evelyn that satisfaction. As her adversary bent over her and shook her roughly, Jenny decided that innocence and bewilderment were her best ploys.

"Here, wake up. I have questions for you. It will be the worse for you if you do not answer me honestly," Evelyn threatened, her hands grasping Jenny's shoulders and, lending emphasis to her words, she slapped the girl across her cheek.

Realizing that she could dissemble no longer, Jenny opened her eyes and looked groggily at the woman bent over her. She adopted a pose of confusion and faintness. "Oh, it is you, Evelyn. What has happened? Where am I? Some horrid man has assaulted and abducted me. Quickly, we must escape before he returns. You must help me, Evelyn, for I am not feeling quite the thing."

"You are going nowhere, you little fool. I ordered your abduction, and you will answer my questions or your death will be a lingering one. I will be glad to see the last of you. Your meddling has caused me a great deal of trouble, and now you will pay the price for your snooping," she warned and then, turning to Black Jack, said, "Jack, here, will have a go at you if you don't cooperate, and I don't think you would find his attentions to your taste. By the time he's through with you, my prosy girl, the fine Lord Trevarris wouldn't touch you. You'll be fit only for the stews and serve you right, with your missish airs and fancy manners. I know your kind, all sweetness and light, then trying to wrap a man around your finger. You are a menace, but you will soon be regretting your interference," Evelyn stormed, her former grievances and real hatred of Jenny surfacing.

Appalled by the woman's harsh words and the baleful light in her eyes, Jenny repressed a shiver. She would not give way before this harridan. Not only was the woman a traitor, inspired to her treachery by imagined slights and a desire for revenge against the world, but she was verging on insanity. Why else would she behave so?

"I don't know what you mean. I have no information you want," Jenny protested weakly, not yet ready to challenge Evelyn and her confederate. But the implication of what would happen to her at Black Jack's hands had almost sent her into a panic. And she had no reason to believe Evelyn was speaking idly. Looking at the burly smuggler as he lounged against the wall, eyeing her with a knowing and evil grin, Jenny hardened her spirit. She would not cringe before these villains.

"You found the body of the Frenchwoman. She washed ashore the night of the big storm with valuable information from the other side, information I must have immediately. Now, what did you find on her body?" Evelyn asked, tightening her grasp on Jenny's arm and pulling it meanly.

"What body? I have no idea what you are talking about, but I think you must be mad to think that you can speak to me in this way and threaten me. How dare you behave so?" Jenny protested, indignation in every line of her body.

"Don't try to gull me, you little fool. You were always hanging about that cove, and one of Jack's men saw you leave and scurry into town with the news of your find. But we foiled you, got the body out and away so that that pompous Bosworth thought you were imagining the whole business. And I almost sent you to join the woman in the Trevarris tomb, when my credulous brother interrupted us. But no one will bother us here and I will have it out of you no matter how long it takes," Evelyn insisted darkly.

Although her situation was desperate, Jenny refused to surrender to panic. Perhaps, if she admitted to finding the body but denied discovering any revelation of secret messages she might delay the inevitable. She had no doubts about what Evelyn and Black Jack intended, but the thought of that lout Black Jack laying his hands on her was too horrible to contemplate.

"I did find the poor woman's body, but she was cold and long gone when I came across her quite by accident. I just concluded she was a victim of the storm, off some boat which had tried to ride out the weather," Jenny temporized, wiggling her hands surreptitiously and wondering if there was any hope of bargaining with her captors.

"It is possible the wench had only a message to deliver and nothing written down which might compromise her," Evelyn said after a moment's reflexion.

"'Tis unlikely. I wouldn't trust this one an inch. She's been nosing around the quay and mixing herself in my business since she arrived. She knows something, I vow." Black Jack was eager to have his chance to force Jenny to an admission.

"Perhaps. At any rate she cannot be allowed to live with what she knows now. You can dispatch her, Jack," Evelyn said callously.

"After I have had a little fun, eh?" he insisted, still lounging against the wall, his hand stuck in his belt, his eyes raking over Jenny's form with lecherous intent.

"You men, you are all the same. Always trying to get some woman on her back and work your will. Well, I care not a pin about that, but I still think she knows more than she's telling. Perhaps a little persuasion might induce her to tell us," Evelyn suggested. "I must know that date."

Jenny had no doubts that the date she was referring to was the month, day, and time of the long-awaited invasion. How could this dreadful woman contemplate delivering her country over to its enemies in retaliation for some personal disappointment?

"Surely you have some compunction about aiding Napoleon to conquer your country. Not that he has a chance of accomplishing such a task," Jenny jeered, anger overcoming prudence.

"What do you know about it, you little fool? Napoleon has power and has brought most of the world under his hand. He rewards those who serve him well, which is more than this stupid government will do, a bunch of timid vacillating old women. I would love to see the likes of Major Bosworth and the high and mighty lords like your precious Trevarris brought to their knees. I will enjoy their humiliation," Evelyn replied, a fanatical light in her eyes.

"But enough of this chatter. You are just trying to delay your own degradation. Black Jack will enjoy your favors and then slit your throat, a fitting end to your meddling," Evelyn laughed, her mouth twisting into an evil grimace. Turning to her confederate, she said, "You will put her in the crypt when you are done. She can moulder there with the other fine lords and ladies."

"You are insane to think that you can get away with murder. My disappearance will raise a hue and cry. Do you think you can just kill me and expect no investigation?" Jenny argued, holding on to her calm with difficulty. "Black Jack will be the first to be suspected, and do you think he will protect you, his coconspirator?"

"Who would suspect the vicar's sister? I have deluded my stupid brother all these months, and Black Jack can disappear for a time. We are safe enough. But I have no more time to waste on you." She laughed again, the mad chortle chilling Jenny's heart. She knew there was little hope now.

"Here you are, Jack. Take her and enjoy her." Evelyn pushed Jenny toward the smuggler and he grasped her eagerly. For a dreadful moment Jenny felt his hands roam her body and then the door of the moor house flew open with a resounding crash.

"Let her go, you cur, or I will put a bullet through your black heart," Piers cried, standing motionless in the entrance, his pistol cocked.

Black Jack, stunned, tried to get his knife loose from his belt, but Jenny, her hands finally free, knocked his paw away, and Piers, turning to his companion who loomed behind him, ordered, "Watch them both." Handing his weapon to de Lisle, he pulled Jenny into his arms, frantic to assure her safety.

"Has he harmed you, Jenny dear?" he asked in anxious tones, as she buried her head in his shoulder, her body shuddering.

"Not yet, but you came just in time. They intended to kill me and put me in the crypt with the dead lady. But first he was to ravage me and she was going to watch. Evelyn Herron is your master conspirator, Piers. Don't let her escape," Jenny sobbed, seeing Evelyn sidle toward the door. But she could not escape de Lisle's stalwart figure blocking her exit.

"I think you had better remain, madam," de Lisle said coldly, gesturing with his gun. Evelyn began to laugh maniacally and beat upon him with her fists. But de Lisle subdued her and heard with relief the sounds of Bosworth and his troops dismounting outside. Within minutes the moor house was crowded with soldiers who quickly seized the smuggler and bound his hands firmly. Evelyn Herron resisted violently, but she, too, was subdued and the two were brought under restraint, while Piers tried to comfort the distraught Jenny, now overcome with relief and unable to repress her emotions.

"Come now, Jenny, it's all right. You are a brave girl and the danger is past. Wait here just a moment while I confer with Bosworth about the disposition of these villains and then I will take you home. It's all over now," Piers soothed her.

Gasping, Jenny threw her arms around Piers's neck, holding tight to her rescuer. Then, realizing that the major, de Lisle, and several soldiers were witnessing her abandoned behavior, she flushed and regained some measure of sensibility.

"Forgive me. I cannot believe it is over. I was so frightened," she admitted a bit shamefacedly.

She retreated from Piers and watched wide-eyed as the men ushered Evelyn and Black Jack, cursing and struggling, out of the moor house. Piers said a few words to Bosworth and then, taking Jenny by the arm, gently escorted her from the sinister place. He could not comfort her as he wished before all these onlookers.

Outside all was confusion, stamping horses,

shouting men, and, a little apart, Maritza, holding Jenny's mare and gazing with vengeful satisfaction at the downfall of Black Jack as he was thrown on a trooper's horse and led away. Evelyn, her arms pinned behind her, was put on the major's horse and Bosworth jumped up behind her. As Jenny watched, the troop galloped away toward the village. She could hardly believe her amazing rescue, unable to take in the fact that Piers had arrived so opportunely to save her. Her legs felt weak and she trembled violently. Piers, seeing her condition, hurried to her side.

"Maritza here was your guardian angel. And she will be rewarded, but now we must get you back to Pencairn. Come, Jenny. Time to sort it all out after you have regained your composure. And I have several matters to discuss with you," Piers informed her a bit grimly. But his touch was gentle as he helped her onto his horse and jumped up behind her, holding her firmly in his arms as they rode swiftly away from the horrifying scene.

Chapter Twenty

At Pencairn, Piers and Jenny's arrival was greeted with cries of relief and frantic questions by a worried and confused Francis and Amy. The Marquess de Lisle had informed them of Jenny's kidnapping and subsequent rescue but his terse message had left much unanswered. Piers would not allow them to quiz Jenny in her exhausted state and insisted she be put to bed after some food and a bath. She needed quiet and rest to recover from her ordeal.

Amy, appalled by the little she had heard of Jenny's escape from death, and feeling a certain amount of guilt for not chaperoning her cousin more faithfully, shepherded Jenny away, eager to make up for her lapses. Piers crossed the hall with them and stopped Jenny as she was preparing to leave.

"I must explain this all to Francis, Jenny, and then confer with the authorities, but I will be back this evening to settle affairs between us. We have a lot to discuss when you have put this dreadful business behind you," he promised, a look in his eyes which brought a warm glow of reassurance to the weary girl. Surely she could not be mistaken. His expression revealed more than just compassionate concern. Bemused, she protested a bit at being denied the chance to hear what he had to say, but there was no gainsaying Amy.

Struggling with aching feet up the stairs, she turned at the top to look down where Piers still stood watching her halting progress. He must care for her. What else could that yearning look mean? Feeling lightheaded but satisfied, she followed Amy docilely into the bedroom.

The excitement of her rescue from death and the expectation she had seen in Piers's eyes had taxed her last resources. After Polly and Amy had superintended her bath, she tried to eat the light meal they insisted on providing, but, in fact, yearned to be alone and sleep.

Amy, sensing her need for privacy, shooed Polly from the room and bustled about tucking Jenny under a comforter and drawing the draperies so no unwelcome light could disturb her slumbers. Jenny watched her from beneath leaden eyes but felt some explanation should be offered.

"You must have the tact and patience of a saint, Amy, not to ply me with questions about what has been happening," Jenny said drowsily, much touched by Amy's care and concern.

"Of course I have. I have an insatiable curiosity, but I can wait until Francis and Piers explain all these puzzling and dreadful events. And you can add the colorful details when you feel more the thing.

Just now you need to sleep. We will celebrate at dinner. Piers promises he will have settled all the complications by then, and I have a feeling we will be toasting more than your rescue," Amy answered with a complacent air which mystified Jenny, not able to concentrate on nuances in conversation. "And Jenny, I must tell you all is now resolved between Francis and me. I was foolish to think he did not care. I know you were worried."

Jenny smiled in response and Amy had barely glided from the room when the girl was fathoms deep in sleep.

Evening was drawing when Jenny awakened after a few hours sleep to find Babs staring at her round-eyed from her precarious perch at the foot of the bed.

"I didn't wake you, did I, Jenny? I promised Mother I would be quiet as a mouse, but you must have felt the power of my mind in your sleep and now you are awake and can answer all my questions. You have a lot to thank me for, you know. You might be a cold stark corpse by now without my telling Lord Trevarris of your direction."

"Ugh, Babs, don't remind me. And I know nothing of your role in all my adventures, so you can enlighten me," Jenny said, smiling at the little girl who yearned to be included in the serious affairs of the day.

Babs recounted her knowledge of the events, her eyes agog, embellishing the story which Jenny felt was dramatic enough without the little girl's additions.

"And how have you discovered all this, Babs? I am

sure neither your mama nor papa described the recent events in such a lurid fashion," Jenny reprimanded, but without much heat, now that the horror was behind her. She knew that when she was Babs's age she would have enjoyed the excitement in just such a fashion and could not fault the little girl.

"The Peabodys were telling Nurse all about it in the kitchen. They were so enthralled and drinking so much tea that they forgot all about me. I was able to eat six rock cakes before Nurse remembered I was there and meanly dragged me off to the nursery," Babs complained.

"Most unfair, I agree. I hope the rock cakes are not causing you indigestion. But, really, Babs, it was not quite so exciting as frightening. And I was in danger of losing my life at the hands of Black Jack and Evelyn Herron, who really is quite mad, I think."

But she must not burden Babs with her fears. To the little girl it was a thrilling tale with Jenny in the role of heroine, a part she felt she had played poorly.

"She is a spy and a traitor and deserves to be shot or maybe hanged, drawn, and quartered, but I don't think they do that to traitors anymore. More's the pity," Babs mourned.

"Really, Babs, I had no idea you entertained such bloodthirsty thoughts. Evelyn is to be pitied, although she must pay for her sins, I fear. It is poor Robert, her brother, I feel for in this dreadful coil," Jenny said with compassion.

"Pooh. If he hadn't been so busy reading scripture and teaching me horrid mathematics, he would have seen that she was fit for Bedlam," Babs concluded firmly, if inaccurately.

"Perhaps, but let us not discuss it anymore. I must get dressed for dinner, for Piers is coming to report on what will be done with Evelyn and Black Jack, and I can't miss his arrival. And surely it is almost bedtime for you," Jenny said briskly. Then noticing Babs's disappointment, she promised, "If any more exciting details are revealed I will inform you forthwith. Now, will you ring for Polly? I must not dally any longer." Jenny rose from her bed and crossed to the window, where Babs, against orders, had pulled the draperies to look out on the fading daylight, thankful for her safety within the walls of Pencairn.

"You haven't forgotten the badgers, Jenny. If you had taken me to see the set, you would have missed all the excitement, so I won't be too angry. But perhaps tomorrow you will have time." Jenny could not resist her little cousin's entreaty.

"Quite right, Babs, and badgers are far more important than all these nasty incidents. We will definitely see the set tomorrow. Now scamper away for here is Polly to help me dress," Jenny insisted, but feeling much cheered by her insouciant little cousin. Babs had banished her unpleasant memories of those terrible moments facing the maddened Evelyn and the gloating Black Jack. Jenny felt almost up to the ordeal of meeting Piers at dinner, for she had an embarrassed sense that she had revealed too much when he had held her in his arms after the rescue.

To strengthen her defenses, she selected her favorite gown, a simple cherry silk, which flattered her complexion, still a bit pale from her ordeal. Turning before the mirror after Polly had dressed her hair, she decided that she looked demure and young, not at all the picture she wanted to present, but there was no help for it. Taking a deep breath, she descended the stairs, a flutter of anxiety and apprehension dampening her usual ebullient spirits.

Entering the drawing room a bit shyly, she was relieved to see only Amy and Francis there to receive her. They greeted her with gentle concern, Francis teasing her with compliments on her looks.

"Obviously chasing spies and fending off villains agrees with you, Jenny. You look quite sparkling. I am happy to see that you suffer few ill effects from your ordeal," he said, guiding her to a chair near the fireplace. "But I think you need some restorative. Here is a glass of sherry. We will dine as soon as Piers arrives. He will be here shortly."

Jenny hoped the blush she felt rising to her cheeks at the mention of Piers's name was not too noticeable, but she distracted her cousins by asking about Robert Herron.

"Of course, Robert has been informed. How shocked and unhappy he must be," she lamented, knowing that the vicar must be suffering agonies of reproach and confused anxiety.

Amy was not so charitable. "He should have noticed that his sister was up to no good. She certainly behaved in a most suspicious fashion. I never liked her. She had a *farouche* and disagreeable manner, all the time conspiring in the most heinous way. You suspected her from the start, didn't you, Jenny?" she finished with admiration.

"Not really. But you know I have this strange talent for drawing people as animals, almost without my knowledge, and from the first I saw Evelyn as a ferret, a nasty mean animal I have never liked. My brother used to keep ferrets," she added disarmingly.

"And she was always rude and meanspirited," Amy added.

"I think she believed I had designs on her brother and so excused her rudeness because I knew she was frightened of sharing him with another woman. I must admit I did not think she had so lost her sanity as to betray her country," Jenny conceded, sipping her sherry, grateful for the comfort and support of her relatives. She could so easily never have seen them or Pencairn again.

"It is difficult to think that a woman would be so despicable. And to enlist Black Jack, too! He has always been a brutal, nasty customer," Francis agreed. "But you never should have left Pencairn in answer to that note, Jenny. Foolish of you when you had been warned. If I had known how precarious your situation was, I would have prevented it, or at least accompanied you," he reproached her gently.

"I didn't think, I just rushed off," Jenny admitted.

"She has a tendency to do that," Piers said, entering the room before he could be announced and hearing Francis's complaint.

"Well, how could she have known that that wicked woman had filched writing paper from Arthmore to make her request look genuine? She really was abominable," Amy defended Jenny vehemently. "And it was brave of Jenny to challenge her in that dreadful moor house with Black Jack threatening all kinds of horrible things."

Jenny shuddered, remembering Black Jack's intentions and Evelyn's salacious enjoyment of her possible degredation.

"Never mind, Jenny. You are safe now," Piers soothed, realizing that she would have dark memories of that encounter for a long while. He hoped his offer would banish those wretched moments and hoped, too, that her reaction to his arrival was more than just relief at her rescue from a nasty fate.

"I have a lot of questions about this disgraceful business, Piers," Francis said, eager to hear how the aristocrat had settled affairs with the authorities, mindful of his duty as a magistrate.

"We all do, Francis, but let us discuss it over dinner. I fear the food will be spoiled if we don't repair to the table immediately," Amy insisted. "Although it is very informal this evening, just the four of us," she finished a bit archly. Taking Piers's arm, she led the way into the dining room.

Jenny, noticing that Piers looked tired and worried, determined not to prod him with queries during the meal. And indeed, it was not until the savoury was served and Peabody had withdrawn that Piers attempted any explanations.

"It will be very difficult to prosecute a madwoman and there is no doubt that the scene in the moor house drove Evelyn Herron over the brink of sanity. I suspect she has been teetering on the edge for some time, but she had directed her conspiracy so successfully for so long, eluding any suspicion, that she imagined her cleverness would always triumph," Piers explained.

"But why did she begin in the first place?" Amy asked, puzzled by Evelyn's motivations.

"She seems to have had some sort of lust for power and was frustrated by her former betrothed's rejection and her tame role as the vicar's sister here. I understand from Robert that she behaved very strangely after the broken engagement, vowing all kinds of revenge, which was why he decided to leave Surrey and come here. He thought a complete change of scene would help her forget and recover."

"Yes, well, other women have been rejected without turning to such dire reprisals," Amy protested. Then remembering Jenny's reason for visiting them, broke off in some confusion.

However, Jenny was not at all embarrassed. "I was among them, Amy. I feel a certain sisterly sympathy for Evelyn about her unhappy situation, but cannot imagine why she felt betraying her country would heal that disappointment."

"Well, you may be hotheaded and impulsive, Jenny, but you are far from mad. We cannot view Evelyn Herron in the same light as a normal person, poor soul, for she could have caused grave harm," Piers insisted.

Before Jenny could take issue with him on his analysis of her character, which she suspected he had deliberately thrown out to distract her, Francis asked, "I believe you suspected an entirely different villain, Piers?"

"Yes, I thought Henri was our man. He behaved oddly, dashing off to Penzance to meet fellow émigrés, and then my house guests were convinced his tale of lost property and wealth was bogus. Henri may be a dissembler and an opportunist, but not a spy. I had to acquit him, his sister, and brother-in-law, who also merited distrust. But Jenny muddied the waters by not confiding all she knew," he said sternly. He was still shaken by how he had nearly lost her, just when he had discovered how much she meant to him.

"I should have told you about what I overheard in the church, but I was sulking because of the way you had been treating me," Jenny admitted a bit shamefacedly, but always willing to confess her impetuosity.

"What will happen now, Piers? Will the Army arrive to repel any invasion?" Francis asked.

"I don't think Napoleon will chance it once he knows we are waiting for him. And there are ways to leak that information."

Francis, still not completely satisfied with Piers's explanations, probed further. "How in the world did Evelyn make the French contact which enabled her to organize all this? She seems to have spun a fairly intricate web, importing spies, dispersing them from here to do their nasty jobs, and helping to plan an invasion. Pretty formidable work for a country spinster."

"I believe Henri was inadvertently responsible for introducing her to her primary contact. Fouché is always on the watch for a possible conspirator. Black Jack is confessing to a great deal in hope of saving his neck, but, of course, Evelyn Herron is incapable of telling us anything. She sits in her cell singing the

Marseillaise, I understand," Piers explained briefly, remembering his last sight of the wretched woman, and not wanting to remind Jenny of the episode in the moor house. Fortunately, she appeared more interested in the climax of their investigations than dwelling on her own perilous situation.

"Well, it has all turned out most happily, except for poor Robert. We must try to ease his unhappiness," Jenny suggested.

"I am not sure that I will permit that," Piers replied a bit arrogantly.

"Really, Piers, you have nothing to say about it," Jenny argued, her temper up at what she considered his managing ways.

"But I intend to have a great deal, and if Amy and Francis will excuse me, I will say it now before you take it into your head to throw yourself into any more disastrous escapades," Piers answered coolly. And getting no demur from his hosts, he grasped Jenny's arm ruthlessly and escorted her from the room.

The night was warm with only a slight breeze and Piers decided that for the privacy he required only the terrace behind the drawing room was suitable. Not permitting Jenny to elude his grasp, not even conceding she might need a shawl against the evening chill, he hurried her out the French doors onto the terrace.

"Really, Piers, you are quite rude. What must Amy and Francis think?" Jenny protested. But the warmth of Piers's glance just before he lowered his eyelids to mask his feeling gave her more than a suspicion of what she faced.

"They are thinking that my patience is exhausted and I cannot wait one more second to tell you that I love you, maddening baggage that you are, without the common sense of a pea goose. I want to marry you forthwith before you wander off into another ghastly episode. I am too old to play the knight errant often," he proposed, without the slightest attempt at romance.

But before Jenny could criticize his manner, he had taken her firmly in his arms and stopped her words with a kiss which overwhelmed her with its passion. As his hands roamed over her body she gasped with delight and returned his caresses with as much enthusiasm as she could.

Pausing for a breath, but not allowing her to leave his arms, he looked at her quizzically. "Do I take it that this effusive reception of my kisses means that you are content to become Lady Trevarris?" Despite his effort at mockery Jenny sensed the uncertainty beneath the insouciant words and hastened to reassure him.

Raising her head from his shoulder, she looked at him soberly. "I love you, Piers, you must know that. I am not good at dissembling. Of course, I want to marry you." And then, with the artless honesty which was so typical, "As soon as possible, please."

Piers laughed. "There is no one like you, Jenny. Any other woman would have pretended surprise and received my offer with coy modesty, but not you. That's why I love you, among other reasons. But are you sure?" he asked, a frown furrowing his brow.

Jenny, knowing instinctively what he was too

reticent to ask, answered briskly. "If you mean do I feel any lingering affection for Harry, you are the goose. I will always remember him kindly for our childhood ties, but what I feel for you is far different than the rather tepid emotion Harry inspired."

In truth Jenny was surprised by the passion which rose in her to meet Piers's expert kisses. There was no resemblance in the feeling Piers inspired in her to her almost forgotten reaction to Harry's caresses. She knew that Piers would try to dominate her, manage her for her own good, and she would resist, but their relationship was founded on a deep love and understanding.

"I am glad you are being sensible about a wedding date. I do not want to wait, Jenny, for you are much too enticing for a long engagement. I suggest we travel to Wiltshire within the week, so I can meet your parents. And you will want to marry in your father's church, I suspect. We should be able to clear up all the details of this Herron matter quickly. So there is no reason to wait," Piers insisted, kissing her with forceful authority to underline his desire.

"Will I have to testify?" Jenny asked, a bit awed by the thought.

"No, both de Lisle and I heard enough to insure Black Jack's conviction and I fear that Miss Herron will never stand trial, but be incarcerated in some hospital like Bedlam," he explained.

"Poor woman! Poor Robert!" Jenny could not completely forget the tragedy in her own happiness.

"Enough of them. I want you to concentrate on me, Jenny. I will be a very demanding husband."

Piers made some of those demands apparent on Jenny's trembling lips.

"I can quite see that and will be happy to oblige with some demands of my own," Jenny agreed, responding ardently and delighting Piers with her final words. "I wish we were married right now. I am very impatient."

Laughing, he released her, prepared to return to the drawing room to tell the Morstans their news. "Curb your appetite for adventure until the wedding night, Jenny. That will be all the excitement you need, I promise you."

Willing to give him the surrender he sought, Jenny nodded, and some weeks later had to admit that he had more than fulfilled that promise.

The new Zebra Regency Romance logo that you see on the cover is a photograph of an actual regency "tuzzy-muzzy." The fashionable regency lady often wore a tuzzy-muzzy tied with a satin or velvet riband around her wrist to carry a fragrant nosegay. Usually made of gold or silver, tuzzy-muzzies varied in design from the elegantly simple to the exquisitely ornate. The Zebra Regency Romance tuzzy-muzzy is made of alabaster with a silver filigree edging.

A FASCINATING STRANGER

Suddenly Jenny was recalled to the late hour and the impropriety of her sitting up in this inn with a strange man, exciting though the encounter had been.

Giving a sigh of regret she rose and thanked him prettily.

"You have been most kind and forebearing to entertain me so well, sir, but I must retire now. Thank you for your hospitality."

But Piers, who had been dipping deep into the claret, was not about to let the evening end so tamely.

"The thanks are all on my side, my dear. This has been an unexpectedly delightful evening. Since it is doubtful we will meet again, let me give you an experience to compare to your Harry's callow lovemaking," he drawled.

Before she could protest he had drawn her into his arms and kissed her. . . .